Corpses Say The Darndest Things

Corpses Say The Darndest Things

Nod Blake Mysteries Book 1

Doug Lamoreux

Large Print Edition
Copyright (C) 2013 Doug Lamoreux
Layout design and Copyright (C) 2019 by Next Chapter
Published 2019 by Next Chapter
Cover art by Cover Mint

Dedicated to -
Edwin Lamoreux,
and the Lamoreux clan, with love.

Acknowledgements

- Jenny McDonnell - My rock; my shelter in the storm.

- Carole Gill – For asking the question that led to The End

- The folks buying and selling Geraniums at the flower stand at Post & Kearny.

Chapter One

Imagine, if you will, an all but washed-up private detective pursuing a uniformed cop down the street as fast as either of us could run. Yeah, we were a sight.

Not that it mattered to anyone. In The Windy City like any other metropolis, with a million people passing at any given time, few bothered to look and nobody put in a hand. No, sisters and brothers, I was on my own and chasing him for all I was worth. I'm the private dick. I could describe the sounds, the smells. I could name the streets, the twists and turns, the folks we almost knocked down, the things we ran around, jumped over, the vehicles that nearly hit us. What would be the point? We ran until I could barely breathe and wished the same for him and then some. We ran till he made a mistake.

He was passing two hookers, a skinny blonde with roots that matched her vinyl knee-high boots and a tall apple-bottomed girl the color of rich dark chocolate wearing gold and green zebra-striped spandex loitering near a deserted building on North Avenue, when he shouted and turned into an alley that I knew was a dead end. The sap. As sure as a frog has delicious legs, I had him. I passed the working girls myself, too fast to take real notice, turned the corner, and nearly collided with a dumpster that smelled like fish hell at low tide. The man in blue was just ahead. From one of the open windows above, as if pleading his case for him, the Electric Light Orchestra begged *Don't Bring Me Down*. Nuts to that. Sucking wind, my heart ready to explode, I leapt and landed on his back.

He couldn't just go down of course. Because luck is non-existent in my life, and good fortune only a fantasy, the cop took a header. I rolled ass over tea kettle over him onto the pavement and, as I still had a grip, he returned the favor. Garbage, newsprint, cardboard and, I'm sorry to say, gravel flew. I rang my own bell on an inconveniently discarded concrete block using the back of my skull as a clapper. A conjoined scream, our pain, my anger, his fear, went up like a mushroom cloud. Before the noise and dust settled, and despite my blurred vision and bleeding road rash, I scrambled to my feet.

He did too. Then he went for the holstered gun on his hip.

"Willie," I screamed. There was no time to think, just enough to kick him hard in the groin. He collapsed like a marionette with cut strings and rocked on the ground in a fetal position. "No guns, Willie, ever," I barked. "I hate guns."

Then, and only then, did they show up.

By *they* I mean Detective Lieutenant Frank Wenders and his sidekick Detective Dave Mason, two more frauds passing themselves off as real cops; these paid by the city. Wenders, a few years short of retirement but ages past his sell-by date, belonged in New Orleans rather than Chicago. He was made for Mardi Gras. For him, every day was Fat Tuesday and he could chomp a king cake whole and never taste the baby Jesus. His shadow outweighed his partner. Speaking of which, Mason, who was too young for his promotion out of patrol, had not failed to make the worst of it. In no time at all he'd become every bit the jerk Wenders was, only stupider. Together they were always a day late and a dollar short; two scabs constantly picking at me.

"You… all… right, Blake?" Wenders asked. I thought I was breathless. He was huffing like a paint junkie. I nodded. (Okay, I was winded myself.) Between gasps, I pointed at the little man in blue, still suffering on the alley floor, and told the city boys, "For a sawbuck, tell you where he got the uniform. He looks better than your guys."

Wenders gawped at the fake cop, balled up like a baby, cupping his package with both hands and whimpering like a whipped dog, and seemed to decide that (outside of Willie's white socks) he couldn't disagree with my assessment. The rest of the costume looked genuine. Still he frowned. Apparently he didn't need a wise-acre like me pointing it out to him.

As long as I had him annoyed, I kept going. "Frank," I said, because the lieutenant loved it when I got chummy, "meet Willie Banks. Willie," I told the whining slug on the pavement, "this is Detective Lieutenant Wenders. He'll be your arresting officer this morning." The smoke rolled from Wenders' ears. Apparently he didn't need me introducing him to low level perps like we were all guests at a garden party either. He stared daggers at me then told Mason, "Scoop him up."

The counterfeit cop went without resistance and only a little crying. The barely real junior detective followed behind yanking on the handcuffs and shoving him like he was less than human. As they reached the mouth of the alley, in a high, nasally voice, Willie shouted back over his shoulder, "Blake, take care of my car, will ya?"

That didn't help. Wenders looked at me like I was a bug. He shook his head in dismay (but not surprise). A lifetime ago, when I was a cop, the pre-lieutenant Wenders, along with the rest of the boys in the precinct, gave me a bad time because of my habit of picking up strays. My heart, to hear them tell it, bled all over for one scumbag after another. I couldn't say they were wrong and I don't pretend things have changed. Things never change.

Wenders noticed the gun on the pavement and grunted as he picked it up. He didn't know much but he knew it wasn't his. Without thinking he held the weapon out to me. "Yours?" My vision was only just clearing, my head was still vibrating like a drum, and I wasn't in the mood.

I growled and turned as if the weapon smelled bad. I couldn't help it. It was automatic like the kick after a quack taps your knee with a rubber hammer. Knowing what he knew, Wenders couldn't blame me. "Sorry," he said. "Must be his, huh?" He tucked the gun in his belt (a trick with his gut). Then he took another swipe, "You know, Blake, you ain't Broderick Crawford. You gotta quit acting like a cop."

I lit a smoke (which, truth be told, didn't help my dizziness) and blew it in his face. "You could say, Thanks," I said, "for helping us get the guy."

"You're not a cop anymore," he said, pretending he hadn't heard me. "You're a lousy *gumshoe*."

That wasn't nice but, then again, neither was Wenders. He rotated his girth and, trailing Mason and their phoney cop prisoner, walked away like the bovine he was. Always one to look on the bright side, I noted with thanks that he didn't raise his tail. "You're welcome," I told his back.

There are three theories as to how the word *gumshoe* became a stand-in for private investigator. The first suggests the term was a tribute to the unflappable sticking power of the detective.

Like gum, you can't shake us. The second says private dicks spend so much time poking around bad neighborhoods they end up with gum on their shoes. While neither of these are absolutely untrue, as to word origin they are highly suspect and probably half-baked. The third theory, the one that holds water if you ask me, says the name came from the gum-rubber soles on shoes worn in the late 1800's. They walked quiet and a gumshoe could sneak around. Handy if you wanted to avoid detection or take a run-out powder with somebody's stuff because, yeah, a gumshoe was a thief. By 1910 or so, and don't ask me how, I'm no historian, the term had come over to the other side of the law and from then on referred to those who quietly went about detecting crime.

Seventy years later (it's 1979 as I confess this to you), with shoe power all but replaced by high-tech security firms, personal computers, a Fotomat in every car lot, news eighteen hours a day, and a half-dozen law enforcement agencies holding concurrent jurisdiction over every inch of the U.S., the hard working private detective (and his gumshoes) had, like pre-Star Wars special effects and backroom book-making, gone the way of the dodo. With the exception, that is, of me.

My name, as you've already heard, is Blake. Don't ask about the first name. Yeah, I have one. No, I don't use it; and it's not because I want to be all private dick-*ish*. That name alone proves my parents were child abusers. My old man paid for his crime ages ago and is serving his sentence in the city cemetery with no possibility of parole. My mother, on the other hand, what with the world so full of Bingo parlors and people she's yet to annoy, has so far managed to push back her trial date. Some day I'll see justice done; enough said. In a modern Chicago, filled with agents, cops, and rent-a-cops, I'm still just a private eye. I admit, I've out-lived my time. As the eighties approach and the new age shoves the old out and over the hill, I still smoke, I drink before, during, and after business hours, I still think of women as dames though I rarely say it aloud. (While I often find trouble, I'm not as a rule *looking* for it.) And I still wear gumshoes. They're quiet, as comfortable as can be expected for a job where the only time you're off your feet is when you're knocked on your can, and they're handy for those times when it's necessary for a middle-aged, out of shape, throwback to a by-gone era of detecting on the mean streets to move fast, like that morning.

I headed, slowly and painfully, out of the alley but was stopped before I reached the sidewalk by the little blonde hooker. "Hey, Blake," she exclaimed. "I thought that was you I seen running." She was twitching like Howdy Doody, involuntary muscle spasms proclaiming her addiction. Fucking junk. Suddenly, it dawned and I could have kicked myself. I knew the girl, knew her well, but hadn't recognized her for the hell the street was beating out of her. She was still in her early twenties, but couldn't have passed for forty.

"You look awful," I told her.

She took me in with her huge doe eyes and I can only imagine what she saw from her side; a thickening gut, thinning salt and pepper hair, a dirt and blood-caked, sweaty, dated suit of clothes hung on a rumpled knot-headed former cop that was now... What was I anymore? "You think you're Gregory Peck?" she asked. "Have you looked in a mirror lately?"

I took her point and changed the subject. "Have you been eating?"

"I get by," she said with a twitch.

I pulled a twenty from my pocket and pushed it into her shaking hand. "Don't smoke it up," I told her. "Buy some food." She nodded without looking me in the eye.

"Hey, Charisma!" The shout came from the other girl, her huskier, flashier co-worker, who'd moved their trollop shop to the corner across the street. "Who's the boyfriend?"

I looked from the loud one in the distance to the soiled dove beside me. "Charisma?"

"I found a book of names at the library," she said with a shrug. "I'm trying it out."

"Okay. But I'm still calling you Connie."

She pecked my cheek, turned and, zigging as the traffic zagged, headed back to her girlfriend shouting "Love ya'" over her shoulder as she went.

As I watched her, skinny and street-worn, heading back into the hell that made up her existence, I shook my head and wondered at how lousy life could be. That led to thoughts of the crap week I'd had so far and to the dandy morning it had been. Like most ruminations of the past, these thoughts in no way altered the present and in no way put me wise to two vital facts: One, that though I had not fatally injured myself, the head shot I had just taken was the first of several I had coming over the next eleven days that would permanently scramble my brains and forever alter my future. And two, that one week prior, almost to the minute, a heavily guarded gate at the Stateville prison near Joliet had ratcheted open and disgorged my worst nightmare.

Chapter Two

Smoke billowed in great gray swirls from the exhaust of Willie Banks' old Ford as I pulled it into the lot outside of my office. I suppose I should have been grateful, with the bald tires, shattered left headlight, dented green left and rusted blue right quarter panels to highlight the faded Madagascar Orange of the Mustang's original body, I might well have been pushing it in. With the things I let myself in for a sucker like me ought to have a hook in his mouth. Anyway, somewhere behind the smoke was the small red-brick two-story building I rented, and sometimes paid the rent on, on the near southwest side; the former campaign headquarters of someone running for something. It featured a vestibule that was too tight to change your mind in, an outer office for my secretary, an inner office where I thought great thoughts, met clients, and hid from bill collectors, and a one-room second floor filled with boxes of long-forgotten junk. Someday I'll hire a detective to see what's up there.

Though I shut it off, Willie's car continued to cough. Finally the engine gave a great last gasp and shuddered to a halt. I sighed, grabbed an envelope from the seat beside me and, as beat as Grandma's rug, went inside.

Lisa was at her desk. That's Lisa Solomon, my secretary. When she stood she was a tall brunette drink of water. Sitting or standing, she was as bright as light, efficient as a well-oiled machine, and nearly as awkward as she was gorgeous. As usual, one long, boney hand scribbled madly on one of the piled papers on her desk while the other dug, equally as madly, into a bag of five and dime candy. I saw Lisa once when she wasn't eating; once. How she stayed so skinny is one of the world's great mysteries. She looked up when I entered, offered no discernible expression from behind her big owl-like glasses, but said, "You look like a lump of Grade A ground chuck."

I gave the comment all the consideration it was due, meaning, I ignored it. "Willie Banks is in the jug," I told her. "If his mother wants to spring him, and I would assume that's a big *if*, we should let her know." I handed her the envelope. "Add that to the bill and remind her I don't take checks." I tossed his keys on the desk. "Those are Willie's, to that wreck outside lowering the property values."

"Is that what that was?" She glanced out the window. "I thought the Sydney ghost train rekindled."

I ignored that too. "Ask her what she wants done with it. I'm going home and..."

Some detective I was. It was only then, from the corner of my eye, I saw the blonde sitting crossed-legged in one of the two chairs in my waiting room. The chair never had it so good and my eyes were feeling better about the day too. If Lisa was gorgeous but awkward, this dame was just gorgeous. She smiled and what could I do but smile back. Her smart, if business-like, skirt and jacket, in soft canary yellow, deserved attention but I couldn't supply it because her legs were hogging the show. Then she stood and, as if they hadn't caused enough trouble, the legs made a perfect ass of themselves. Outside of my aching skull I heard Lisa mumbling. "Huh?"

"I said," Lisa said, "this is Gina Bridges."

"Blake," I said, taking her hand. I indicated the door to my office with my free mitt. "Please." She followed directions like a champ and I champed to follow her. Behind me, under her breath, I could have sworn I heard Lisa ask, "Who do you think you are, William Holden?" I ignored that too.

*

For the uninitiated, entering my office must be something like walking onto the set of a Skid Row stage production of The Front Page. The massive oak desk, no doubt gorgeous in the first three or four offices it had served, was so buried by stacks of paper it could have passed for the working space of a haggard newspaper editor. I'm not a news editor of course, I'm merely disorganized. And, though I wasn't much of a writer, that day at least I was certainly haggard. A book shelf behind held stacked files, phone books, atlases and outdated city directories. None had been touched since we'd moved the new computer in and a fine layer of dust had settled. Beneath another stack of files, a fire proof safe sat like a rock in the far corner protecting papers of importance, a frosted brownie I'd hidden from

Lisa then forgotten, and my gun. (Just because I hate the damned things doesn't mean I don't have one. It is, after all, a tool of the trade.) A small refrigerator, from a motel that went bust, sat next to the safe cooling mixers and limes and holding up its own stack of files. Beside that, ready for action, was the liquor cabinet, the top of which was the only cleared flat surface in the room. There are two framed photos on my wall; one of a cabin I stayed in outside of Mammoth Hot Springs, and one of a woman I do not know. The first reminds me of one of the only weeks in my life I want to remember. The other came with the frame and tries, but fails, to remind me to replace her with my detective's license. Both bring the same phrase to mind; some day… Miss Bridges gave no indication she was bowled over by the opulence, but she didn't look ready to run either. I took it as a sign she meant to go through with whatever it was she'd come for, shut the door, and showed her to a chair.

"I'm sorry," she said, sounding as if she was, with a voice that could float a yacht. "I missed your first name."

The voice could stay, the question had to go and I waved it away. "Don't worry about it; I don't use it. Call me, Blake, everyone does." I smiled so she wouldn't take offense (my parents weren't her fault) and found my chair behind the desk. Aching, feeling as on the ball as a ceramic bobblehead, and out of respect for the first-rate job the alley had done on my other parts, I sat gingerly. "Now, what can I do for you?"

"Well," she said, "I'm the executive secretary for the Reverend Conrad Delp." She paused, waiting for my reaction. When I didn't offer one, she proceeded. "The Reverend has a crusade appearance in Atlanta tonight." She checked a stylish watch on her slim white wrist. "The advance team is already there and set up, we'll be flying out shortly. Usually the Reverend's wife, Katherine, goes along but she isn't feeling up to it this evening."

Any other day a drop-dead beautiful woman like that could sit in my office talking until the cows came home and I'd listen without interruption trying merely to swallow my saliva before it reached my shirt. But, truth be told, just at that moment, it hurt to sit and focusing my

18

eyes wasn't a *gimme* either. "Miss Bridges," I said, smiling but squirming forward in my chair. "I apologize if I seem abrupt," I bit my lower lip, adjusting, "but, I've had a rare morning." I found a position that offered some relief and exhaled to prove it (which just made me dizzier). "How, specifically, can I help you?"

"I'm sorry. The Reverend would like his wife looked after."

There weren't any crickets but there should have been. "Now I'm sorry. He wants what?"

"He wants to hire you to make sure his wife is safe... while he's gone."

"Oh, I see." I needed the work, I could always use the money, and I was amenable to sniffing her perfume until my Medicare kicked in, but without knowing it she had just given me an out and, the way I was feeling, I was gratefully taking it. "I don't do that sort of thing," I told her. "Some private investigators do; bigger firms with more manpower. I work alone. What you're looking for is a security firm or a private bodyguard."

"You don't understand, Mr. Blake."

"Blake. Just... Blake, please. My old man was *Mister* and he took it with him."

She smiled. She understood me. She'd do any-thing to please me. "Blake." See, I told you. "I know this is short notice but it isn't just anyone we want looked after. It's Reverend Delp's wife. He needs someone he can trust. I've been told he can trust you. You come highly recommended."

"I do?" It took an effort not to laugh but I made it. "By whom?"

"Mr. Blake… Blake… I don't know." I'd have felt bad, but she sounded so defeated herself I let it go. She took a breath deep enough to test the top two, insanely-secure, buttons on her blouse and championed on. "I'm doing as I was in-structed and telling you what I was told. Among the things I was told was that you come highly recommended."

I nodded to demonstrate how much the com-pliment meant to me. Then I stood, turned, and opened my little fridge. With effort, I ignored all the fixings inside that might have contributed to a lovely and well-deserved late morning toddy and, instead, grabbed a handful of ice from the freezer box. "Would you excuse me a moment?" I took a last look to remember her by, enjoyed a fleeting dirty thought about the girl who looked like Bo Derek but acted like Bo Peep, and left the office pulling the door closed behind me.

Lisa swiveled her chair. "The first rule of being a detective," she said, proudly shoving a sheet of paper at me. "Investigate the client first."

Holding the ice to the back of my head, I took the paper with my dry hand. "She's not the client. The client is Conrad Delp."

"Reverend Delp?"

I nodded and scanned the sheet. Ice water ran down the back of my neck. I didn't mind at all. "You know him?"

"Everyone who *isn't* going to hell knows him," Lisa said. She bit several inches off a black licorice whip to emphasize her disgust at my ignorance. You've got to be hateful and mean to eat black licorice. Then she talked around it while she chewed. "He's a biggie in the television preacher industry – and not just in Chicago. He's huge all over the country; TV specials, weekly radio show, books, newsletter. He's his own cottage industry, and you ought to see the marble cottage God gave him in thanks. My mother dotes on him. In fact, that VCR you tried to bribe her with really comes in handy; she tapes all his crusades, never misses a radio broadcast." She paused to suck candied spit.

I'd been studying the bare-bones sketch of Miss Bridges but I turned from it to ogle my secretary. I have as many prejudices as the next guy, but I'm way too lazy to be an -ist and too contemptuous of society in general to form specific -isms, still I couldn't help myself and asked, in genuine confusion, "Aren't you Jewish?"

"Oy," she answered. "But Reverend Delp is special. He makes Mom cry. And, for an older man, he is kinda hunky." Sometimes my arched brows and dismal head shakes (even pained dizzy ones) just happened on their own, like then. "It's a girl thing," she explained.

I raised one hand in surrender while I chucked the last of the ice bits into the wastebasket with the other. "It doesn't matter," I said, drying my hand on my pants. "It's babysitting. You know I don't…"

"I know you don't," she cut in quickly, nearly lashing me with licorice in her excitement. "But it sounded simple and you could use the money. Besides…" Lisa had that frightening gleam in her eye and, believe me, if you haven't seen it, you just can't know. Worse, beneath the gleam she was still talking. "I thought, if you didn't want to do it, it'd be a good case for me to get my feet wet."

I hate that gleam. Did I mention Lisa wanted to be a detective? Yeah, well, she did. Like Ahab wanted fish for dinner, Lisa wanted to be a detective. "We've had this talk before," I said with a sigh. "You're not an investigator. You're barely a secretary."

"Well, what am I then?"

"The word *thorn* comes to mind. Or bane, burden, irritant. Nuisance, pest, plague. Oh, and pain, of course; you're definitely a pain." I handed the paper back. "I'm going to cab over and get my car, if it isn't already, 'Please God, No,' up on blocks. Then I'm going home to soak in hot water; very hot water, for a very long time. Explain my departure to Miss Bridges, please, offer her our deepest apologies that we cannot be of service, and send her on her way."

Done with my secretary, fed up with the day, the back of my head throbbing, I turned to exit. As I opened the outer door, from behind, Lisa said, "Don't you think, since Reverend Delp is who he is?"

"Lisa Solomon," I said, cutting her off like a naughty child. "I am turning down this job."

"Even," she asked, "at the risk of your immortal soul?"

"I'm closing the door now," I said. And did, as I left.

Chapter Three

I found my Jaguar exactly where I'd left it and, to my astonishment, unmolested. No, I'm not rich. I'm a working-stiff (just then a stiff working-stiff) like, I imagine, most of you. One of the few things in this world I'd ever really wanted was a Jag and, like the fabled merchant and his pearl of great price, I'd given most of what I had to buy it, used. Imagine the sexiest 150-mph super car ever, an erection on wheels, and you have the '61 Jaguar. Now, add power-sapping Federal emission controls, discontinue the elegant fixed-head coupe for a long wheelbase, perfection stretched on a medieval rack. Replace the reliable 4.2-liter six for a monstrous 5.3 V12 that's a bitch to keep tuned and makes the front anchor-heavy. Spoil the smooth lines and sleek contours with plumped fenders. Then nail the coffin closed with horrendous rubber pads to meet senseless 5-mph bumper standards. And, *voilà*, you have my deep blue '74 Jaguar. It will go down in history as one of the worst cars of all time, but it was still a Jag and it was mine. Now you understand my relief at finding it intact. Without further ado, I fired it up and took it and my battered self home.

Much later that night, soothed if not softened by a hot bath and partially recharged by several hours shut-eye, but with my head still aching and my senses tingling from a feeling that something was just *not right*, I gave Lisa a call. No, I was not receiving any psychic messages, I just had a hunch. I got her answering machine, considered the fact she never went anywhere, then got a chill. Hating myself for it, I dressed again and drove, not to her place, but to the north side of town or, financially speaking, to the other side of the tracks. I turned down the winding road that fronted the residence of Chicago's (perhaps even the Almighty's) gift to television worshipers everywhere, the Reverend Conrad Delp. What little of the columned mansion could be seen from the peasant's side of the ornate wrought-iron gate and walled fence, beyond the curve of the substantial drive, through the myriad trees was, I'll admit, impressive, and I whistled to show my respect as I slowly cruised by. Then I came abreast of a speck of a car, a 1970-something Volkswagen Cabriolet, an electric-yellow roller skate fueled by lead-free gas and pretension, that was parked at the curb. I stomped on my brakes.

"Son of a bitch." It was Lisa's car.

I only thought I'd had a headache before. Now it was pounding. On top of that I was deeply annoyed but not in the least surprised. The reason I was there, seeing her car, was because I had somehow known my eager secretary was going to ignore my direct order. And, as sure as the Ayatollah Khomeini was back in Iran, there she was. Chewing my lower lip in frustration, I continued on and parked in the shadows down the street.

I walked back to Delp's estate, scaled the wall and slipped into the yard. I wound through the trees and bushes, playing commando from one shadow to the next until, within shouting distance of the mansion, I made out the thin but graceless form of Lisa standing beside a tree. She was dressed in black like a Ninja, pointlessly, because she was leaning directly into an amber pool of light from one of the windows of the house. She was sucking on a blue and white swirled lollipop (raspberry ripple?) that, when she pulled it from her maw, was as big around as a bar coaster. She held a metal file, doing her nails between licks of her candy and, I imagine, telling herself she was watching the house.

Sue me. I sneaked up behind her.

"What are you doing?"

Lisa jumped. She rammed the file under her fingernail and had herself a moment. Then she recognized me, got mad, recognized the injury she'd done to herself, felt the pain, recognized she was caught where she had no business being, and raced from embarrassment to defensiveness faster than a pimply teen reaches his first orgasm. "God!" she shouted in a whisper. "Who do you think you are, Chuck Norris? You scared me half to death!"

"Yes," I said without a hint of compassion. "What are you doing here?"

"What are *you* doing here?" she shot back indignantly.

"I'm a licensed private investigator. I'm trained to know when someone is doing something really stupid. Now, I repeat, what…?"

"You're here." She was angry but still whispering. "So you know why I'm here. I took the job."

"You can't take the job. You're not…"

"An investigator, I know. I took the job for you."

"Without telling me?"

"You wouldn't take it." She furled her brow. I stared back so hard that, had I had a couple more chins and forty rolls of fat, she'd have thought I was Frank Wenders. She cocked her head, an embarrassed coquette owl behind the glasses, and raised one corner of her mouth to smile. "I thought it could be a really good case," Lisa said. "Not too hard but really interesting."

"What's interesting about it?" I asked doubtfully.

"You left too soon," she exclaimed. "There was more to Gina's story."

"Gina? The last time we talked it was Miss Bridges."

She ignored that. "Reverend Delp has been getting threatening letters, so he didn't want his wife left alone."

"What sort of threats? From whom?"

"Gina didn't know. Just threats, I guess."

"She didn't show them to you?" Lisa had a habit of gaining speed as she talked. My questions were as much to slow her down as to harvest information.

"She couldn't show them to me, she hasn't seen them. She's just heard about them."

"Rumors? Gossip?"

She clicked her tongue because I wasn't playing fair; asking questions to which she didn't know the answers. "Gina said they weren't the kind of thing Reverend Delp would speak about." For emphasis, she added, "He is a powerful and influential man."

"Yes, so you've said repeatedly. But you don't know anything about these threats? Whether they were mailed or from where? Cut from newsprint? Written in blood?"

Lisa shook her head. I was spritzing her with questions about unimportant details and she was trying to keep the windshield clear enough to barrel forward. "All I know is Katherine, eh Mrs. Delp, was unaware of the threats and the reverend wanted it to stay that way because of her delicate nature."

"Her delicate nature?"

"That's the way Gina, eh Miss Bridges, put it. Because of her delicate nature. That's why I'm out here. He doesn't want her to be alone but he doesn't want her to know she's being watched either. I'm just supposed to make sure she's safe. Once she's asleep, I'm done and I can leave. I mean, you're done and you can leave."

"Does Reverend Delp know you're here?"

"No, remember, he's in Atlanta," Lisa said. Then under her breath she added, "He understands that... you're... here."

I sighed and looked to the heavens. There were a few stars up there beyond the leaves and a lot of clouds but not a thing that looked like help. "Go home, Lisa." She started to say something but I cut her off. "I'll see Mrs. Delp is tucked in. Go home."

She made one last offer to stay and help, tap danced a final *shuffle-ball-change* on my nerves, then decided she'd pushed her luck as far as it would go. She said goodnight and headed in the direction of the street. It was just after eleven o'clock at night. I watched her disappear into the dark then, resigned to the evening my secretary had selected for me, moved into the shadows near the house.

I looked through a window and for the first time saw Katherine Delp. More accurately, I saw the woman that presumably was Mrs. Delp. (I'd never seen her and wouldn't have known her had she bit me.) She was well worth the look (and welcome to bite me anytime). She was slender and tall from the shag white carpeting to her short-styled blonde hair. In-between, though her figure wasn't exactly an hour-glass it still knew what time it was. Aside from her obvious personal attractions, two things about Katherine Delp stood out. One, for a homebody at that time of night, the lady was exceptionally well-dressed in a clinging red drape that more than hinted at the firm contours beneath. Two, she was visibly on edge, pacing like a caged panther, and stealing uncounted looks at a bold Broccato wall clock I could have hocked for my rent. She paced the length of an inviting couch the same non-color as the carpet, threw a cube of ice into a cut-glass tumbler, and gave it a bath in Tanqueray and tonic. She wet her whistle, examined the clock again, and went right back to pacing.

She kept it up, the pacing and the drinking, for a long time as if waiting on a late train. Something was on her nerves and she was getting on mine. Then the phone rang and we both started.

The minister's wife snatched the instrument from the end table so quickly she nearly spilled her drink. She put the glass down and, forgetting the gin altogether, lifted the receiver to answer. Trailing the cord, Mrs. Delp and her phone disappeared from the room and my view.

*

She was gone for several minutes during which, as far as I could see, absolutely nothing happened. I was bored to tears. Little did I know they would be the last few *quiet* moments I would have for the next week and a half and that my life was about to become a soup sandwich.

I heard a car motor at the front of the property and saw fingers of light, headlights bisected by the iron bars of the front gate, stealing through the trees. I couldn't see the car itself but it was there. There followed a barely audible clank of metal and the grating swing of the gate. The engine revved and the car started up the crescent of the paved drive. I'd had to move forward to a new position to clearly see the visitor without being seen. He made that easier when the headlights suddenly went out. The motor continued to purr softly and, moving slowly in the dark, the vehicle, a dark sedan, came into view. It was brought to a stop by the wide columned front porch and shut off. The lone occupant, the driver, a tall athletic-looking man in his late twenties got out. He took the front steps in two brisk hops and the porch in three long strides; an eager beaver. But, if he was champing at the bit, he had nothing on Mrs. Delp. Before he could even take aim at the doorbell, the minister's wife opened the door, grabbed him like a dog latching onto a meaty bone, and hauled him inside.

I checked my luminous watch, saw 1:00 am straight up (an interesting time for visitors when your hubby was away preaching), then headed back to the side of the house. Flickering shadows showed they'd returned to the living room in which I'd first seen our client's wife. But now I really needed a closer look. I entered and navigated, as best I could by the spill light, a small

34

rock garden to a spot just beneath the window. I was almost in place – when I tripped. I'd been fairly successful up to that point in keeping the noise to a minimum but I knew I'd make a hell of a racket if I fell and, sisters and brothers, I was falling. I grabbed the sill to catch myself. Then, quick as I could, ducked back from the window into the shadows. I leaned there, against the house in the dark with my eyes closed, trying to quietly catch my breath, hoping I hadn't given myself away. I wasn't at all confident because, as one does sometimes, I had the feeling I was being watched.

Outside of the window's light the yard was dark. Outside of a gentle breeze all was quiet. The shadows inside remained constant. Whatever they were doing in the living room, neither had come my way. Apparently this time I'd gotten away with being a klutz. I carefully edged back to the window, stole a look in, and found I'd been worrying about nothing. Mrs. Delp and her young man were locked in a passionate embrace and wouldn't have given a rat's ass if I'd been blowing a trumpet.

The right Reverend Conrad Delp would have been delighted. He'd gone to the trouble of hiring a gumshoe to ensure his delicate wife wasn't alone and he'd gotten his wish. He'd seen to it – and so had she. Whether or not I'm a pervert may be debatable, but I'm not an idiot. I could have stood there in the shadows watching the two of them grope each other for all they were worth but everything about that situation screamed *tit in a wringer.* The only question ultimately would be, hers or mine? I needed to get a handle on whatever the heck was happening there, for my client, for whatever protection I could give his wife, and for myself. It was time for the first rule of detecting: keep the detective safe (out of jail, out of the hospital, out of the morgue). I quietly escaped the rock garden, retraced my steps across the deep wooded property, and slipped back over the wall to the street. No, I wasn't running away (have faith, faithful readers). I dug into a satchel I kept hidden in the trunk of my car, a goodie bag filled with many of the fun things a private dick would love to have with him on a caper but usually can't; camera, latent printing gear, business card printer, and other handy devices, and lock jimmies, slim jims, and other completely illegal accoutrement. This looked to be one of those rare times when my toys would prove, not only useful, but lifesaving.

I returned to the house with a few choice items and, admittedly outside of the law, popped the door lock on the visitor's car. I didn't think he'd mind. And, even if he did, I didn't think he'd be out soon enough to know I'd done it. I didn't bother with ancillary details (what did I care if the guy's insurance was current), just checked the registration for his name and gave the interior a once-over for anything incriminating or informative. For all I knew Nicholas Nikitin, that was our guest, was nothing more than Mrs. Delp's passing fancy or rent-a-date. (In which case, I didn't care who he was.) I found nothing outside of his name and address that qualified as earth shattering. But at least I knew the players, or guessed I did (I was still taking it on faith the woman was Katherine). In the know, but no wiser, I returned to the side of the house to see how the game was going.

The lights were out downstairs, suggesting play had continued without me, and one was now burning in an upstairs window that had been dark. Certain where things were headed, and eager for another disappointment, I looked the yard over. No ladders, no walls, no rises in topography whatsoever. There was probably a garage somewhere on the estate, deep in the dark back forty, but I had neither the urge nor the inclination. There were, I noted, plenty of trees. I'm not an arborist, wouldn't know my oak from my ash, but as a kid running from his insane mother on a tear I learned that trees were tall and you could hide in them. The game was afoot or, by that time probably abed, and I needed to either use it or get off the pot. I sighed, shook my head in dismay and, camera over the shoulder, picked one and started climbing.

Midway up, I heard something somewhere in the yard below. The snap of a twig? The rustle of leaves on a moving branch? I didn't know for sure. From my precarious position, I took in the shadowed surroundings, the expansive grounds, the trees and bushes swaying in the breeze but saw nothing of consequence. I resumed climbing and reached a limb level with the mansion's lighted upstairs window. It was a bedroom, hers surely by the silk, satin, and opulent softness of the surroundings. Katherine and Nicholas were there, in equal stages of undress and again in a clinch. Her physical promises, hidden by the red dress, were splendidly fulfilled. Nicholas' bronzed body brought back memories of a sculpted youth that I would never see again (if I'd ever seen it at all). I might have stewed in a broth of jealousy had I not been so worried I was going to fall out of the fucking tree. Instead, I situated myself in relation to the window and bedroom beyond, threw a leg lock on the limb to secure my perch, and found and focused on the lovers in the camera's viewfinder. The young man had a hold of Katherine's breasts from behind and was biting her back. She seemed to be enjoying it.

"Because of her delicate nature," I mumbled. Then, because I didn't know what else to do, telling myself I was collecting evidence, I started taking pictures.

Chapter Four

It was after 3 am when I got back to my apartment. My head was aching from the tumble I'd taken the previous morning wrapping up Willie Banks, the *faux* police officer, and it was full to overflowing from the X-rated scene it had just witnessed at Delp's palatial mansion. Between sips of gin, it occurred that vultures made a cleaner living than I did. I went to bed and didn't sleep.

The morning took me to AC's, a friend who developed all my film for me, then to my office to examine in detail the results. I sat looking at the photos of Katherine Delp and Nicholas Nikitin, whoever he was, and was, I must say, impressed. Not with my photography, that was only passable, but with the gymnastics on display in the pictures. Nikitin looked like the captain of the copulating team ready for the Olympics in Moscow, while Katherine did a fine job representing thirty-something ministers' wives everywhere. I was whistling, wondering at the physics involved in a particularly interesting shot, when a sledge hammer hit me in the back of the head. That's what it felt like. A pain smacked the tender part of my skull so severely I had to hunch my shoulders. It was followed by a flash of heat that raced around to my face. I felt the flush. I nearly cried out. I did drop the pictures onto my desk. My vision blurred. Though it lasted only seconds, it seemed longer and scared the living hell out of me. I thought I was going blind. When it cleared, through tears, I looked the office round grateful to see it was still there. I didn't know if I was crying owing to an acute physical problem, the pain, or just good old-fashioned fear. As I wiped them on my sleeve, my eyes fell on the photos that I'd dropped. You wouldn't believe it. I didn't. The top picture had changed.

I mean just that. The picture I had been looking at had undergone a complete change. It was the same setting, angle, distance but the guy, Nikitin, was gone from the image. Katherine Delp remained in the photograph, alone, surrounded by a bright blue, pulsating aura as if she were a character in that Star Trek movie they were making. I know it sounds idiotic. Had it not been for the pain in my head, I would have laughed. But that's what I saw. Then things got really stupid. Katherine looked up. No, that's not it. The image of Katherine, glowing with this otherworldly blue outline, looked out of the photograph, staring right at me, and cried, "Help me!"

No, I couldn't and wouldn't argue with what you're thinking; send in the nets. Worse, I can't prove any of it. For just then, after the picture of Katherine Delp had called for help, like snapping your fingers, the sharp pain was gone. The heat flash went with it. I felt a huge sense of relief like a prisoner unbound. I caught my breath and, when I had my wits about me again, looked back to my desk. The photo was exactly as before with Katherine and her young lover having at each other with wild abandon. The blue science fiction haze was gone and neither of the characters in the image were paying me the slightest notice. All was as it was when I took the shots.

It was the damnedest thing I'd ever seen; not to mention felt. I rifled the pictures and saw plenty, but only plenty of the same tits and tongues I'd seen when I took them; nothing from the Outer Limits. I shook my head wondering whether or not I was cracking up. I was still wondering, so deeply that I jumped, when Lisa stuck her head in the office door.

She looked a little sheepish, it was the first time I'd seen her since chasing her out of the reverend's yard the previous night, and even more concerned. "You all right?" she asked, licking frosting from her fingers.

"Ye-ah," I said, stuffing the pictures back into their envelope. "Yeah, I'm fine."

"Gr-eat. Okay. Uh, sorry to barge," she said, "but Lieutenant Wenders..."

She barely got that out and I barely got the photos slid into the top desk drawer when the Chicago Police Department's only indigenous water buffalo shoved past my secretary and in. Maybe I should pause and sweeten the pot with Wenders' full description so you can be as sick to your stomach as I was. He was five foot-nine and, though he wasn't quite there, was working on a corresponding circumference. He was wearing the same threadbare gray suit he was born in, with a gut like a broken barrel of jello, a disposition like a bucket of bent nails, and two mean and beady black eyes that shot holes through you like you were a paper target. What little of his once-red hair remained had gone gray. Dave Mason, his left hand man, as always, followed on his heels like a humping Chihuahua. There's no point adding to his description, in the flesh Mason was practically invisible.

"Blake," the detective lieutenant grunted, reminding himself who he'd come to harass. He had a rolled newspaper tucked under his arm and he snatched it free with his puffy pink hand as he plonked his quarter-beef butt in the chair opposite my desk, all familiar territory to Wenders.

Lisa disappeared and Mason, none too subtly, started sniffing around my office like a drug dog in a waterfront warehouse. I noted it, then ignored it. "Well, Frank," I said instead, giving the lieutenant the attention he so desperately sought. "What brings you out in the sunlight?"

"Oh, I don't know," he lied, rolling the newspaper tightly in his hands as if he intended to swat something. "Just thought we'd have a little chat."

The notion of me chatting with any but a handful of cops still on the department amused me greatly. The idea of chatting with Wenders darn near split my sides. I controlled it and smiled pleasantly (though the back of my head still ached). Mason was starting to make noise as he snooped through my stuff, sliding things around, lifting and peeking, not putting anything back. That amused me less but I kept it to myself and returned to my fascinating conversation with his boss. "I'm intrigued, Lieutenant," I told him. "About what are we going to chat?"

"I just thought we'd chat."

Like talking to a puddle. I continued to smile. "Well, that would be special," I agreed, "but, as you're so fond of pointing out, I'm not a cop anymore, Frank. I have to spend my time working. So, if you could point to the general area on the map we're going... that would be just grand. While you're at it, unless you brought a search warrant, tell your chimp to stop looking around my office."

"Dave," Wenders said without looking at his second, "go hit on Blake's secretary for awhile."

Like the good little brown-shirt he was, Mason obediently made his exit to the outer office. I watched him go and, when the door had closed behind him, couldn't help but ask, "Is he any good?"

Wenders shrugged his disinterest. "I don't carry a watch. Dave keeps time for me."

Hey, whatever works. In response to the weird morning it was quickly turning into, I rose and opened the small, well-stocked and equally well-used liquor cabinet. It was the closest I had to an island get-away and just then I needed a vacation.

"Where were you last night?" Wenders asked my back.

Emily Post insisted I ignore his rude personal question and who was I to argue with her? I withdrew a bottle of whiskey instead, making Emily and I both happy. Then, remembering the baboon in the chair I usually reserved for paying clients, I made a friendly offer in spite of myself, "Drink?"

"Jesus, Blake, it's ten o'clock in the morning."

I frowned. "I thought telling time was Dave's job?" I waved the bottle, renewing the offer.

"No, thanks."

I shrugged, poured a double into a tumbler that thinks it's a shot glass (who am I to argue with it either?), and kneed the cabinet closed with the bottle still on my side.

"So," Wenders said, reminding me he was still there, "where were you last night?" It was awful early in the day for my first lie. And I wanted to be helpful. While I tried to think of some version of the truth that wouldn't tell him anything he got impatient. "What? Suddenly you're the quiet type? You think you're Lee Marvin or something?"

I downed the drink, clenched my teeth while it exploded in my chest, exhaled (surprisingly without breathing fire) and, when I was able, took in a bushel of air. My, that stuff was good. Yet, Wenders was still there. "Try a different question."

"All right," he said, studying me. "How about: Have you seen this morning's city edition?"

In what had to have been the moment he was waiting for, the lieutenant unrolled his flyswatter and laid the world's greatest newspaper (by its own admission) front page up. Then he oozed back in the chair with a cold stare and a palpable satisfaction as if he'd thrown the switch and was really looking forward to my catching fire. It was routine to see Wenders full of himself but this had a different smell to it. I set the glass down and, warily, stole a look at the newspaper. Like tacks to a magnet, my eyes went straight to the bold above the fold headline. I could not believe it said... what it said.

EVANGELIST'S WIFE FOUND MURDERED.

I read it three times, my eyes desperately trying to convince my brain (for the second time that morning) they were seeing what they saw, before I moved to the kicker line below: *Katherine Delp Bludgeoned.* I sat, my mind doing a mental lap around the fact I'd just been handed, coupled with the bizarre image (Wenders knew nothing about) that I'd seen in the photograph a few minutes before, and finally mumbled, "Holy shit."

"How'd you know her?"

"I didn't know her."

Wenders snorted like a pig. "It's a little late for that answer."

"I didn't know her." I rose again and brought both glass and bottle back with me. "I've heard of her husband." I poured, sat, and returned my attention to the news article.

"You've heard of him?" Wenders didn't bother to hide his incredulity. "Come on, Blake, let go of my crank. No horseshit, what were you doin' at her place last night?"

I'd like to think that few things catch me off guard. But that did. I looked up, examining Wenders, wondering just how in hell the fat *s.o.b.* could have known I was… I didn't finish the thought because the lieutenant was studying me. I got my face back under control, changed the look of surprise to one of pure snowy innocence, then took another drink without saying a word.

Wenders sighed like an aggravated bear. "I'm slippin' right out of *friendly* mode," he said. "An informant called in the license number of a butt-ugly Jaguar leaving the scene…" When I showed no sign of life, he asked, "What, I gotta finish that sentence?"

"You know," I said brightly, "come to think of it, I was driving down Del Mar last night. The Delps, they live on Del Mar, don't they?" I stole a look at the paper. "Yeah, Del Mar, it's right there. That's a hell of a coincidence, huh?"

"What time?"

"I don't know."

"Ballpark it."

"Late. I'm certain of that. It was late. Or early, I guess, depending on your point of view." I smiled, taking pride in being so much help. "How did she die?"

Wenders hesitated but not long. Figuring, I guess, that he might as well give me some rope, he said, "She was found in her bed. Her head was beat in with a rock."

"That's a strange way to die in your bed."

"Yeah, ain't it just," Wenders agreed. "That's why your bein' there made so much sense to me. You working a case, Blake?"

I shrugged because how the hell would I know.

"Or were you just fixin' her hair for her?"

"Now," I warned, "be nice."

"Nice my ass. What were you doin' at the Delp mansion last night? And what do you know about this murder?"

"I don't know anything about this murder," I told him, one detective to another. "That is the god's honest truth. I know nothing of it, other than that my presence on Del Mar had nothing to do with it. Eh meaning, of course, that the reason for my presence there is none of your business."

"Damn it, Blake. Katherine Delp ain't even cold yet and I'm gettin' heat from upstairs."

"You're exaggerating."

"The hell I am. We're not talking about the wife of some Skid Row missionary. The Reverend Delp has got connections all around town."

"You can say that about a sewer pipe."

"I'm not laughin'," Wenders said. And he wasn't. "Delp rubs noses with all the muckety-mucks, you see. And the police commissioner, who the reverend numbers among his friends, is so beside himself this morning there are two of him calling to chew on my ass. I need everything you got on this woman from last night and I need it yesterday. Now how is that exaggeratin'?"

"You said Mrs. Delp wasn't cold yet. That's just silly. If this is right," I flipped the newspaper across the desk at him, "by now she's room temperature at most." If Wenders got the joke he was keeping it to himself. No matter. "Was it a robbery?" I asked.

In answer, the cop pulled himself up from the chair like a hippo from a swamp and headed for the door. He'd apparently given out all the information on the murder of Katherine Delp that he intended to. "Play it your way, Blake," he said. "For now." He left with a slam of the door.

I was a whole lot of emotions shook up in a burlap bag. Who or what had done the shaking, and why? Who had killed the beautiful, sleeping Mrs. Delp? Was it all a rotten coincidence that had nothing to do with me? Or had somebody used the head of the minister's wife to knock on my door? Not to belittle her sad end but, as far as heads went, what the hell was wrong with mine? Was the pain from the spill I'd taken with Willie Banks? Or was there something wrong with me? And what had gone on with the picture? Had a dead woman in a photograph actually spoken to me? Called for help? Before I'd known she was dead? The whole thing made as much sense as an eight-fingered glove. I finished my drink. Then, because I couldn't think of anything worthwhile to do, I poured another. I retrieved the envelope from my desk and extracted the photos I'd taken the night before. I drank and studied the images of the couple, the young and handsome Nicholas Nikitin, whose presence at the scene Wenders either was keeping to himself or didn't know about, and the smoking sexy and unbelievably dead Katherine Delp.

*

The Delp mansion and estate looked altogether different in the cold light of day. You'd think it might look smaller when you could take it all in but the opposite was true; there was a lot of house and garden there and the late morning sunlight only made it look grander than ever. While I had nothing against wealth and power, I wasn't awed by it either. That said, it was impressive. The manicured lawn climbed a steep slope in three bush-framed tiers before it met the sprawling house. A horseshoe drive kissed the sweeping steps. Slowly pitched roofs adorned three red brick squares, the main and an east and west wing. Black shuttered windows all around, chimneys competing above. Four massive two-story white columns braced the roof up front and provided protection from the elements to a second story balcony above the porch and entrance.

I made a slow pass by the front gate and saw no evidence of the police. Apparently they'd done their thing and gone. But they had certainly been. The porch was surrounded with yellow *crime scene* tape and a red-printed sign had been tacked on the door. I couldn't read it from that distance (I could barely see it), but was well aware of what it said. Entrance was *verboten* by order of *Das Polizeichef.* I'm paraphrasing but, what it sadly boiled down to was, my notion of pretending I'd been authorized to look around was shot in the butt and entering to snoop now would be illegal. On the other hand, with the officers and scientists done and dusted, it also meant that when I went ahead and did it I had a good chance of being undisturbed. I just needed to make certain there were no stray cops still in attendance. I located the nearest pay phone, patted my pockets until I found Delp's scribbled number (I'll win no awards for memory) and let it ring thirty times. A shiny newly-Academized probationary officer would have answered in half that and even a lazy blob like Wenders would have snatched it up by the thirtieth ring. The house was, at least temporarily, unoccupied. I hurried back, parked a block away and hoofed it to the grounds of stately Delp Manor.

I didn't need to worry about closed-circuit television cameras. They were suddenly up and coming all over the place for security purposes but I'd seen no evidence of them at Delp's place. Just the same, the estate's driveway gate was secured and I saw no reason to present myself to passers-by while I tampered with it. Scaling the wall had worked before and I saw no reason for a change. Once over and in the yard, I hurried from tree to bush toward the house. I slipped under the yellow tape stretched between the two center columns on the porch, ignoring it's message, pulled several tools from a small kit in my pocket, picked the lock, and committed breaking and entering as spelled out by our esteemed Springfield lawmakers. Nuts to 'em.

I looked the first floor of the main mansion over quickly to ensure I was alone. I paused briefly to examine the living room, the focus of my surveillance by way of the rock garden window the night before, seeing it now from the money side of the tracks. I took most of it in, the wall clock Mrs. Delp had been breathing by, the phone by which she'd assured her visitor the coast was clear, the remnants of print powder dusted from here to there and back again as evidence Chicago's finest had done their forensic best. I didn't bother ogling the furniture and nick-knacks. What did I care how the other half lived (especially when they were dead)? I headed upstairs.

Katherine Delp's bedroom would have been described, once upon a time, as flirty and sophisticated. Everything had, until last night, been black and white in what was, I guess, a designer's conception of trendy. On the far side of the room, well outside of the area of the crime, stood a solid white dresser, apparently undisturbed and topped as all women's dressers are by a handful of personal effects, a music box – closed, a jewelry box – open and suggestively still laden with a number of shiny baubles, several bottles of perfume, a hand mirror, brush, and comb, and a Holy Bible – also open, to the 17th chapter of the book of Deuteronomy. (If that matters to you. It didn't to me.) Back on the grisly side of the room stood a black wood-framed headboard and bed complimented and book-ended by two like-framed floor-length mirrors. Above the bed, three black floating shelves created space for accessories. To the sides, white matching end tables, despite their obvious expense, looked like up-ended apple crates. Crowning all, adding sleekness, balance and (no doubt high on Mrs. Delp's list of needful things) youthful elegance, were two crystal chandeliers. They were grand, but the elegance of the night before was as dead as the room's mistress and now they might just as well have been cheap glass.

Elegance wasn't all that had vanished with Katherine. The black and white coverlet, matching covers, pillows, and sheets were missing too. The bed had been stripped, its coverings spirited away by the boys in lab coats. Splashes of dried blood in shades of maroon and brown marred the headboard and wall. Fingerprint dust covered some part of everything as if the pixies had had an orgy; black, white and silver smudges on the bed frame, walls, end tables, lamps, clock radio, and telephone near the bed. So much so it looked to be part of the decor. Without thinking, I laid a hand on the mattress – and there came the sledge hammer again.

The pain – the same pain I'd experienced that morning – came again out of nowhere and shot through the back of my head. At the same time came the heat flash I'd experienced earlier and, as if that weren't enough, a low-toned hum came with it, vibrating through my ears. I realized instantly I'd been wrong. It wasn't a hammer. King Kong had smacked me from behind with a tuning fork. (Yes, it sounds stupid. It felt stupid, with pain.) Like before, the blurred vision followed and this time I did cry out. Then my vision cleared and, sisters and brothers, everything was altered; the blankets, the pillows, all back as they had been the night before but covered in bright red running blood. The splotches were still on the wall, but in dripping crimson instead of the dried maroon. And Katherine was there, naked and sprawled across the bed with her gorgeous head bashed in. I don't have to tell you *that* scared the hell out of me. I blinked and spun on my heels, taking in the changes in the room and trying to see if anyone else was taking them in with me. The sound and pain made it tough but a quick assessment showed there was no one there but Katherine and I, and she offered no threat. I closed my eyes and, suddenly nauseous, gulped for air. With my peepers pinched shut, the pain in my head, the ringing in my ears began to sub-side. A moment more and they disappeared al-together. When I opened my eyes, the body, the bedding, and the fresh blood were gone. All was as it had been when I'd entered the room.

Something was grossly wrong inside my skull. I was afraid, terrified that I was cracking up. I wanted to be out of there. I couldn't control much else but I could make that happen. With one quick last look around, I did.

Chapter Five

I'd learned squat at the scene of the crime and had come away with nothing more than a strong feeling that I was losing my mind. I was a drinker and over the years had had my share of hangovers. Who outside of the Amish hadn't? But, as far as I knew, I'd never had a blackout or an alcohol induced hallucination. If these experiences were hallucinations, that is. If they weren't, what were they? I didn't believe in ghosts, didn't know what precognition was, and had never been accused of having sense let alone extra senses. So why was a dead woman bugging me? The question alone sounded batty, but really, why? That was just the first question. There were plenty of others even without the spooky malarkey. Like... Someone had gone to the trouble to kill my client's wife. Why? Who gained? Gained what? Why had whoever it was dropped twenty cents for the call and tossed me to the cops as a great place to start their investigation? Who gained there? I'd bounced Wenders with a wink on his first try at me but I was fooling myself if I thought that would be the end of it. He'd be back all right and, if I didn't have real answers then, he'd climb up my keister with a microscope. I needed those answers fast. But, outside of the knowledge that some sheik named Nicholas Nikitin had swung his scimitar in Katherine's bedroom on the night of the murder, I didn't have any more than the cops did. And, as she was alive and swimming in after-glow when Nikitin left, I had nothing at all. The pictures I'd taken, which at the moment felt like wasted film, were the only place I had to start. But if they wound up being of any value as evidence in a murder case, I was committing a felony by not turning them over. I had to find out if they told me anything. The only way I could do that, and not let it out that they existed, was to show them to the one group of people that might want to keep them as tight a secret as I did.

I parked, stepped from the car with my photo envelope, and approached the monstrous edifice that was Delp's Temple of Majesty Church. I gave myself a once over, as if that might help, but I belonged in a church like a seal belongs running the 100 meter hurdles. The tops of my shoes were my shiniest spot and they were just okay. Doubting they had a floor mat absorbent enough to wipe my soul on, they'd have to take the rest of me as it came – plenty scuffed up. Finding the front doors locked, I began a search around the outside of the building and, finally, spotted Gina Bridges through an office window. Even with the glare on the glass trying to horn in, she was yummy.

As my last incident of window peeping hadn't turned out so well, I cut this one short and rapped to get her attention. I have to say she looked as good startled as she did serene. She pointed behind me, indicating the doors I'd just left, and headed out of the office. I backtracked and met her out front. She let me in, then led me in, to a cavernous foyer that made the offices of Blake Investigations look like a clothes closet. It would have been foreboding had it not been so brightly painted. The church secretary, on the other hand, looked tired rather than bright. Still tired never looked so good.

"Mr. Blake." She stopped and went back, correcting herself without my help. "Blake." She seemed surprised to see me there and not all that pleased. Who could blame her? She also seemed lost for what to say next. Her luscious mouth hung uselessly open a moment before she finally managed, "What can I do for you?"

"Actually, Miss Bridges, I came to see Reverend Delp."

Her surprise shifted immediately to defensiveness. "He isn't here."

"Do you know where I could find him?"

She scowled, her eyes silently asking whether or not I understood English. "I'm sure you can understand," she said, "The Reverend is indisposed. You've heard about his wife, I imagine?"

"Certainly I've heard. That's what I need to talk with him about."

"With the exception of the police, he isn't seeing anyone this morning. I can't disturb him. If there's any way at all that I can help?"

"I do understand," I assured her. "You may or may not be able to help me. But, if you can, I warn you the subject matter is confidential and, more than that, extremely unpleasant."

"Yes, of course. Everything this morning is unpleasant." She tried to smile but came up short.

"Please, come in." She led me to her office. Like her, the room was attractive (framed photos on every wall) without frilly adornments. Still I felt cut off from the real world. Her first question, after offering a chair, deepened the feeling. "Can you tell me, please, what went wrong?"

"Wrong? If you mean what went wrong with our surveillance, the answer is nothing. The way I understood the job, a watch was to be kept on Mrs. Delp, without her being aware. I was to ensure she was safe at home and, when she went to sleep, I was done. Is that correct?"

She nodded. "Yes, of course."

"Then everything was hunky-dory on my end. Mrs. Delp turned out the lights at 2:40 am and went to bed, safe and sound. Then I left."

"There was no trouble during the evening?"

"Ahh," I said. "That would depend upon your definition of trouble. But, and I mean no offense, I really shouldn't be discussing this with you. It's a private matter for Mr. Delp."

"Reverend Delp," she said, correcting me in no uncertain terms. "I'm Reverend Delp's private secretary. I am a part of everything said or done for, to, or concerning the Reverend and the Temple of Majesty Ministries. I am, I assure you, the chief guardian of his privacy. I'm the one that hired you."

"All right," I said with a shrug. "You've convinced me." It was no skin off my nose. "So, you were aware then that Mrs. Delp was seeing someone?"

She didn't scream, run in circles, or puke, but if I had to guess I'd say the sudden widening of her eyes was genuine surprise. "What do you mean 'seeing someone'?" she asked. That ruined it.

I smiled, because though she was starting to annoy me she was still well worth smiling at, and told her, "You can't have it both ways, Miss Bridges. I can try to phrase things like a gentleman and you can get the hints. Or I can just tell you where the bear craps in the woods and you can deal with the cold facts. But you can't insist I tell you everything and be obtuse at the same time. It's a waste of time trying to wake up someone that's pretending to be asleep. I'm asking if you were aware that Mrs. Delp was having an affair?"

"But you must be mistaken. Katherine Delp was…"

"Pulling the wool over your eyes, apparently," I said. I'm a crumby politician. It's nothing to me if folks construct opinions out of baloney and air but I see no point in arguing facts. I opened the envelope, extracted several of my favorite photos of Katherine and her lover, and held them out to the woman who'd hired me (or, at least, hired my secretary).

She hesitated before taking them. The tiny crow's feet at the corners of her green eyes, visible no doubt because she was exhausted, burgeoned into claws as she squinted to make sense of what she was seeing. I heard an intake of air and her mouth became an O as recognition dawned. Katherine Delp had apparently succeeded in keeping her secret because, sisters and brothers, Gina Bridges was experiencing genuine shock. I'd have bet the old homestead on it. She squeaked an, "Oh, my heavens," or something along those lines, but didn't go beyond the first picture. She just stared at it in horror as if I'd handed her a road-kill skunk. She closed her eyes, turned and wandered, still clutching the photographs, to the wall of windows beyond her desk. I don't know when she opened her peepers for sure but she must have because she stopped before she hit the glass. A silence fell over us like a pall and I let it lay there. Finally, with a dry throat, she croaked, "This was taken last night?"

"Yes."

"How…" Still staring out at the luxurious landscape, she took a moment to generate some spit then tried it again. "How could you?"

"How could I?" I felt for her, I really did, but I had to stifle a laugh. "Miss Bridges, I apologize for what might be a shocking revelation…" If she noticed I'd just questioned her veracity, she didn't show it. "But," I continued, "I think you're bright enough to appreciate I was put in a rather uncomfortable position myself. Now, you need to either focus on the here and now or you need to tell me where I can find Reverend Delp because I have a couple of questions that require answers."

She squared her shoulders, lifted her head, and said, "Of course," still staring outside.

"Are those pictures of Mrs. Delp?"

"They were taken at her house weren't they?"

"Yes. But I never met her."

"You're right," she said turning back to me. "I'm sorry." She took a breath and forced an answer. "Yes, that's Katherine."

"And her friend? Do you know him?"

"His name is Nicholas Nikitin."

"How do you know Nicholas Nikitin?"

"We just called him Nick."

"How do you know Nick?"

"He's a member of our local congregation." She stopped herself. "He was a member, I mean. He worked part time as our bookkeeper. He left the church four or five months ago. No one was really sure why." She shook the pictures in her hand without looking at them. "I guess now I know."

I stepped forward and gently relieved her of the burdensome images. No sense giving her the opportunity to rid the world of pornography at my expense. I slid the photographs back into the envelope and asked, "You didn't know about the affair?"

"Of course not. I never could have... Nobody knew."

"You can't really know that, can you?" I asked. "Maybe if I could speak to Reverend Delp?"

"No! You couldn't. Not with this. Not now."

"You don't think he knows?"

"Of course he doesn't know!"

"He'll have to be told. The police will have to be told."

"They don't know about this? About Nick? About these pictures?"

"No one knows any of it, yet."

"Blake, please let me to tell him." She approached as she spoke, took my arm in both of her hands, and I'm here to tell you it was like getting an electrical shock. She let go almost immediately, hesitating just long enough that I had to wonder whether or not I'd imagined it. Then she went on as if she hadn't cardioverted me. "The Reverend, I mean. Please let me tell him. It would be better."

"All right," I said. I was still inexplicably shaken. I cleared my throat and found my balance. "But it will have to be soon. I'll have to let the police know about this soon. And I will need to speak to the reverend myself."

"Of course. I'll arrange that as soon as he's able."

"Thank you. Now… I need to switch subjects, if you don't mind. You told my secretary that the reverend had been threatened. That he'd been getting threatening letters. Could I see those letters?"

She thought about it. "Of course. I haven't any idea where they are but I'll speak with Reverend Delp and get them for you as soon as I can."

"Please do." With that, having done all of the damage I could for the moment, I let Miss Bridges show me from her office and back to the vestibule.

If Frank Wenders were to discover I had photos of his latest murder victim, on the night of her death, having sex with a gentleman without the benefit of a conjugal connection, and that I'd failed to turn them over to him, he'd have come down on me with every ounce of his considerable weight. If he'd known that I not only had them but was showing them to others he'd have just shot me. Showing them to Gina Bridges had been a risk and admittedly I'd wound up with little for taking it. But I did at least now know for certain who the first set of players were as the identities of Katherine Delp and Nicholas Nikitin had been confirmed. I had to hope, for the present, that embarrassment and potential ruin for the Temple church might help Miss Bridges, and Delp once he knew, to keep my secret. With this on my mind, I was actually surprised when the church secretary paused on the way out.

"Mr. Blake…"

"Blake," I corrected (unhappy that we'd regressed).

"Blake," she said as we reached the doors, "about those pictures; a scandal could ruin the Delp Ministries."

"I'm sure it could," I agreed. She was staring at me with something like fear in her eyes and it suddenly dawned she was questioning my veracity. I smiled to show her we were all on the same team. "I think I started this conversation by telling you it was confidential. I assure you, Miss Bridges, I am the soul of discretion. It's part of my business."

"Part?"

"Yes. I'm also partial to the truth. If you're worried about me showing them to anyone, I'm not ready to do that. If you're worried about me blackmailing the reverend or the church, shake your head real hard, the feeling will go away. I'm too busy and too lazy to be a blackmailer. Delp hired me and he's going to get a bill; per diem and expenses, including film and developing. I don't charge for content. When the case is finished, the photographs are his to do with as he pleases."

"But I don't understand. Your case is finished, isn't it?"

"If that's what you call a joke," I told her. "I don't get it. This case has only just begun."

Chapter Six

I entered my office, feeling behind schedule as usual, shouting directions over my shoulder as I passed Lisa's desk. "Get a hold of Large," I told her, referring to a friend and informant of mine who was all that his name implied, plus nosy, who on occasion gave me a hand with everything from threading administrative needles to poking into lions' dens with a stick. "Have him check with his mole in the Department of Corrections, will you? See if they have any history on a Nicholas Nikitin; N – I – K – I – T – I – N."

Lisa pushed her glasses up on her nose, pushed a pizza-by-the-slice box to the corner of her desk, began scribbling atop her pile and, through masticated pepperoni and cheese, asked, "Is he Russian?"

"I don't know. He sounds it. Maybe Large can tell us."

"Right."

"Then see if Willie Banks has been bailed out yet." I paused at the door to my office. "If he has, get a hold of him and get him over here. His car is already drawing flies and I expect peasants with pitchforks soon. Tell him to get it off my lot."

"Right." She held up a fistful of pink and blue note slips. "Do you want your messages from this morning?"

"Are any of them reporting this building on fire?"

"No."

"Then, no." I pointed at her phone. "Large. Tell him I need speed."

"Wenders didn't look happy this morning."

I didn't know if she was changing the subject in order to stop me or stopping me in order to change the subject. It didn't matter. I'm not an ogre, I paused again. "How does Wenders not looking happy make today different from every other day?"

She ducked the question and asked another. "Are you in trouble again?"

"I think I should resent that."

"That was a non-denial denial."

I gave her the stare, made a noise of derision, slipped into my office, and closed the door. I poked the speed dial button on my phone as I sat.

It was answered uptown in the DMV's office. "Illinois Department of Motors Vehicles. This is Miss Laney, how can I help you?" Though we'd dealt with each other on and off for years over the phone, Kellie Laney and I had never actually met. It was probably just as well. She had a voice as warm as a melted cheese sandwich and, with the images I'd created in my head, meeting her, even if she was a knock-out, might be a letdown for me and surely would have been for her.

"How's your love life?"

"You would be the last one I'd tell," she said. "What are you doing, Blake? I heard they pulled your license and threw you out of the city."

"They will when they catch me. But that is neither here nor there. Right now I need a favor, beautiful."

"That's obvious, you called."

"It hurts when you talk that way."

"What do you want, you pest?"

"You. But you're holding out on me."

"And will continue to do so. Now that that's settled, anything else?"

"I need the skinny on a Nicholas Nikitin."

"Nicholas," she repeated. I could hear typing. "N – I – K..."

"I – T – I – N. Nikitin."

"Is he a bad man?" Laney asked.

"Aren't we all?"

"You don't even want to go there," she said. My cheese sandwich had gone cold. "When's dinner?" she added. "You've been promising me a dinner for two years. You still owe me."

"Of course I do. The anticipation *is* the excitement," I told her. She made a noise. "Hey, that's not nice. I was sincere."

"You sincere?" She made another noise. "Are you ready?"

I grabbed a pen. "Ye-ah, more than ready." She talked and I scribbled – all that she had. "Thanks, doll face." She asked a question and I couldn't help but wonder if some weird new club was forming. "Well, yes," I answered. "Now that you ask, I do think I'm Humphrey Bogart."

She must have been a Bogie fan and, based upon where she told me I could go, must have known he'd starred in King of the Underworld. I decided not to ask, offered a simple "*Uh huh*" in reply, and quietly set down the receiver.

*

I entered the lobby of the swanky Lake Shore Apartments building just off Lake Shore Drive; the address I'd found on the vehicle registration of the virile Nicholas Nikitin, now verified by Kellie Laney. Locked glass doors and a humorless security guard stood between me and the elevators. She was short, square, and bumping fifty hard enough to break bones; everything I loved in a woman. I waved to her and smiled, making it clear I offered no threat and that she'd probably really enjoy my company. Without any indication she was convinced or that we'd established a life-long friendship, she buzzed me in.

"Hey, how are you?" I asked approaching the desk. "I'm looking for a tenant, Nicholas Nikitin."

Glowering beneath a protruding forehead and a single eyebrow, the guard said, "We don't give out tenant information."

I brightened the smile. "Not even for me?"

"Who do you think you are?" she asked staring icicles, "Sam Elliott? We don't give out tenant information."

"Well, of course you don't. I'm not looking for information, just your tenant." I handed her a business card. "I'm Mark Pullman," I lied, "Illinois State Lottery. Nikitin is a multimillion dollar winner and he hasn't responded to our letters. Guys a millionaire, but doesn't answer his mail."

"Really?" Finally, life in her eyes. "A millionaire, here? Damn!"

"You said it. I go home every night to an arthritic dog and a wife and dinner that are both frozen."

She scowled. "We all got problems."

Ah, the motherly type. "Sure, but before I go home to my problems, I spend my whole day handing out four, five, and six figure checks to complete strangers."

"Yeah, that would suck. What d'you say this guy's name is?"

"Nikitin. Nick Nikitin. Course, now he's a millionaire, he'll probably stick with Nicholas."

The guard began to hunt and peck on her computer keyboard. "No. He ain't here. Wait a minute." More hunting. More pecking. The green screen didn't help her sour complexion. "Yeah.

No wonder I don't know him. He moved out six months ago. How long ago did he win?"

"I've been looking for a while. In fact, he's about to expire. You know, if you don't claim your winnings in a year, it's bye-bye winnings. You wouldn't have a forwarding address, would you? I know it's probably breaking the rules but, if he knew you helped him out, and if you wanted I could let him know that, and then he'd probably show his appreciation."

"Sure." She looked again and, a minute later, though it couldn't afford to, her face fell. "No. Nothing." She was disappointed but not nearly as much as I was. I thanked her pleasantly, escaped the confines of the glass cage, and paused outside to consider my next move.

Chapter Seven

I was back at the office before I planned or wanted to be with absolutely nothing to show for my sortie. Willie's car was still in my lot. I entered, pushed through to the outer office and stopped at Lisa's desk. The cupcake she was eating looked good, chocolate cake, chocolate frosting, but the two-cake package on her desk was already empty and it was, presumably, the second of the pair she was making short work of. Oh, well.

"Any luck finding Nikitin?" she asked, through creamy filling.

"About as much as you had finding Willie Banks," I said. "But, moving on, I had a thought. You said your mother taped the Delp television crusades. Would she let me borrow those tapes?"

She looked at me like I'd grown a third eye. "Getting religion, Blake?"

"Not just yet."

"Good." I did a take, but let it go. Sometimes it was best to just let it go. "He's supposed to be on television tonight," Lisa said, making the last of the cupcake vanish like she was Harry Blackstone Jr.

"Who's supposed to be on television tonight?"

"Who were we talking about? Delp. He has a special on tonight. Mother's probably already making her popcorn."

"Really?" That was interesting. The guy hadn't been able to see me that morning because he was indisposed by his wife's death. But he wasn't so far gone he couldn't preach tonight. Call me cynical, or just hard to convince, but I wasn't overwhelmed by his show of grief. Still, as the vice-president of the Solomon family's Reverend Delp fan club was right there in front of me, I kept my doubts to myself. "I'll have to tune in," I told Lisa. "Don't forget to ask your mom about those tapes for me."

The telephone rang as I headed into my office. I shut the door, and just got sat down, when Lisa opened it again and poked in her head. "Miss Bridges is on the phone."

"Thank you."

"You know, if you put in an intercom, you'd save me a lot of time, not to mention the wear and tear on my shoes."

"I also know that if I got rid of you and hired an answering service, though it would send Hostess into bankruptcy, I'd save me a lot of money, not to mention the wear and tear on my last nerve."

Lisa turned, mumbled something about me being "No Mike Connors," and left, closing the door behind her.

I picked up the phone. "Blake. Yes, Miss Bridges." She was calling to let me know she'd broken the awful news about Nicholas and Katherine to the good reverend. "How did he take it?" She didn't like that question a bit and told me so. "I'm not implying anything, Miss Bridges, I'm asking questions. That's what I do, I ask questions."

There was a good long pause while she sorted out how she wanted to deal with the disagreeable detective. At least that's what I guessed was happening. She finally put forward a demurrer, saying she didn't intend to discuss Reverend Delp's personal life on the telephone. I apologized, assuring her my secretary would be firmly spoken to because I'd been led to believe that she, Miss Bridges, had called me. There followed another long pause. Hell, you might as well hear the rest yourself.

"You're doing this on purpose, I suppose?"

"Miss Bridges?"

"Being objectionable. You're doing it on purpose for some reason?"

I considered the first rule of being a detective (and staying alive): admit nothing, deny everything, demand proof. The poor thing was struggling to deal with me and she wasn't the Lone Ranger there. I took pity on her. "I'm not being purposefully objectionable," I assured her. "But let's start over."

"All right," she agreed. "The real reason for my call, Blake... Reverend Delp has asked me to secure your services to find Nick Nikitin."

That set my nerves a-twitching. "Has the reverend spoken with the police since you and I last talked?"

"Well, yes. They've spoken, briefly."

Oh Christ. I'd just gotten her back in the buggy and now this. I hated to even ask, but I needed to know if the cat was out of the bag. "If he's told them about Katherine's affair," I said, "the police are already looking for Nick. You won't need me. I couldn't compete with their manpower." I kept it to myself that the coppers were probably already on their way to scoop me up and toss me in the can.

"He hasn't told them," she said.

"He hasn't?"

"No. He hasn't."

I started breathing again. "Nothing about the photographs or the..."

"The Reverend didn't mentioned the... situation you brought to our attention. The situation we're not going to talk about on the phone. He agreed with you. In fact, the Reverend thought that if you found Nick first, before the police..."

"That things could be wrapped up more quietly?" Her silence told me I was right. It also told me my execution at the hands of an irate Lieutenant Wenders had perhaps been postponed. "All right," I told her. "I can certainly try to find him. But, failing that," *sigh*, "the police may have to be notified."

"That's a last resort?"

"I can assure you on that. You wouldn't happen to have an address for Nikitin?"

"I checked," she said. "He was living at the Lake Shore Apartments."

I thought of a curse word. "Is that the most current address?"

"Yes, for him. But his emergency contact information has an address for his brothers, John and Mike Nikitin, sharing a place on Racine Avenue. I don't know if that's up-to-date either."

"Could you give me that address?" I scribbled the number down. "All right, Miss Bridges, I'll take a look."

That's when the change came. That's when, in a voice that came right out of the oven, she told me to call her Gina. If we were going to be working together, she said, closely together, I should definitely call her Gina. How could I not? She asked what she should call me, assuming, I guess, the relationship had changed on this end of the line as well. Maybe it had and maybe it hadn't. Maybe it would and maybe it wouldn't. But I told her, with a smile in my voice, that Blake was working out just peachy for me. She took it like a trooper.

I hung up and opened the door to the outer office. "Lisa, I'll need another contract drawn up for Delp." She shot me one of her patented looks, made all the more questioning by her huge glasses. "He's hiring me again," I told her, "to look for Nick Nikitin."

"You're already looking for Nick Nikitin."

"Right. In which case I might as well let someone else pay for it."

She shrugged her thin shoulders. "Can't argue with that. By the way," she said, "you were so fast with the sarcasm earlier, you didn't give me a chance to tell you; Willie Banks is still a guest of the tax-payers. His mother wanted to know if you could drop his car off at her place."

"You told her, No, right?"

"Sort of."

I leaned against the door frame, sorry before I even asked, "What do you mean, sort of?"

"Well, actually, I told her, yes."

*

Clouds encircled me as if I was a god. That's the way it will be when they draw the comic book of my life. Actually, I was just a down-and-out detective arriving in Willie's smoking, piece of crap car. I'd gotten a ridiculous, time-saving idea of killing two birds with one stone and had decided to take the wrecked Mustang back to Mother Bank's place, with a stop en route on Racine Avenue to flush Nicholas Nikitin out of the weeds. I'd checked with the city and found the house jointly owned by Iancu and Mikhail (Americanized as John and Mike) Nikitin; Nicholas' older brothers.

As I climbed out of Willie's wreck, coughed, fanned the gray air, and started across the street, a hand parted the front window blinds. I saw it, but acted as if I hadn't and headed for the front door. As I climbed the steps, I heard a side door slam and caught a glimpse of someone bolting through the back yard. He looked a whole lot like Nick Nikitin (though I didn't know him well with his clothes on). With a not particularly well thought out shout of, "Hey," I took after him.

For the rest of the telling, I might as well get on a first name basis with the guy. After all, once I'm chasing you, we're friends. Nicholas jumped the wooden fence at the rear of the property.

I went over the fence after him and found myself in a gravel alley between the back yards of two residential blocks; poorly kept fences, grass that needed mowing, several unseen dogs barking. To my left, Nicholas was on the hop, shoe soles and elbows. He appeared to be just as good a runner as he was a sexual swordsman and I didn't have a Chinaman's chance in hell of catching him. So, of course, I took off after him again. At the end of the alley, he turned the corner to the right and vanished from sight behind a garage. I got there, turned the same corner, and was immediately struck in the face by what was probably a meaty fist. Not that I knew for sure, not that it mattered in the slightest. What mattered for me was, despite it being the middle of a bright sunny day, the lights went out.

Chapter Eight

It would be inaccurate to say I woke up. I hadn't been asleep, I had been unconscious; knocked colder than a big daddy cat at the Delta Fish Market (without the dreamy blues jams). Believe me, sisters and brothers, the two were not the same. I guess the best way to put it was, *I came to*, to discover I was no longer in an alley.

I didn't move. It took a few minutes to get my bearings, to figure out I wasn't dead, to recall what had happened during my last seconds of consciousness, to put two and two together and guess where I was now. I let it. *Ooohh.* I was on my back, being swallowed by couch cushions that had all-but given up the ghost, in a gloomy living room. It was late afternoon or early evening; muted amber rays of an approaching dusk were stealing in through carelessly closed blinds and curtains. My vision was foggy from the blow I'd taken and partially blocked by a plastic bag of ice balanced on my beak. Instead of a blues combo, there was an army of percussionists in my head, shivering from the cold, fighting their way through a confused arrangement of Fleetwood Mac's *Tusk*. The walls of my noggin throbbed to the beat. I moved my bottom lip to groan only to find it was split, as big as one of Charo's boobs, and caked in dried blood. My teeth were bloodied too. My mouth tasted of iron and felt like cotton. I'm not a doctor, but if I hadn't already had a concussion when I'd arrived, I had one now.

"Wait," someone anxiously declared. "Look. He is awake." The observation proved two things. One, I hadn't regained consciousness in the middle of a Mensa meeting. And two, the speaker was a foreigner, Russian probably, eastern European certainly. He had a screwy accent with his w's sounding like v's, his o's like u's. ("Vait. Luke. He is a-vake.") That's the last time I spell it for you. You know what Russians sound like and these two were, put it in yourself.

I turned to the speaker and the ice bag toppled from my face. I paused, pretty much regretting I was still alive, and slowly opened my eyes. A matching pair of gorillas hovered above me. I didn't know them from Adam but a silly wild-assed guess told me they were Nicholas Nikitin's brothers. I would soon discover I had been made a guest, of sorts, in their clean but sparse two-story home.

It will stun you to realize that between this and my last bout of laying battered in the dirt I had actually found a moment or two to do some investigating and to chat with my snoops. Digging into the Department of Corrections, Large had come up blank on Nick Nikitin (he'd never been convicted of anything here). Digging elsewhere, my immense informer had snagged a lot of ancillary details about his family, including corroboration that Mike, the middle brother, and John, the eldest, were co-owners of the house on Racine where I was currently laid out. I called in chits from several other associates that know a lot about some things and a little about everything, gathering facts and rumors as time allowed. Nothing startling surfaced. Nikitin's older brothers kept a low profile. They were union iron workers, and looked it. The only real difference between them, I was led to understand, other than a calendar year, was their tempers. Mike was supposedly a reasonable human being while

John, it was said, was a prick. Lying on their couch I couldn't tell them apart but, it occurred, if I got under their skins they would quickly show me which was which.

"Who are you?" one of them asked.

I made an attempt to sit but the old pain in the back of my head, coupled with the new pain in my nose, attached to the other pains running from my hair to my knees, was excruciating. (Oddly, for once, my feet *didn't* hurt.) I settled back into the couch wallow and took a breath. The place was okay for a couple of bachelors; nothing special, clean carpets, recently painted walls dotted with framed pictures of these two apes and young Nicholas on a beach, in a gym, at a lake, in the snow...

The question came again, demanded in a growl. "I said, who are you?"

I gritted my teeth and, despite the pain, tried again and kept at it until I was sitting. I'd been right. Everything hurt but my feet. I took another breath, inhaling deeply, held it as long as I could, and then exhaled. The one barking at me was wearing a green polo shirt. "You first," I said, returning his stare.

His reddening face clashed with the shirt. "We are asking the questions."

The other one wore a yellow button-down. "You have forty different identifications here," he said calmly. "Do you mind telling us which one you are?"

"Mind hell!" Green shirt growled. "Who are you?"

Voilà, kids. Have you located the prick yet?

I turned from John's livid eyes to Mike's curious ones. Mike pointed with his Landjäger finger to a worn coffee table. There the contents of my pockets; keys, receipts, a stick of gum, a wad of money (a small wad, mostly singles), and my wallet, and its contents; a PI's license, driver's license, and FOID card in my name, two dozen IDs ranging from attic insulator to zoo guard with my picture and a grab bag of phoney names (I never know who I'll have to be), and the hastily scribbled phone number of a cocktail waitress at the Cape Cod Room on the Gold Coast who talks naughty when she's horizontal, lay spread out and gone through. I frowned. "I feel so violated."

"What is your fucking name?"

Hearing the F-bomb in a Russian accent was precious. Then again, maybe it was just the effect of the yelling on my headache. "Blake. I'm a private dick on a case."

John grunted. "Not much of one by the car you are driving."

I screwed my eyes up wondering what he was talking about. Then it dawned, I'd come in Willie's crap Ford. John was a jerk but I couldn't argue with his acute assessment of automobiles. That being the case, I changed the subject. "You got a tissue?"

Mike lifted a box of Kleenex. I took one and dabbed at my nose. He tossed the box on the table in front of me. "What do you want?" he asked.

"With you; nothing."

John grunted again. "He thinks he is Arnold Schwarzenegger." He was wrong. Whoever Arnold was, I'd never heard of the guy. But I digress. John was still growling. "He wants another ass whipping, yes, smart guy?"

"No, thank you," I said. "I'm real satisfied with the last one." I slowly started to push my cards back into my wallet. It was tougher than you'd think on account of one minute there was one wallet and the next there were two. Blinking helped a little.

"You are looking for Nick?" Mike asked. I nodded. "What do you want with Nick?"

"That's between me and Nick."

"We should kill this smart son of bitch."

I'm telling you, precious. But not impressive. To show it, I gave John my coldest stare; both of him. Then I blinked until there was only one. Trust me, one Iancu Nikitin was enough. I cracked my neck (The sound always gets them and, to be honest, my neck needed it). "You don't look like the killing type to me," I told him and added, "Then again neither did Nick. Unless I'm wrong?"

Mike jumped in, excited, "Nick did not kill anybody!"

"Then I'm not wrong!" *Oohh.* My yelling wasn't helping either. "So how about we three tough guys let the tide go out on the testosterone, huh? Let's figure out what's going on."

"You say you are private investigator? For who?" John was shouting again. "Who hired you?"

"The names of my clients are confidential and
_"

"Who hired you?"

I took a deep breath and started over. "The names of my clients are confidential and completely beside the point, John. Or do you prefer Iancu?" I turned to the other. "And while we're at it, is it Mikhail or Mike?"

"How do y-you..." he stammered. "How do you know our names?"

"I told you, I'm a private investigator."

"Then why did you ask who we were?"

"It's the first rule of being a detective: ask questions to which you already know the answers. It's a quick way to find out if you're talking to a liar. Now can we skip the lessons? I already told you, I don't think your brother killed anybody. That's why I need to talk to him."

The reasonable one, who did go by Mike by the way, asked, "Are the police looking for Nick?"

"They don't know about him yet. They'll have his prints and eh samples of his work but, with no police record, those will lead nowhere for the time being."

"What are you talking about?" John bellowed.

"Forget it. The cops are investigating the Delp murder and Nick's name will eventually surface. That's why he should stop running and talk to me. I'm looking for the real killer. If that isn't Nick, and I don't think it is, I might be able to help him. Running is a miserable way to prove he's not guilty."

We talked for a while longer but, sadly, didn't end the conversation with any great meeting of the minds. The brothers Nikitin were more worried about Nick than they were trusting of me. Nothing I said altered that to any great extent. The best I managed was a promise from them that they'd talk to Nick and, maybe, get back to me. I left them a card with my real name and number. Then I departed in Willie's smoke-belching rattle trap with a brand spanking new set of aches and pains. All in all, it had been a mostly fruitless but memorable visit. As far as I could see, the only thing I'd gained with any certainty was more brain damage.

*

Aware that I was fresh out of bandages and alcohol, both isopropyl and distilled, I did some quick shopping (ignoring the alarmed stares of my fellow consumers and the cashier's helpful suggestion, "Ya' better put somethin' on that, man," as she grimaced at my face). I'd had every minute of that day I could stand and decided then and there to skip a stop at the office. To soothe my conscience, I found a phone booth and called Lisa, who stopped chewing long enough to assure me nothing was happening. Relieved, I told her I was headed home and that she could lock up and go play. I wasn't hungry but, as I hadn't eaten, knew I'd better put something in my gut. To prove I'm never too sore or tired to make another bad decision, I cruised the drive-through of a greasy spoon. My teeth hurt all the way to my heels so I ordered a cup of soup and told them to hold the crackers. They wouldn't open the window because of the smoke from Willie's car and, aching as I was, I had to park and walk inside to be handed my drive-through. Yeah, another rare day. I dragged back to my apartment with my soup, fully intending to give myself indigestion just before I died.

No sooner did I set the soup down than the wisp of an idea struck me. I could tell right away the notion was going to nag until I did something about it. I left my supper go cold to start searching. Failing to find what I was after in my apartment, and determined to pick at the thread in my brain, I ventured into the hall and started rapping on my neighbors' doors. The details of the next few minutes aren't important, just the results, and they were; one slammed door, one "Go away" shouted through a door that never opened, three silent glares of varied description and uncertain meaning, one invitation to tea and whiskey from a woman old enough to be my mother (It couldn't have been my mother; she doesn't share her whiskey) and, finally, one unabridged copy of The Holy Scriptures. Before you laugh too hard, just know, that's what I was after. Yeah, I needed a Bible. I hadn't been able to find mine, assuming I still had it there someplace, and needed to borrow one. I probably could have done better, faster, had I not forgotten I'd just come from my meet and greet with the Nikitin brothers. Next time I visit my neighbors, I'll wash the dried blood off my gob first.

Later, leaning over my bathroom sink, being watched by the frightening reflection in the mirror, I polished my lip with rubbing alcohol and screamed like a colicky baby. Having caused as much pain there as I could, I moved on, dabbing my nose with a washcloth. That was fun too. Finished and satisfied I'd live, I headed down the short hall.

Melodic choir song (yeah, you heard right), the sound of a singing church choir filled my small living room, over-stuffed with books, a computer with accoutrement, television and video equipment, and rumpled clothes. Atop the island, separating the living room from the economy kitchen, sat a glass of gin and, already open, the Bible I'd borrowed from the neighbor. I don't think I'm overstating it to say that, when the idea hit me, a light went on in my battered brain. What could I do but follow it to the end of the tunnel? I scooped up both on the way to the couch. I sat, gently, studying the scripture text, sipping my gin, and mulling my notion.

I paused, thinking (if you can believe that), then turned my attention to the television screen. There, a small group of people, surrounded by an impressively large audience, oc-cupied a platform beneath a boldly colored ban-ner reading: Temple of Majesty. That's where the choir music was coming from. Behind the speak-ers' dais, sitting in the center of a row of folding metal chairs, yet in no uncertain terms standing out from the others around him, was the unde-niably handsome (or as Lisa would have it, kinda hunky) Conrad Delp. A young Latin couple sat immediately to his left looking distracted, to say the least, and not at all a part of the wide-smiling joy being exhibited by the others. On Delp's right looking, I had to admit, absolutely smashing, was Gina Bridges. (Confessions of a sad sack private eye, though it hurt my lip, I smiled too when I saw her.) The chorus finished on an inspira-tional high and Gina rose from her seat. She laid a friendly (maybe more, or was I reading into it?), hand on Reverend Delp's shoulder then ap-proached the dais and the microphone.

"Praise God for that joyful noise," she said. The crowd laughed pleasantly and applauded. "It's wonderful to be back home," Gina contin-ued, "and it's wonderful to be a party to bringing you something... someone very special. It is my privilege to say, ladies and gentleman, the Reverend Conrad Delp."

They traded places. Gina, and the others on the platform now standing, joined the audience in thunderous applause as Delp, all quiet dignity, took to the microphone. He cleared his throat. Then his voice rang out with a tenor that would have humbled Cecil B. DeMille. "There has been a tremendous outpouring for me in my grief. Many personal gestures and much love sent my way; and I appreciate them all. There are those astonished by my determination to go on with this service. There are those in awe that I stand before you tonight. My grief weighs heavy on my heart. My pain runs deeper than you can know. All I can offer as an explanation for my ability to carry on is the 9th chapter of Luke, verses 59 and 60." And he quoted, " 'He said to another man, 'Follow me.' But the man replied, 'Lord, first let me go and bury my father.' Jesus said to him, 'Let the dead bury their own dead, but you go and proclaim the kingdom of God.' "

That was it for me. I gave a fleeting thought to Lisa's mother gushing over that self-aggrandizing schmaltz and shook my head. I didn't have anything against the scripture. It didn't sound pompous coming from Jesus, but Delp gave it a twist... Okay, I didn't know the guy from Adam, and maybe he was *all that* to those in on the joke, but he sanded me against the grain. I shut the television off. I hit Stop on the video recording I was making, then Eject and pulled the tape from the machine. I weighed it in my hand, thinking harder, then tossed it on the coffee table. It had been an interesting, if not particularly informative, first day on the Katherine Delp murder case. My head was throbbing (front and back). I gulped my gin and, frowning, refilled my glass.

Chapter Nine

The Bible and I had been strangers since the Sunday School classes of my youth went into storage in the seldom visited halls of my memory. There may or may not be a song in that but it was true all the same. My notion, as mentioned, to wander back into scripture after all those years surprised me as much as it could have anyone. I'm relieved to report the exercise did not appear to have been in vain. My reading had shown a light unto my path which, in turn, stirred additional late night activity on my part; the kind of activity that often spurred new questions. The next morning found me pulling back into the parking lot of Delp's church intent on getting some answers.

I should, I imagine, give you just a brief description of Reverend Delp's Temple of Majesty. You've already been there once without it but, now I've settled into the telling, it might help. But how to go about it? How does one briefly describe the treasures of Egypt? The Hope Dia-

mond? The Holy Grail? I could tell you it was impressive but that would miss the mark. It was imposing; overwhelming. It would have been awe-
inspiring were it not for the first rule of detecting: always remain fresh out of awe; it's health-
ier. Still, that's why I saved this until the second visit, to help you feel a little of what I felt
every time I stopped. The eye was immediately
drawn, no matter the direction of your approach,
to the looming skyline. Unlike every other Chris-
tian church in the city, the Temple did not have
a spire or bell tower, it had a dome as if it belonged in the center of power in Washington
and, towering over this, *three* spires. The combination was an architect's recreation of Calvary
with the dome standing in for the hill outside of
Jerusalem's wall. The tallest spire, at center, represented the cross upon which Christ was crucified and the shorter outer spires those of the
two thieves who died at his sides. Below, the
campus was a landscaper's dream of what the
garden of Gethsemane might have looked like
(had the Jerusalem city council had hundreds
of thousands of dollars to piss away for con-
struction and up-keep); sculpted marble statues,

benches, columns, a lawn mowed in alternating stripes of shamrock and pine green, ash trees and lilacs (Chicago isn't exactly temperate enough for olive trees to thrive). You made your way from the sprawling parking lot along a wide and winding flagstone pathway through the garden. As you neared the church entrance you were made to pass, and wonder at, a huge dark gray boulder. I wouldn't know a Middle East import from Lake Michigan rip-rap but a shiny fixed plaque insisted this represented the Rock of the Agony where the Lord prayed, and his disciples failed him, before his arrest. Certainly beautiful… and even more certainly, for me, all a bit much.

My presence was decidedly incongruous as I coaxed Willie's car into the manicured lot. Once again I was on my way to his mother's house, making an attempt to return the damned thing, when I veered off to the home of the Delp ministries with an itch to get those earlier mentioned questions answered. Perhaps it was a metaphor for my soul, or a prelude to any attempt I might make to pass through the Pearly Gates at some distant time; sleek white marble overlooking gold-paved streets, soothing harp music and pious serenity… Then I'd crash the party, sputtering and belching fire.

My appearance was god-awful but my timing couldn't have been better. Gina was in the lot, just climbing from her car, when I arrived back-firing in a cloud of smoke. The initial look on her face was one of mixed shock and amusement but she moved quickly to hide that behind the patented Delp Ministries' smile. She returned to her task, the better not to witness my stutter-ing halt, and opened her back door. I abandoned Willie's ship of fools before it caught fire, fell apart, or exploded, and started toward her, carry-ing a new photo envelope with a different set of pictures. These promised to be less shocking but, I hoped, more revealing. Gina was bent over re-trieving cardboard boxes from her back seat and – let's just say I'm a pig and leave it. I should have been ashamed of myself (but wasn't). Gina rose with her burden of boxes and turned as the smoke cloud from Willie's folly reached us. She coughed and tried unsuccessfully to fan the smoke away. "The detective business a little slow, is it?"

"I'll say," I agreed, stifling a cough myself. "I've been trying to return it to the rightful owner for several days without much luck. Let me give you a hand." Taking care not to bend my envelope, I took a share of her boxes (office supplies, it looked like) and together we started down the stone path for the church. "I saw you on television."

"You did? You don't strike me as someone who watches religious programming."

"Oh, I'm full of surprises."

"I'll just bet you are."

Had it not been for the glint in my eye, I would have sworn I saw one in hers.

We rounded the Rock of the Agony, she on the path to the right, me to the left (what can I say, it's my nature to be different) and met on the other side approaching the doors. She was laughing but, again, tried to hide it. "Any luck finding Nicholas?"

"No." It wasn't really a lie. I'd seen Nick, yes, but I hadn't actually spoken with him. "Not yet. But he's out there somewhere."

With a sympathetic smile, she balanced her boxes atop mine, used her keys, and unsealed the

Holy of Holies. (Sorry if my cynicism is showing.) Inside, Gina relocked it, reclaimed her share of the load, and led us to her office. She placed her boxes on her desk and directed me to a clear spot atop a file cabinet where mine stacked nicely. She thanked me politely, then frowned. "I'm sorry," she said, "I can't get used to just calling you Blake. Please, what is your first name?"

I frowned. Oh well, it was still true, my parents were not her fault. "It's Nod."

She squinted, apparently trying to see it. "Nod? You mean…"

"Nod. My name is Nod, as in a slight affirmative movement of the head. Wynken and Blynken's little brother. Before you ask, no, I neither own nor have I ever sailed the stars in a wooden shoe. And there's no middle name or initial to fall back on. Just Nod Blake." I smiled my special smile, the one with the clamped lips.

Gina's were clamped as well so I couldn't actually see her biting her tongue. "You had fun in school, didn't you?"

"Now you know why I don't use it."

"Well… Blake," she said. "What can I do for you?"

"You can answer a few questions. The first of which is, why was I originally hired?"

Her eyes took on a weary, then a wary, look. "Your secretary and I went over that in detail."

"Yes. But it's in the details that I have a problem, Gina. What exactly did Reverend Delp tell you when he asked you to hire me?"

"He didn't tell me anything." She was searching for words and looked it. "What I mean is Reverend Delp didn't ask me to hire you. Reggie Riaz did."

I didn't yell 'Aha!' like some demented road-company performer doing Sherlock Holmes, but I wanted to. Instead, I merely smiled and asked, "Who is Reggie Riaz?"

"He doesn't have a title so much. He's Reverend Delp's right hand man, I guess you'd say."

"I was told I was hired by the reverend. My secretary was led to believe I was being hired by the reverend."

"Well, I certainly didn't mean to mislead. Reggie told me to hire you. So I hired you."

"To watch Delp's wife?"

"Are you asking if I lied?" To my surprise, she seemed genuinely hurt. To my greater surprise, I noticed. I made a mental note to cut it out then returned my attention to Gina who, though wounded, was putting up a solid front. "I wouldn't do that, Blake. I wouldn't lie to you or anyone. Reggie handles all of Reverend Delp's affairs. Everything he does here, Reggie, I mean, is done in the Reverend's name. He said Reverend Delp wanted you to watch his wife and that's what I told you."

I opened the envelope I'd brought with and withdrew a series of pictures, blow-ups of frozen frames from the crusade, or whatever it was, I'd watched and video-taped the night before. (I'm telling you the new technology was better than melted butter on stove-toasted bread; Betamax, a miracle.) I shuffled the photos, found one I was searching for, and held it up. It was a picture of the auditorium platform upon which all of the event stars went about their work; Delp, Gina, the announcer, the colorfully-robed choir, and the Latin couple I'd noticed at the dog and pony show the previous night. I pointed the last (sour-looking?) pair out, then specifically the young man, applauding from their seats behind Delp. "Is that Reggie?"

Gina looked at the photo, smiled, and nodded. "Yes. Where did you get these?"

"Made them," I said simply, stifling the urge to gush about my video equipment. "Eh about Reggie. I'd like to speak to him."

"Reggie Riaz? Oh I'm sorry, you can't. His sabbatical started today."

"Sabbatical?"

"Yes, he's taking some time off. He and his wife both. Taking time away from his work in the church. Sort of a physical restorative."

"They did look a bit *out of sorts* last night," I said. "Did Reggie ask for time off?"

She hesitated. "Yes, of course. Well, actually, I think it was at Reverend Delp's suggestion."

"What makes you think that?"

She offered an *out of sorts* look of her own. "I don't want to talk out of turn…"

"Gina, I've been hired, twice, by your organization. If I'm to do the job for which I'm hired, I need your cooperation."

"I'm trying to cooperate." She sighed and, I swear, I could see the toys turning in her luscious head. She took a deep breath and, apparently decided, said, "Reggie and Rocio were upset last night at the service."

"Rocio?"

"Mrs. Riaz; Reggie's wife." She pointed at the other half of the couple in the picture. "This one. Something was bothering Reggie and his being upset was bothering his wife. I mean, they were trying to hide it, trying to soldier on, but it showed. Reverend Delp is sensitive to these things. He met with Reggie, here, early this morning. They spoke alone in the Reverend's office. I don't know what was said, but it got a little…"

"Heated?"

She frowned. "I don't want to say that."

"I'm sure you don't," I said. "But is that what it was?"

"It was emotional," she said, forcing the frown away. "Understandably emotional. We're like a family here, Blake. Reggie left without speaking to me but, after, Reverend Delp said he and Rocio would be on sabbatical starting immediately. I think it was generous of the Reverend to consider their needs with all he's going through."

"What kind of person is Reggie Riaz?"

"It's hurtful if you're implying something evil."

"I was simply asking a question."

"Reggie Riaz and his wife are warm, friendly people. They're lovely; neither would harm a fly. I haven't any idea at all what Reggie or the Reverend talked about this morning. But there was no fight, as you seem to want to imply, and there is nothing sinister about the Riazs' taking time off. It's just as likely this sabbatical was already scheduled. I'm certainly not told everything."

"I would like to speak to them," I told her. "Reggie and his wife, as soon as possible."

"All right," she said, though I could still hear the hesitation in her voice.

"At your request," I reminded her, "I'm trying to get somewhere before the police do."

"I'll get in touch with Reggie immediately. I'm sure he and Rocio will both be happy to cooperate. That said, you're aware, I'm also sure, that even providing they haven't already arranged a departure, the soonest they could meet with you would be tomorrow. You do know, Blake, we're burying Katherine Delp this afternoon?"

*

I didn't know where Katherine Delp's soul was but, that afternoon, her mortal remains were on an impressive, aggravating last ride. Super-tramp made it worse, annoying me from my radio with *Take the Long Way Home* while, from behind the wheel in the middle of it all, I could see neither the end nor the beginning of the line of traffic down Irving Park Road. The cars stretched for several miles at least, all the way to hell and back, and finally slowly undulated like some weirdly jointed multicolored snake into and through Graceland Cemetery. I thought of the hundreds (maybe thousands) that had been in that crush for over an hour, wondering how many were actually mourning, how many were merely members of the flock dutifully seeing their fallen shepherdess off, and how many were just licking their lips in anticipation of the free chicken salad.

Graceland, the famous Cemetery of Architects, a sprawling 119 acre Victorian park decorated with, of course, architectural masterpieces, was one of the most beautiful places in Chicago, if you could get over the fact it was a grave-yard. Its permanent residents included Chicago's elite, public figures, baseball and boxing greats (from an era when those were *the* great sports), merchants, inventors, and more renowned architects than you could shake a blueprint at. Like the fabled elephants' graveyard, this was where Chicago's rich and famous came for their final rest. Tens of thousands of on-lookers had followed the body of Carter Harrison (Chicago's most popular mayor) there after his fifth term assassination (you can't be popular with everyone) at the Columbian Exposition in 1893. I wasn't sure how today's numbers compared but, trust me, there was a crowd.

As the cars parked and the throng gathered, I found a discreet distant position from which to watch. A talented girl in a long black gown beautifully played a violin at graveside. It was creepy. I occupied myself by considering what music might have been more appropriate. Billy Joel's *My Life*? The Doobie Brothers' *What a Fool Believes*? I was leaning toward The Knack with a lyrics change; *Good Girls Don't, But I Did* when the strings stopped and the burial ritual began. The service was conducted by a big-wig evangelist flown in from California. I'd seen him and his pomp of white hair on television but didn't know his name and, frankly, didn't care. He stood at the foot of the grave and, around him and the burial plot, the heavy hitters were in attendance; the governor, the police commissioner, the police chief, the fire chief, and all the other chiefs that kept the reservation running. All wore stately black like the powerful back row of a chess board, city officials, representatives of the arts, ministers of every stripe. They were all there. Conspicuous by her absence was our recently elected, highly esteemed fiftieth (and first female) mayor. Who knew, perhaps she was busy attacking the Second Amendment or glad-handing at Cabrini-Green? Maybe Delp hadn't voted for her? Her deputy was there instead looking officially grim. Gina was there, of course, making the color black look like fireworks. Beside her stood the real reason I'd come. I was getting my first look at the Reverend Conrad Delp in the flesh.

Oddly, what I didn't see was either Reggie Riaz or his wife Rocio. They were a no show.

Chapter Ten

"I appreciate your coming down," I said and gestured to the empty chair on the other side of my desk. It was the following morning; the third day of the murder case. "Have a seat."

Reggie Riaz looked thinner in the flesh than on television. I guess the claim the camera adds twenty pounds was true. Otherwise he looked like what he was; a handsome Mexican in his late-twenties, three inches shorter than me with black wavy hair, a thin black mustache, and dark copper skin. He wore a button down shirt, jeans, and an expression that said he'd rather have been anywhere else on earth. My invitation to sit didn't alter that. He stared at the chair as if it were the hot squat; which was silly, Illinois hadn't burned a guy since the early sixties. And, in this town, where you could get a lethal injection standing on the wrong street corner, why worry? Despite his hesitation, with no excuse to leave and no other way out, what could the poor guy do but sit? He finally did, uneasily.

"I was hoping you'd bring Mrs. Riaz. I'd like to speak to both of you."

"She's not feeling well." He had a hint of an accent but there was nothing wrong with his English.

"I'm sorry," I told him. "Is that why you folks missed Mrs. Delp's funeral?"

I didn't know what it meant or why, but I'd struck a vein with the first swing of the pick. Reggie looked as if I'd slapped him. He studied the wood grain on the front of my desk while he recovered control of his face then, and only then, nodded in answer to the question.

"I hope she feels better soon."

Reggie nodded again, then looked away like a wall-flower trying to avoid a dance. He might have thought he was going to skate through this interview like the debutante hiding her thick ankles but I didn't have time for it. I needed answers from His Royal Shyness, so I got the cha-cha started. "I understand," I said, "that you're Reverend Delp's *go to* guy?"

"We've..." He cleared his throat. "We've been together a long time. I help where I can."

"You're being modest." I smiled. "The way I hear it told he can't get along without you."

Reggie shrugged. "I guess not."

"So why is he?" He looked up in confusion and, for the first time, looked me in the face. I asked again. "Why is Reverend Delp getting along without you? Why the sabbatical?"

"Rocio and I just needed some time away. That's all."

"You asked for time off? It was your idea?"

"Yeah. It was."

"Strange time to abandon the boss, isn't it? Just after his wife died? You figure he'll be able to carry on without you?"

"He knows how to get by."

If that had been meant as a testimonial, I couldn't help but notice it was a little weak. It was also worthy of more digging. "What about his crusades, Reggie? You're a big part of those aren't you?"

"I organized them."

"Yeah, that's what I mean. The crusades, they're your babies. You got them up and running?"

"Yes."

"So, what, now Gina Bridges handles them?"

That bit him. "What's she got to do with it? She's the reverend's secretary. What's she got to do with the crusades?"

"I'm not telling; I'm asking. That's what I want to know. You organized them but Reverend Delp can handle them without you, can't he?"

That bit him harder. Reggie looked me in the eye. "No, he hasn't. I organized them; staged them. I was right there running the show. Reverend Delp was a... He is a great man but, as far as the revivals are concerned, he's more or less a guest speaker and his secretary..."

"Just stage decoration?"

"I didn't say that. I didn't say nothing like that. She's there for the reverend that's all. The point is... I'm just answering your question. No, I put the crusades up."

"All of them?"

"Yes, all..." He hesitated, dropped his head again, and finished in little more than a whisper. "All of them."

"Tell me. Why did you involve me?"

"Huh?"

"Try and hang on, Reggie, I'll come around again. The night that Mrs. Delp was killed. Why did you hire me?"

I didn't know if he was searching his memory for the correct answer or was busy making one up but he'd stepped away from the microphone. When he came back, his voice had a tremor in it. "Reverend Delp was concerned about his wife. Worried about her. He needed someone he could trust. You came highly recommended."

Oh, my aching sides. He hadn't said it with as much conviction as Gina had but I couldn't blame him. She'd been prepared for it. "Yeah, so I've heard. I'm wondering by whom?"

"I just meant you have a good reputation."

"*Uh-huh.* Take it from me, Reggie. My reputation isn't all that good." I leaned forward intent on the young man across the desk and wanting him to feel it. "How about yours?"

Busy studying the dirt in my carpet, he didn't answer. But I had all the time in the world. I waited patiently. When he couldn't stand it any longer, Reggie looked up. I pointed at the home-made tattoos, a common prison pass-time, decorating his knuckles. "How long were you in the can?"

He pulled his hands off the desk and bunched them in his lap. "I did my time."

"Yeah, we just determined that. How about you fill in some of the details?"

I kept up the stare until something, a fire, rose and gleamed behind his eyes. Finally, in a slow, sharp tone, Reggie said, "I did five years in the roundhouse."

"Stateville? That's maximum security. What was the charge?"

He wet his lips. "Grand Theft Auto. I was dumb. There's nothing else to say. I was dumb and I was with someone who was dumber. He had a weapon I didn't know about and he used it."

"Did you usually work with someone else?"

"What do you mean 'usually work'?" he demanded coming forward in the chair. His feet slid under him as he readied himself to... what? "What's that supposed to mean? I just said I made a dumb mistake. I paid for it. What's that supposed to mean, 'usually work'?"

"I'm just tidying up the shop, Reggie. Keep your shirt on." He eased himself back but he was not at ease. I had him where I wanted him. And, as the first rule of being a detective was: when you've got them, keep pressing, I kept pressing. "Do the Delps have any enemies?"

I don't think Reggie got whiplash but the quick turns were making him miss the corners. He hesitated while his brain caught up. "No-o," he stammered, "I-I don't know anyone who would take her. I-I mean, take her life." I stared. Reggie squirmed. "I'm sorry," he finally said. "I'm sorry I couldn't help you anymore." He started to rise.

"Sit down, Reggie." He didn't want to and, for a minute, I thought he might balk but he considered it and took his seat again. "Is the church having financial problems?"

"I wouldn't know anything about that."

"Did you take a pay cut recently, Reggie?"

"Just a small one. Everyone did."

"Have you seen Nicholas Nikitin recently?"

"Nick? Where you going with all this?"

"I'm just filling in the map; seeing where there is to go. Have you seen Nicholas…?"

"No!" You could see it immediately; he wanted to take that back. Instead, finding his nervous whisper again, he added a caveat. "No. Not since he left the church."

How could I believe him when he so obviously didn't believe himself? "Do you think Nikitin killed Katherine Delp?"

"No."

"You sound sure. How do you know?"

"I just know. Nick couldn't do that."

"Who do you think could?" Reggie shrugged lifelessly. It looked as if his arms weighed a ton. I wasn't sure if he was resigned or merely exhausted but the poor kid did need a vacation. He wasn't getting one just yet. "Did you kill her, Reggie?"

"No!" His eyes began to mist. "I can't even believe she's dead."

"Yeah, it's bad. But I'm not the cops, you know. I want to help you, if I can."

"Help me with what? I've been under a lot of stress. My wife and I were close to Mrs. Delp."

"Is that why you call her Mrs. Delp, because you were so close?"

"I didn't have anything to do with it. Whatever happened. I don't need anyone saying I did. I'm on parole. I've tried to start a new life and it was going good."

"Sure it was. You've got a great wife, a great life. You got the Lord. And you didn't do anything wrong. So why are you twisting like a tuna on a hook?"

"Cause I'm upset. That's all."

"No. It's because there is something that you are not telling." From the look on Reggie's face, I might as well have stuck a fork in him. He was done and so was the interview.

Lisa did her best to discretely close a container of cottage cheese, and choke down the bite already in her maw, as I opened the door and escorted Reggie Riaz from my office. I ignored her and, instead, told Reggie, "You're going to have to trust somebody." I opened the outer door and stepped into the vestibule with him. I handed him a business card and, in the exchange, our hands touched.

Son of a bitch if it didn't happen again. As if by lightning strike, I was standing in Katherine Delp's bedroom. The pain in my head vibrated my teeth. The now too-familiar hum sounded in my ears. Katherine was laying naked on the bed, surrounded by the same blue aura I'd seen in the photograph in my office, alive but with blood pouring from the wound in her head. She turned and looked up at me. Blue tears glowed as they ran down her face and she cried, "Help me."

"How did you get here?" I asked. "How did I get here?" She made no sign, gave no indication at all, that she had heard me. "Are you even real?"

Again, no sign she'd heard my voice. "Help me." Then her plea exploded into a scream. "Dear God, help me!" A hand holding a large rock drove downward through my line of vision. It landed with a crack on the already spattered blonde hair and the convex surface of her scalp became concave. It felt as if I'd received the blow myself – and I screamed in pain.

Just like that I was in the vestibule again. I had one hand on the back of my head where the vibrating pain had been and one on the side of my skull where I'd experienced Katherine's crushing blow. I'd fallen against the paneled wall but the pain was gone, and the ringing with it, as if it had never been. Reggie Riaz was staring, eyes wide, mouth agape; scared to death. He had to have been wondering what my major malfunction was. I couldn't blame him, I wondered myself. But there was more to it than that. He wasn't just surprised by my antics, he was shaken and visibly trembling with a terrified, knowing look in his eyes. Reggie grabbed the outer door. I grabbed his shoulder and am delighted to report that, this time, all that happened was he stared back at me.

Reggie was afraid. So was I, but I made an effort to not let him see it. I took a deep, badly needed breath, and told him, "I'm a lot easier to deal with than the cops. If you don't open up to me, you *will* have to open up to them." I pointed at the card I'd given him. "You've got my numbers, Reggie, here and at home. Call me when you're ready. But don't take too long."

He left without saying another word. I watched him through the window, hoofing it past Willie's car (still in my lot, damn him), and down the street out of sight. My breathing returned to normal but my mind was racing. This case was a millstone but, beyond that, what was happening to me? And why had making contact with Reggie just made it happen again?

I went back in the office and found Lisa staring at me like a two-headed boy in a carnival sideshow. "Are you all right?" she asked. I didn't know, so I nodded. "Blake."

"I said I was all right," I snapped. "Let's get back to work."

A blind man could have seen that I'd hurt her but I didn't know what to do about it. Suddenly I was hurting everyone I spoke to. I headed for my office, changing the subject as I went and hitching a thumb in the general direction of Reggie's departure. "He did a stretch in Stateville," I told her. "Get a hold of Large. I want Reggie Riaz's prison records. And tell him the official stuff alone isn't going to cut it. I need to know what Reggie did in prison; how he behaved, who he hung out with, who he shared a cell with, everything."

The phone rang and Lisa grabbed it. "Blake Investigations." There was a slight pause and, when she spoke again, a noticeable chill in her voice. "Yes, Miss Bridges." I pulled up and turned around. "I'm certain he would. This morning?" I returned to Lisa's desk, reaching for the phone. She didn't actually bite my hand but she swiveled in her seat, turning her back on me, while she continued her conversation. "I'll let him know. You too. And thank you." Lisa hung up.

"What was that all about?" I asked.

"Your girlfriend again. You have an appointment with Reverend Delp at two o'clock this afternoon."

"No, not that." I lifted a finger and drew a downward spiral in the air, recreating the spin of her chair. "That."

"It's my job to make appointments for you," Lisa said, snapping back at me. "I do that on my phone in my office. When the call is actually for you, I will make the cross-country hike to your office and ask you to pick up your phone."

There followed a pregnant pause during which I considered a number of different responses. I decided against them all. I had no right to be angry with her and I knew better than to smile. I said, "Okay," and retreated.

Chapter Eleven

Like a living example of the Sock and Buskin, Gina was a strange mix of comedy and tragedy as I entered her church office. The slump in her shoulders and weary features were due, I imagined, to the previous week (not many laughs when you're fresh from burying someone you cared for). They were coupled with an odd exuberance despite all of the awful and mysterious goings on. She greeted me with chittering small talk, yet seemed anxious to move me along. Don't read me wrong, she wasn't trying to get rid of me, she was bursting to introduce me to her boss. Though I was eager to meet him, it struck that I didn't have any idea of the nature of Gina's relationship, her devotion to Delp. Was it hard to see? Was I pretending blindness? I enjoyed her company, but what did she enjoy? Why did I care? I was lost wondering when, with no noticeable signal, the moment apparently arrived. She excused herself and, with an excited, "Be right back," headed for the massive oak door to the side of her desk, surely the Reverend's private office. There was no echo when the door closed behind her – but there ought to have been.

"Nobody sees the Wizard," I said under my breath. "Not no-body. Not no-how."

I took the opportunity to wander her office, snooping. The walls, as I've already mentioned, were covered with framed photographs of Delp, and not a few with Delp and his secretary, hob-nobbing with senators, congressmen, governors, lesser televangelists, international heads of state (even a social studies wash-out like me recognized Menachem Begin and Margaret Thatcher, the Prime Ministers of Israel and the United Kingdom, respectively), and entertainers. On her desk, suggesting that the girl had a bad case of Delp-itis, was a too-large framed picture of the reverend and Gina alone. There was no question her eyes sparkled and little doubt it was a reflection of the sun shining out of Delp's...

The door came open again and Gina stepped out. "The Reverend will see you now."

Lucky me. I smiled and stepped past her into Delp's office, eager as a beaver to actually meet my client. I heard no declaration I was on holy ground, saw neither flames nor burning bush, so I left my shoes on. That must have been okay because Gina just smiled and, from her side of the frame, closed the door behind me, shutting me in. Jonah was more comfortable inside the whale. That was only my first thought; Hollywood-tainted religious metaphors were tumbling in my head like drumsticks in a Shake 'n Bake bag.

If the sanctuary was the heart of the Temple of Majesty then there was no doubt I'd entered the head. A soft amber glow warmed all. The walls, in some dark wood that I knew was expensive and other materials I imagined was, were decorated like those in Gina's outer office, only more so. Endless leather-bound bookshelves, countless photographs of Delp and staff surrounded by peoples of political power and entertainment might, and a multitude of pricey framed paintings depicting religious figures and scenes. Over a fireplace hung a damned near life-sized painting of the minister. The place seemed equal parts glory to God and glory to Delp. The real living and breathing man sat stone-faced, staring my direction, in a huge carved wooden chair at the far end of what (were it not for the ornate desk between us) looked and felt like nothing short of a throne room. "Mr. Blake." He did not stand. He merely stretched a hand, putting on a show from his seat.

I took the offered chair on the peasants' side of the desk. "Reverend. Thank you for seeing me. I'll try not to use any more of your time than is necessary but there are a few questions I need to have…"

"Tell me," he said, interrupting, "have you located Nicholas Nikitin?"

"Not yet," I lied again. "But I have no doubt I will. In the meantime, as I said, I have a number of questions along a different line of investigation. I apologize if they seem banal but I'm trying to get chisels into a number of places at once. With that in mind, and for the moment assuming it isn't Nikitin that is responsible, I need to ask, did your wife, or do you have, any enemies?"

"I've already told the police. I haven't any enemies, Mr. Blake. I serve the Lord. The Lord certainly has no worldly enemies; only those who are found and those who are lost."

I studied him for a moment. He appeared sincere which, of course, only made me wonder more. Though my mother would disagree, I was born as innocent as the next guy but somewhere along the line I'd become a cynic. My street-honed *bull* detector was always on and usually twitching. I didn't have any particular aversion to organized religion or its practitioners but I didn't like unlicensed junk peddlers. I simply did not believe I had finally met a man with no enemies. "That's commendable, reverend. How about your wife?"

"Why would it be any different for my wife?"

"I don't know."

"Katherine had no enemies. The idea is ridiculous."

"Okay, it's ridiculous, but so is your answer, sir. Your wife was murdered."

"I'm aware of that." He should have been defensive but, oddly, didn't sound it. He was merely stating a fact. "I hired you to find her murderer, not to run down blind alleys."

Ahh, defensiveness. The guy was human after all. I felt better. "You forget, sir," I told him. "We're assuming for a moment that the perpetrator is *not* Nicholas Nikitin."

"I am convinced that it is."

"Are you also convinced Nikitin is the person who was threatening you?"

"I don't think I understand." For the briefest instant Delp looked confused.

"I was led to believe you received a number of threatening letters and it seems unlikely…"

His confusion didn't last long. He interrupted to say, "I'm afraid you're mistaken." He smiled for the first time; an oily smile that… Okay I'll admit, if pressed, that I came in thinking I wasn't going to like the guy. It was about then I decided I'd been right; I didn't like him.

"Mistaken?" I asked. "How?"

"There were no letters. There have been no threats. It's preposterous. I can't even imagine where you heard such a thing."

I didn't know much, but one thing I did know was that Lisa Solomon was not a liar. That took the situation out of the realm of guesswork; someone in that glorious place of enlightenment was spreading manure. Since I didn't know who I shrugged and backed away for the time being. "Forgive me," I told the minister. "In this business, you hear things. And you make mistakes." I decided to circle round and poke the lion elsewhere. "Tell me about Reggie Riaz. You weren't concerned about bringing a convicted felon into your house of worship?"

For a moment his gray brows wanted to frown but the rest of his face overruled them and ordered the works back to their unreadable position. This character was good, in what seemed to me a very bad way. "Even Jesus went to jail," Delp said. "Yes, Reggie's criminal history was brought to my attention when I hired him. And, no, I was not concerned. God forgives, Mr. Blake, and so do I. Reggie is a faithful servant. I have no idea why you are making these inquiries but, if you suspect him of anything other than diligent service to the Lord, you have made another mistake."

I smiled. How could I not, this fellow was a riot. "Hard to believe I dress myself in the morning, isn't it?" I didn't wait for an answer. "I understand he's left you? Reggie, that is. The timing for that seems a little odd."

Delp eased back into his throne like pancake batter spreading across a grill. The relaxed position was belied by his grip on the arms of the chair. "Put it out of your mind." He made it an order in a voice that should have been followed by a hiss but strangely wasn't. It didn't matter, I felt it. "Reggie Riaz has not *left me* as you so rudely put it. He goes on sabbatical at the same time every year. He offered to stay, what with all that has happened, but I insisted he go as usual. Surely, you understand my wish for affairs to return to something akin to normal?"

"Don't you…"

"Mr. Blake, please," he said, interrupting me for the third damned time. It was a habit of his I had already grown tired of. Despite Gina's praise for the sentimental minister, he didn't seem to be attuned to my feelings. "I appreciate what you've attempted on my behalf. But, now that we've had this conversation, I realize I was wrong to ask your help in the first place. I was under a great deal of stress at the time and, I'm sure, you can understand that as well. Your services will no longer be required."

"*Uhmmm.* I don't understand actually."

"I was wrong to hire you. Let us say I should have had more faith. I should have left the affair in God's hands. What happened, happened by

His will. Whatever is going to happen, will also happen by His will. Who are we to intervene?"

"I appreciate your position, Reverend. I hope you can appreciate mine. I intervene in murder cases, among others, for a living. My only experience with being asked to leave a case before its conclusion has been when someone was trying to buy me off or shut me up. My services can be rented, you know that, but I can't be bought off. And I never shut up." I smiled so he received it in the manner it was offered. "Now you understand my reluctance to drop the case."

His steely eyes stared through me. Had he not already annoyed me, I'd have been intimidated. But he was trying. "Allow me to encourage you." Delp indicated a framed picture on his desk; a photo of himself with the country's most over-rated peanut farmer. "That's the President of the United States."

"Yes," I said, "I recognize him." I should have let it go but suddenly I didn't feel like exercising much self-control. "I didn't vote for him."

Yeah. I should have let it go. Delp wrinkled his brow. He twisted his lips. A vein appeared in the center of his forehead. It looked like he was undergoing one of those horror film transformations. I wondered what he was going to become. When the twitching ended, I was disappointed to find the reverend was still just an ass.

"The Governor, the Deputy Mayor, the Police Commissioner (I put it down that way because Delp was suddenly talking in capital letters), they were all at Katherine's funeral. Do you have any friends, Mr. Blake?"

If I didn't know better, I'd swear the guy was trying to hurt my feelings. It didn't deserve it, but I gave his question some thought. "I had a turtle once."

He smiled. "Don't think I don't appreciate all you've done for me."

"Yeah, you said that."

Delp rose from his throne and stepped around his desk. He started the length of the room and it was patently obvious that either he was going for a deep pass (which would have been silly as I had no football) or he was showing me the door. "It isn't about me," he said as he went. "I have an obligation to my congregation, to my ministry around the world. It's time to move on, Mr. Blake."

Call me mule-headed but I remained seated. He reached the door, turned, and was a little taken aback that I hadn't followed. Nothing stunned that bird for long. From across the room he spoke, crisp and slow, "Don't butt heads with me, Blake. I have a hard head."

It had not escaped my notice that I was no longer 'Mister'. I know when I'm not wanted. I stood and started for the door. As I drew near, the minister took pains... "Allow me to point out, Blake, that in spite of your complicity in my wife's murder, you haven't had the decency to apologize for my loss."

That deserved an answer and I obliged. "I'm not at all sure you've suffered one."

He turned to a pillar of salt and I let myself out. The door thudded closed and I was on the outside. I tried not to take it personally as chances were I probably just wasn't used to the sound of an expensive door closing. Back in the land of the mortals, Gina was up, in front of her desk, coming at me wearing that stupid Tabernacle smile, and holding out a slim piece of colored paper. It was a check. "I guess I won't be seeing you anymore?" she said.

"I wouldn't be too sure of that."

Her smile wavered. "But the Reverend said…"

"I know what he said. But I'm not about to drop this case. I have a personal interest."

You'd have thought I kicked her dog. "If you'll forgive my saying so," she said. "I think you have a personal grudge." A gleam appeared behind her eyes that could only be described as scary. Her lips, usually red, round, and moist enough to float a buoy, were pale and stretched to a thin line. "Is it powerful men you have a problem with? Or is it just religion?"

Having both my manhood and my morals questioned was, considering how accommodating I'd been, too much. "Gina, here's a fact you need to glom onto. The coroner's report lists the cause of Katherine's death as homicide by blunt trauma. Somebody busted her skull with a rock." I wasn't telling anything she didn't already know, yet her hand went to her mouth in alarm. No sense stopping there. "You should understand that, for the murderer, it went deeper than that. In their mind, Katherine was righteously executed for her sins. Whoever killed her had, has, an intimate knowledge of scripture. The

Bible on her dresser was left open to Deuteronomy 17, specifically to verse five, charging her, convicting her, of adultery, and passing sentence. 'Take the man or woman who has done this evil deed to your city gate and stone that person to death'."

Gina stared, as unreadable now as her boss. I didn't wait for more.

"I don't take checks," I said. I ripped hers in half and handed the pieces back to her. "I don't like being told what to do. And I don't have a problem with religion. I have a problem with murder."

Chapter Twelve

I was a disgruntled, unfriendly, and bone-weary detective when I forced myself up from the couch to answer my doorbell that night. Following my not very impressive (for either of us) visit to – and impromptu firing by – Reverend Delp that morning, I spent the remainder of the afternoon and evening studying the pile of video tapes supplied by my secretary's obviously obsessed and probably (I always thought) not quite right mother. Like a cryptographer deciphering a coded message, or a brat being made to eat his peas (take your pick), I studied one crusade appearance after another, one tape after another, trying to see, hear, or get a feel for *something*. I took in messages from the good reverend on the subjects of giving, forgiving, sharing, forbearing, abstaining, and not complaining (the detective complained). I watched Delp and his gang pound the hell out of the seven deadly sins, and their illicit progeny, to the wild applause of their tear-drenched stadium and concert hall audiences. I was awash in the (deadly stiff and formal, but admittedly beautiful) solos, duets, quartets, and choirs belting out choruses and hymns from *Absent from Flesh! O Blissful Thought!* to *Zion Mourns in Fear and Anguish.* I found myself bowled over by the organization, as I neared the bottom of the stack, without being any the wiser. More than that, I was just plain sick to death of the show.

I'd collected an impressive number of splinters so far in the search for truth regarding the shortened life and brutal death of Katherine Delp. The cooperation I'd received felt none too cooperative. My luck was running along usual lines, meaning none at all. I knew two things; the killer was a religious wacko and, now that my crusade orgy was nearing an end, absolutely everyone at the Temple of Majesty was still in the frame. (Plus the population of Chicago, eh, and the world.) Reverend Delp whistling me off the scent and back into my cage like a hound that had failed him did nothing for my humor and only deepened my suspicions. As for Gina questioning my motives… My motives are questioned twenty-four, seven, three-sixty-five by everybody from Frank Wenders to my green grocer and they can all run down an alley and holler, "Fish!" But when Gina accused me of malice, it bothered me. I don't know why. The fact that it bothered me, bothered me. That was just the stuff I could talk about.

That other thing. I didn't even know what to call it. Whatever it was that had been happening to me. The pains in my head, the low ringing tone in my ears, the visions or hallucinations I'd been having. I didn't even want to think about them but, of course, had been all day and into the evening. A glowing photograph that spoke to me? The appearance of the murder victim at the scene of the crime long after the body had been removed? And what in God's name had happened when I'd accidentally touched Reggie Riaz's hand? I'd not only returned in an instant to the Delp bedroom, I'd seen the murder first hand and been spoken to again by the victim. Hell, I'd felt the murder. I'd experienced the crushing blow to my own head! And, really, thanks to Willie Banks and the Nikitin brothers, hadn't my head taken enough already? Was I losing my mind? Had I really damaged my brain? It was ridiculous, the whole thing, but it wasn't funny. I couldn't talk about it with anyone and, had I been able to, wouldn't have had the slightest idea what to say.

The point is, when my doorbell rang, I wasn't very goddamned happy. Besides, I'm a bachelor (a longtime divorcee, but we aren't even going into that) and a loner. No good ever comes from my bell ringing and I had no reason to expect a change. In spite of all that, I rose above the call of duty and managed not to growl as I pulled the door open. Then, as miserable as I was, I laughed.

There stood Lisa, back lit by a single dim bulb dangling from bare wires in the hall. Her arms were loaded with, in no particular order, the massive purse she always carried (and the portable grocery it contained), file folders from the office, a black plastic video box, a paper bag of yet-to-be-determined fast food, and a cardboard carrier featuring two tall lidded paper cups with straws (triple-thick shakes, if I knew her). Her massive glasses had slipped and were precariously balanced on her nose making her look like a drunk owl with a question.

"There goes the neighborhood."

"Hi," she replied, her head cocked to keep her glasses from falling.

"Hi. What are you doing?"

"I found another tape in mother's machine and thought I'd better bring it over." She was animated but, with her glasses askew, not to good effect. I took pity and carefully slid the specs back on her honker, giving her the opportunity to straighten her head. "Oh and, by the way," she added, her voice now quiet as if she were sharing a deep secret, "I really, really, hope you are being careful with these videos because my mother will never forgive me if something happens to her tapes." She brightened like throwing a switch. "On the other hand, she's delighted you have finally found religion."

"Thank your mother for me and tell her, Amen. But just between you and me I've had about all of Reverend Delp and his merry band of followers I can stand. I'm crusaded out."

"I think you'll want to see this," she said. She altered her voice again going, I think, for something in the neighborhood of seductive. "I peeked at it..."

148

I won't say I was seduced but, okay, I was curious. "Yes? And?"

"And it's a recording of their most recent revival in beautiful Atlanta, Georgia."

"Atlanta?"

She nodded eagerly as her glasses slipped again. "It's the show they put on the night that Reverend Delp's wife was murdered."

Okay, I was seduced. "Why isn't your mother my secretary?" I took the tape from the pile in her arms and tucked it under mine. Then, because I'm a nicer guy than people think, I relieved her of the drink carrier as well. I started into the living room. Lisa kicked the door closed and followed.

"What else you got?"

She adjusted her purse, poked her glasses, and waved one of the file folders, fanning me. "Reggie Riaz's redacted prison records; with additional notes from one of Large's snoops. Knowing you, you'll probably find it a page turner but what little I waded through was pretty dull reading. Not much *bad guy* stuff at a casual glance."

"Thanks for the book report," I said, taking it from her. "But I'll probably read it anyway." I dropped the file on the coffee table next to the drinks. "And?"

Lisa gave me a questioning look, then remembered the paper bag she was still carrying. "Oh, yeah." She passed her free hand before the printed golden arches like the lovely Carol Merrill before a year's supply of dog food. "I brought supper." She slid my mess over, clearing the working center of the table, and began unpacking burgers and fries. "Sorry," she said. "It's the best I could do. I can't cook."

"Did we just meet or something?" I grabbed the video box, removed the cassette, and headed for the tape machine. I popped it in and pushed Play.

If you don't have a tape player and recorder, you must get one. What I knew about technology could fit in a thimble with room left for my... Let's just say, no detective should be without a video machine. I don't watch TV, it watches me, but that recorder was indispensable. While I pitch a product from which I won't make a dime, keep in mind that smaller will always be bigger. Betamax, baby. VHS will wind up a fart in the breeze.

On the television, the Delp Ministries' Atlanta Crusade appeared in color, pomp, and circumstance. God would have been delighted. Then the whole shooting match took off at a breakneck pace as I continued to play the tape but held down the Fast Forward button. That improved the show.

"Are you," Lisa began through chewed french fries, "looking for anything special?"

The tape, and the devout crusaders, raced onward. There was Delp waving at the substantial crowd. I liked him better on Fast Forward too. Guilt and hypocrisy with music, it seemed, was easier to take in double-time. Lisa repeated her question.

"Yes," I said. "I am looking for something special." I slowed the tape when the esteemed reverend reached the dais to join his slathering entourage. He shook hands, issued hugs, and returned to waving at the gushing auditorium of believers. The television cameras panned the crowd then cut back to the podium and widened out to take in a full view of the stage. I paused the image. "And there it is."

"What?" She jumped up and joined me by the set. "What do you see?"

"It isn't what I see," I said. Then I stopped, unable to proceed with special sauce dripping from Lisa's lip. I stared, tried not to smirk, failed dramatically, smirked – and pointed. She slapped me and asked, "Who are you, John Travolta?" Had it all been a joke, the punch-line would be that we both smoked a cigarette. But it wasn't a joke, it was just Lisa. She licked the milky gob off and, with my secretary's lip again suitable for family viewing, we got back to business.

"It isn't what I see," I repeated. "It's what I do not see. I do not see Reggie Riaz or his wife, Rocio. Neither one is there."

"That's significant?"

"Don't you read Sherlock Holmes?" I asked. "It's inexplicable. That makes it significant. In all of the other tapes," I said, pointing at the television screen, "the Riaz couple are right there, beside Gina Bridges, behind Delp. But they're not in Atlanta."

"What's that mean?" Lisa asked.

"*Ah.* That is the question," I said. "What does it mean? Reggie told me he's never missed a crusade. But he missed this one; the night Katherine Delp was murdered." I couldn't help but smile. I'd finally found a reason.

"Doesn't seem like much to put you onto this Reggie Riaz as a suspect."

"It isn't what put me on to him." It suddenly occurred that, if I didn't shut up, I was going to have to tell her about... things I didn't want to tell anyone about. Don't get me wrong. I trusted Lisa with my life. But I wasn't prepared to foist my questionable mental state on her. She was staring with that patented look of curiosity. "They are all suspects," I told her. "Every praying one, down to the kid who hands out their programs." There came a loud and persistent knock at my door, startling us both. My smile disappeared.

"I'll get it," Lisa said all signs of her smile gone too.

I shut off the tape machine and the television while she opened the door. Standing there in the same dim light was what at first glance looked to be a rabid moose. A closer look showed it was only Frank Wenders stinking up the doorway. If by then Lisa hadn't recognized him, his growl made his identity plain. "Blake here?" The man was little more than a traveling belch.

"Yeah. Come on in, Lieutenant."

Despite Lisa's invitation, the fat bastard still seemed to barge in like a pig through a sale barn gate. He filled up my living room, grimly proud, on display, but I wouldn't have given a wooden nickel for him. In an admittedly weak attempt at playing host, I groaned, "Hello, Frank," then, bowing to an obvious fact, added, "Slumming are you?"

Wenders ignored me and eyeballed my apartment instead. Up until that moment I'd been spared his company. Now that he'd crossed the threshold, he took it in from kitchen, to hall, to living room and gave no indication he was impressed. He stopped snooping when he spotted our food. He grunted. "Sorry to interrupt your dinner."

"Think nothing of it," I told him. "But why aren't you out planting evidence in the Temple of Majesty choir loft or hitting Delp's newsboy with a rubber hose?"

"We are," he said, turning to me. "Now it's your turn. You and I gotta talk."

"Pull up a french fry," I told him.

Other than his chins, he was a statue. Eventually he said, "We need to talk alone."

That didn't appeal to me at all. I held up my end of the stare-down for nearly a full minute before admitting to myself it was useless. He wasn't going to go away until *we* had his talk. Both of us turned to Lisa. One of the many things I like best about her is she usually gets it and she certainly did that time. "I'll get my things." She did, hiding whatever frustrations (if any) she had. With her jacket back on and her half of the meal gathered back up, she turned and forced a smile. "I'll see you at the office. Good night, Lieutenant."

After she'd gone I asked Wenders if he'd like a drink.

"I'd like an explanation."

I shrugged that off. "I can only guarantee a drink."

"I can guarantee you an arrest and an indictment for murder if you don't play ball with me."

If I hadn't been so tired, I'd have stared incredulously. As it was I just stared. "When did I become a murder suspect?"

"You're wasting all that innocence. You've been a suspect since the morning Katherine Delp was found."

"Oh, come on."

"You know, Blake, your explanation for your car being spotted outside of Delp's place was so lame that I can't wait, I am absolutely dyin', for you to tell me why your prints are at the murder scene?"

"My prints?"

"Yeah. It's actually none of your business until your trial, but your left hand print was on the window sill outside of Delp's living room. You're a naughty boy. You was lookin' through the window. Now, what was you lookin' at?"

I stared like Willie Mays judging a tricky one. The difference being that Say Hey played center and I was all alone in left field.

"This can get shittier, ya' know," Wenders assured me. "Any clue why we might dust an exterior window sill?"

"Clueless."

"Oh, now you come on. That was the easy question. I expected more from a street savvy Private Eye. The murderer went in through the window. Now, do you have any idea why your footing was so bad you needed the sill for balance? Don't ya' remember where you were standing?"

I was sucking hind tit but it finally dawned on me. "A rock garden?"

"See, now you're cookin' with gas. The same rock garden from which," he pointed at me, "the murderer picked up the weapon. One large rock with which," he pointed at me again, "the murderer bashed in Katherine Delp's once fairly attractive noggin. Now, would you like to share information? Or shall we take a ride together?"

"This is bull, Frank."

"I swear to God I'll arrest you and hand you over to that prick DA for an indictment."

"You could indict that chair. You know I didn't kill Katherine Delp." I might as well have been talking to my shoe. I sighed in partial (which from me to Wenders is complete) surrender. "What do you want?"

"Before I walk out that door, I'm gonna find out what you were doin' at the scene of a murder."

"I wasn't at the scene of a murder. That's what I've told you all along. I was at the mansion to keep an eye on Mrs. Delp. That was it; babysit her and the house until she went safely to bed. She did so at 2:40 am o'clock. Then I went home."

"You left out the murder."

"There was no murder while I was there. I repeat, she went safely to bed."

"It won't do. I find your facts devoid of facts."

"You couldn't *find* a walrus in a phone booth, Wenders. The story is going to have to do because, as far as I was concerned, that was all there was to it. Now I'm a clam."

"Go ahead, Blake, do everything ya' can to give yourself a hard time. When it all collapses on you, I'll piss myself laughing." He shook his thick head as if he found it all so very disappointing. "I'm telling you now, if we weren't friends –"

I cut him off. I could take a lot of things, but I couldn't take that. "We're not friends, Frank. We've never been friends."

With such terse remarks on my part, I did as promised and showed him how pretty my lips were when they didn't move. He blustered and barked, threatened and growled, but in the end having nothing more than my hand print at a place where I admitted being, Wenders managed to collect enough sense to leave. Good riddance.

Chapter Thirteen

That was twice I'd squirted out of the lieutenant's hands but, if I knew Wenders, the third time was going to be the charm. Those pictures were burning a hole in my desk and I still didn't know whether or not I was withholding evidence in a murder case. I had to corral Nicholas Nikitin. It was almost a miracle that the police had not stumbled onto him yet, had not interviewed anyone from the church that knew what Katherine had been up to and had mentioned him, or analyzed a spot on the bed linens that wasn't what it ought to have been. Okay, maybe it's overstating it to use the word *miracle*. Wenders couldn't find a hippo in a turnstile – but eventually even he'd get there. Sooner rather than later the young man's name, if not his relationship to the victim, would pop up and the lazy lieutenant would go a-hunting. If he was hidden in the city, tucked away in some rat hole, the cops – even a single-celled animal like Wenders – would find him before I could. That was just math and common sense. But my guess was Nikitin was a thinker. Admittedly he'd gotten into this mess by thinking with his little head instead of his big one, but a thinker just the same. If my theory that he wasn't a killer was accurate, then he wasn't a rat either. So he wasn't hiding in a rat hole. Which meant he wasn't in the city. Asking his brothers for help was pointless. Had they been of a mind, they'd have gotten a hold of me and they hadn't. They didn't trust me and my nose was too sore to try to change their minds.

Then again, I suddenly had a hunch and, if it was right, the Nikitins had helped already – by their interior decorating. Among the items I'd taken in during our short and not too sweet confab had been a picture on the wall beside the fake fireplace. A homey snap of the brothers three, standing in snow smiling before a rustic lakeside cabin. It could have been any cabin anywhere, and would have been useless, had it not been for what I remembered in the background; the stylized, conic roofs of, not one but two, old-world Russian buildings. If it had been taken in Russia, I was screwed. But, there was one place, the only place anywhere near Chicago, where those two examples of the pre-communist fatherland might have existed in that wooded setting. A tiny community that had gone about its business for over a century with few on the outside being any the wiser; a place called Lost Lake, one hundred miles straight west over the river and through the woods.

Lost Lake was perfectly named. At just over 300 yards long, running northwest to southeast, and just over 80 yards at its widest, to those that didn't know it was there, this serene little puddle was certainly lost. A transplanted Russian village, the residential section of which, on the east side of the lake, featured three streets running north and south, Tchaikovsky, Igor Sikorsky, and Turchin streets, each two short blocks long. These were bisected by the one and only east-west street, Pushkin, which was also the village's only access and egress by automobile. A scant few houses stood on the west side of the lake including, if I remembered correctly, the homes of the descendants of the original Orthodox Catholic and Orthodox Jew who started the community. They built their homes side by side in order for each to have their enemy in sight. They fought like rabid wolves ever after and passed their feelings on to their children. Americanized, it would be the Hatfields and McCoys living next to each other. Outside of these, the west side made up the recreational and business arms of the community, the Community house and Post Office, churches, playground, bath house, and beach. And on the shoreline to the south, several rustic log cabins. You reached these on an unnamed gravel path, from a poorly paved country road to the north, by entering beneath a red stone arch hidden in the trees, replete with Russian writing that could have said absolutely anything as far as I knew.

It might have been a huge waste of time, an hour-long-plus drive into the country, but a lot of detective work was. Nikitin had to be hiding somewhere and I felt good enough about my hunch to make it worth the trip. I actually enjoyed the escape from the city and the drive. It was nice to open the Jag up, after so many days in Willie's embarrassing rattle-trap, and would have been more-so had so many dickheads on the road not been trying to obey the ridiculous National Maximum Speed Limit of 55. Law-abiding citizens, what were you going to do with them?

It took the better part of an otherwise wasted day to come up with my brainstorm. In consequence, I reached Lost Lake in the dark of night, put out my lights as I turned in not to draw attention, and slowly eased my way under the arch on the western side of the village and started up the rise. Then, because the adventure was apparently going too smoothly, my head decided to attack me again. First came the familiar vibration in the back of my skull, then the low hum in my ears, neither as painful as before but absolutely insistent and impossible to ignore. A brilliant blue flash went off inside my eyes and I was instantly blinded. The flash ebbed and there, floating in front of my car, were two human-shaped figures of gold outlined in intensely bright blue floating just above the road. I cranked the wheel hard to the right not to hit them, slammed the brakes, and barely avoided hitting a tree instead. I threw the transmission into park and jumped out. The figures were gone.

I realized I wasn't breathing, gasped, and then inhaled deeply. As I did it hit again, the vibration, the ringing hum, the pain – more intense this time. Suddenly everything around me was on fire. I mean fire; thick smoke, licking flames, intense heat, an inferno. It should come as no surprise, I screamed. Someone shouted, "No!" A second voice, deeper, more angry than afraid, shouted, "Who are you?" Then, from which of them I didn't know, came an all-out scream of pain and terror. I heard a shot, the report of a gun, and something hit my chest like a sledge hammer. I screamed. I was falling backward, the pain in my head overwhelming, the pain in my chest beyond belief, and all about me – flames. It dawned that the feeling in my chest was not unfamiliar. I'd been shot. If that wasn't enough, all of my surroundings were on fire. God, what was happening to me?

Then it was gone. All of it. The flames, the pain in my chest, the ache in my head, the ringing buzz. My car sat idling, the driver's door standing open, off to my right. I was on my ass on the cold ground surrounded by the real country darkness of the Russian lake village. I'd had another – what? Vision? Hallucination? Or maybe I was just losing my mind.

There came an excited murmur from some-where nearby, I wasn't exactly sure where, as I picked myself up off the ground. There fol-lowed several frightened shouts, different voices entirely from the ones I'd heard in the vision. I looked up the rise, expecting to see a crowd gath-ering. Wasn't that what I was hearing? Instead I saw an orange glow topping the hill. It fluctu-ated to red, to yellow, again to glowing orange, backed by a swirling cloud of smoke. At least that's what I thought I was seeing. How could I know anymore? I was dizzy and, though the sense of burning and the pain in my chest had vanished, my head hurt plenty. I wiped my eyes, blinked, and looked again. The horizon, over the berm, which on my arrival had been black as pitch was brilliant with flickering orange. I fol-lowed the drive up, running, crested the hill and stopped. I looked below, down to the lake, the cabins, and what was indeed a small but excited gathering crowd. I couldn't believe my eyes. One of the cabins, what could only be the Nikitin's cabin, was on fire.

I raced down as fast as I could run in the condi-tion my vision had left me, past the crowd, some dressed, some in night clothes, trading excited Russian and English exclamations among themselves, and to the cabin. The fire had already vented through the roof and lit up the night. The heat was stifling and seemed intent on keeping me back. Orange blazed in the small windows, at the seals of the wooden front door on the lake side, and in scattered spots between the logs where the shrinking mortar clay fell out. Then I saw them, at the top and bottom of the door, chocks driven into the gaps to deliberately block it and hold the door closed from the outside. I knew instantly this was no accident.

Nobody inside, if anyone was inside, could have gotten out. Then I grew terrified that my guess had been right; that Nicholas Nikitin had been hiding in the cabin. I had come too late; someone else had found him first. I grew furious. I searched the ground before the cabin and found a heavy rock in the grass. Ignoring the heat and flame, I advanced and knocked the chocks from the door. I pulled it open, screaming, "Nicholas!" and was struck by the blue flash again.

There they were; the same two figures, glowing golden men, one larger than the other, with a bright blue aura encircling each, standing, screaming amid the flames. "No!" one shouted. "Who are you?" yelled the other. Both turned to me, as if they saw me from within that blast furnace. "Blake!" one cried out. "Help us!" yelled the other. They floated there for a moment, just above the burning floor, and then they were gone.

I didn't have time to be amazed or frightened. As if someone had pushed Play on an insane video machine, suddenly all of the events I'd experienced on the far side of the village hill went into motion again. The vibration, the ringing tone, the pain – and, without taking a step, I was standing inside the cabin, enveloped in fire. I was screaming; another voice (one of them? I didn't know) was screaming beside me. A gun went off. A bullet (the same bullet?) struck me in the chest again. I toppled back into the flames. A heavy, burning rafter let loose above and fell on me. The crushing blow, the searing pain, the terror was indescribable. How my heart continued to beat, I don't know.

Just as suddenly, the hallucination ended, and I was back outside of the cabin. The fire was still roaring, the flames still tearing away at the building, but in comparison, even the heated night air was like a cool bath. It was then, as I stood there breathlessly looking into the cabin, wondering how I could grab hold of reality again, reality grabbed hold of me.

Within the flames, I saw the bodies. Not the gold and blue space creatures I witnessed earlier, the actual physical bodies of two grown men. Both were doing the long sleep on the living area floor to the left of the door. Making it, I guessed, a pretty good dying area as well. Guessing who they had once belonged to, Nick, John, or Mike, or a combination of two Nikitin brothers, or any combination of any two people on earth for that matter, was out of the question. They were not burned black like you see in the movies, yet, but they were as *up in smoke* as any weed Cheech and Chong ever rolled. The flames had reached them, their clothes were alight, and both were officially homicide victims. The chocks in the door and, I had a bad feeling, a yet to be discovered bullet, would seal the deal. I knew, like nobody could ever know, that was more than an arson fire, it was the scene of a double murder.

I couldn't stay in the doorway any longer. The blazing light, the mind-numbing heat, the terrible black rolling smoke were all too much. The crowd of residents from the houses up the hill, and those that had crossed or circumvented the small lake, had grown; with it their ruckus and their stares. It occurred that if I didn't get the hell out of there I would quickly become an object of their attention. That would have been bad. Scorched and sweating, hacking and coughing, but needing to escape, I faced the fire but staggered backward, using a technique developed at the age of twelve for sneaking into movie theaters by walking backward against the flow as the early show let out. It worked great guns as a kid and would have worked there had I not been so near the lake. I slipped and fell to my knees in mud. I crawled to the lee side of the roaring structure to escape the heat and catch some air. I fought to my feet and wiped my caked hands on my pants (my mother would have had the vapors). I fought for a breath, lit a cigarette (because that's what smokers did under stress), and wondered what to do next. Those bodies inside, added to the Katherine Delp murder, put the whole thing beyond church choir intrigue. I had trouble in a major key.

The cabin, the roof completely gone, roared, a black shell of flame-licked logs; a hellish inferno. I left the envelope of heat and smoke, backed into the cool darkness, and got out of there.

Chapter Fourteen

I'd worn a groove in my brain – just thinking – on the trip back from the sticks to my Chicago apartment. I showered letting the hot water treat the aches and the soap eliminate the mud, carbon and stink of smoke, then showered again because the first time hadn't done the trick. It was like scrubbing your kid's face only to discover the real problem was he was ugly. I couldn't wash off what was soiling me. I collapsed into bed with no plans to wake up and a firm belief my life couldn't get any worse. Somehow I slept through the biggest part of the next day but, in the early evening, the pounding on my door gave every indication my imagination was about to be expanded and my life, I had the sinking feeling, was about to head right down the crapper. I opened it to a hungry-looking, viciously grinning hyena, but that was only positive thinking. A closer look showed it was just a bad penny minted by the local police department. What Frank Wenders wanted, again, I couldn't even guess. "Either ante up your half of the rent," I told him, "or get lost. You're here more than I am."

"Is that nice?" he asked with a growl. "Here I go out of my way to bring you a message."

"Not a singing telegram, I hope? You're not going to dance or take your clothes off?"

"No, smart guy, I'm gonna to make you sing."

Speechless with anticipation, I walked away. But I left the door open because I got manners. Unable to take a hint, Wenders crossed to my side of the frame before he closed it and followed me into the living room.

"So what's the message?"

"It's a long one. Ya' ready? I've been asked to thank you for the bar-b-que. To tell you that you left last night before the fun started. And, if I think it's appropriate, to grab you by the balls and drag you someplace where you'll be safe and ready-at-hand for extradition."

It was a strange feeling, my throat instantly going dry while the rest of me felt as if I'd been doused with cold water. Wenders just stared, licking his teeth like a cat measuring a mouse. I'd gone out to Lost Lake on a whim. I had told no one I was going, spoken to no one while I was there (been spoken to by nobody but the dead), and had spoken to no one since I'd returned. Of the uncounted billions of things in this world that Frank Wenders didn't and couldn't know anything about, at the top of the list had to be the Nikitin cabin fire. If somehow he did, he still couldn't have known I was there. But if he wasn't talking about the fire, what the hell was he talking about?

"The Stephenson County sheriff was disappointed you left so early," Wenders said. "By the time he and his boys and the fire department got there, you'd already done your killing and left. He missed you; asked me to pass on his regrets. Then to haul you in on a first degree murder charge."

Okay, he knew about the cabin. How (as big a question as it was) no longer mattered. What mattered was how I was going to answer him. Deny everything because he was just throwing mud to see what would stick, or come clean and show him that, as distasteful as it was to the both of us, we were on the same side? As was my nature, I decided to obfuscate, to tread water until I had a better idea of where I stood. "I'm as happy as the next guy to be a part of this great melting pot, Lieutenant," I said. "But why don't you give me a hint? What language are you speaking?"

"Oh, it's going to be that way, is it? You don't know nothing from nobody. You're innocent as the virgin Mary."

I forced a yawn. "Wake me up when you get somewhere I'd recognize."

He opened his trench coat, a scary maneuver with his gut, produced a roll of papers from an inside pocket, and unrolled them. "Recognize this?" He stuck them in my phiz, the top sheet showing a black and white facsimile of a picture of a burned out log cabin. Yeah, the Nikitin brothers' cabin, taken just as the sun came up. It was every bit as horrifying as it had been in person, a ruin of terror and despair. Of course, that was none of Wenders' business. Speaking of which, he was still talking, "Pretty lake, huh? I always wanted a cabin by a lake. Course it was awful hot while you were there."

"Your sheriff steered you wrong."

"I've got that down as a lie, Blake. If you take it back, right now, I won't even ask for an apology. You were there and all God's law enforcement agencies know it. So, do yourself a favor and help the real police out and maybe, just maybe, you can save yourself a lethal injection."

"Here we go again. I didn't murder anyone and you know it. Help you with what?"

"They got two bodies out there. Course, I'm not telling you anything you don't already know. The neighbors say they're a couple of brothers named Nikitin, Iancu and Nicholas, but we won't know for sure till the medical examiner scrapes 'em like toast and sees what's underneath. Why don't you do us a favor, do yourself one at the same time. Beat the egg-heads with their lab tests; tell us who they are for sure. Then tell me what you have to do with these two dead Russian brothers?"

I gave him nothing. Not even a look of innocence.

"While you're making up a story for that one," Wenders said. "Tell us what you meant by this." He shuffled the pages of the roll, moving the cabin photograph to the rear and replacing it with a second fax, which he shoved in my face.

"Mud?" What else could I ask? I said Wenders had been throwing it when he came in. Now he handed me a picture of it; mud, the puddle and muddy lake bank that I'd slipped in.

"He-Haw," Wenders said. "You being an artist, and me an art lover, we both know the mud was just your medium. I'm interested in your message."

I looked again, closer, then grabbed a magnifying glass from my desk. He guffawed from across the room, "Just like a real detective." I ignored Wenders and studied the picture. Sure enough, though somebody had to have pointed it out to the lieutenant in the first place, there was some kind of message scratched in the mud.

"Tee-something-oh," I read, straining eyes that not only weren't as young as they once were but that still had sleep in them. "Tee-aitch-something... ess... ess? Then, I don't know, the last looks like a number. One? Eight? Eighteen? What is that?"

"You're supposed to tell me, genius. You wrote it."

"I wrote it?"

"Good, we agree."

"It was a question. What do you mean I wrote it?"

"Don't be modest. Below and beside the message, aren't those your hand and shoe prints dancing all around like you were playing Grauman's Chinese Theater? Who'd you think you were, Frank Sinatra?"

I brought the glass up and gave the photo another look. The fat bastard was right again; near the cryptic message (scratched with a proud flare in the mud) were a jumbled collection of hand and shoe prints that, if checked, would certainly be found to have been made by me. But how could he have known that?

"Why were you there, Blake? At the scene of a double homicide? One murder here at home ain't good enough for ya'?"

"Shoe prints? And an unreadable message? This is your evidence I was there? It's laughable."

"Then go ahead and laugh. And, no, future convict, this isn't my evidence. This is just a taste to see how big a lie you're going to tell. You're shaking your head No, Blake. Why are you shaking your head No? You were there. Stephenson County's got a village of excitable Russkies made the trip all the way to America just to put the finger on you. Their lab gurus played mud pies and moulage all morning and, as we speak, they are checking their results against your detective's license. Eh, we'll collect your shoes later." He smiled like the Cheshire hog. "Yeah, I'm betting this week's pay check they're yours."

"Wake up, Wenders, you're dreaming."

"I'm dreamin'? How 'bout I turn it into a wet dream? Wait till ya' hear the best part. That crappy Jag you drive? Yeah, it was there too. Ya' know how we know? You hit a tree, remember?"

He was waiting for my reaction. I could feel it. But I couldn't really see it because my eyes had spun round in my skull and were staring at my brain, wanting to see for themselves what the hell it was going to do next. I hadn't hit a tree at Lost Lake; *had not*. I'd almost hit a tree, when the blue and gold things, the ghosts, the vision of the Nikitin brothers appeared from out of nowhere in front of my car. But I stopped in time. I hadn't hit a tree. What was Wenders talking about? And, now, why was the big ape laughing?

"Get this," he said with a roar. "You knocked off your front license plate. Swear to God. They got your license plate, Blake. Can you imagine anyone being so damned stupid?" He laughed till he was empty, which you might imagine took a while, then turned on me with deadly serious, iced-eyes. "Now, I am asking you officially, for the record, are you denying being at Lost Lake in Stephenson County last night?"

Rule number one of being a detective: when you're caught in a trap, don't wriggle. I had not hit a tree at Lost Lake. Be that as it may, there was a good chance Wenders wasn't lying for once and, in that event, they had my license plate, and prints (again), and I really was caught. "No," I said. "I don't deny it. I was there."

"Get your coat."

"Hold on. I don't need my coat."

"I warned you. You're sticking your nose in every murder in Illinois and I'm going to find out why."

"My nose was already in it. It's the same murder case you brought to me five days ago."

He stopped to think. That took a minute. "The Delp thing?"

"Yeah, the Delp murder. There's nothing I can tell you at the station I can't tell you here. In fact, I can tell you more here." Though I dreaded it as much as I had ever dreaded anything, I took a deep breath as I went to my desk and pulled out the envelope of photos I'd taken the night of the first murder; the pictures of Katherine Delp and Nick Nikitin at play. After all, with Nikitin a victim and not a suspect they could no longer send me to jail so he might just as well know they existed. "Mrs. Delp never knew I was there; outside of her house that night," I told Wenders. "If she had, she probably wouldn't have had a visitor."

"What visitor?"

"You can ask that with all the evidence collected by your lab boys. The sperm donor."

"So Delp had sex with his wife before he left, so what?"

"You took his word for that?"

"He can't be the murderer, he was out of town. I ain't asking Chicago's most famous minister to jerk off in a cup, when he *can't* be the perp."

He had a point. Right on top of his head. I stretched the pictures in Wenders' direction. "Here," I told him. "Pull your hat down tight or don't blame me if your skull explodes."

He snatched the envelope and tore into it like Master Henry Jekyll opening his first chemistry set at Christmas. He swore when he saw the first picture. "If this is one of their church services," he said, "I'm joinin'. If it ain't, Blake, you're going to jail."

He quickly rifled the rest of the stack, giving himself an eyeful, a headache and, for all I knew, wood. I filled him in as he neared the last photograph. "Delp's old lady was being porked by an ex-church member, Nicholas Nikitin."

"That's one of the –"

"Victims from the cabin fire last night," I said, finishing it for him. "Yes. It will be when they finish with the autopsies." I pointed back to the pictures in Wenders' fat hands. "Back to the night of the first murder. Nikitin showed up there, at the Delp mansion, around 1 am –"

"The night of Katherine Delp's murder?"

Quick as frozen mercury. "Right," I said. "They bumped uglies and he left around 2:30."

My warning that Wenders control his temper had been entirely wasted. He turned red as a beet and it looked as if his head had no choice but to explode. "I don't believe this."

"What's not to believe?"

"You, Blake! Who do you think you are withholding evidence?"

"Evidence of what?"

"What the hell do you think? Murder."

"Don't get your hopes up, Frank. He didn't do it; the guy was innocent."

"How do you know he was innocent? You hearing voices?"

I let that one go without comment. Not that Wenders noticed. He was at full roar. "You didn't know he was innocent when you took these!"

"No one was dead when I took those. All they are is evidence the reverend's wife was cheating on him. So unless Homicide has gone into investigating adultery, give your pump a rest."

"How do you know this guy wasn't the killer?"

"His murder last night should suggest an answer if nothing else does. He's the second victim."

"Second victim?"

"Or third, depends how you're counting." He stared. I sighed. "I'll come round again, Frank, hold on this time. He's one of the two bodies in that cabin."

"I got that. I already said that! But just 'cause he's dead now don't mean he didn't kill her then?"

183

"It's certainly suggestive, don't you think?" Still the dull stare like a dinosaur taxing his pea-sized brain. "Look, Wenders, when he saw the paper and read about Katherine Delp's murder, Nikitin got scared and took off. His brothers got him out of town; hid him in their cabin at the Russian lake. I traced them there but I was too late. The killer found them first." I paused to edit the actual events in my mind before letting them reach my big mouth. Wenders could only handle so much truth from me. Any mention of the other things I'd seen at Lost Lake wouldn't do anybody any good. I only half believed it myself and understood it not one bit. There wasn't one chance in hell he was going to get it. Wenders wanted to stick me in jail something fierce, but he would have settled for locking me away in a nut house any day of the week. I wouldn't hand him the chance. "The cabin was totally engulfed when I got there. The doors were rigged outside so no one could get out and there were two bodies inside. Nick Nikitin and, I assumed, one of his brothers; one shot and both burned up."

"How do you know one was shot?" Oops. Stepped on my joint there. "How the hell do you know one of them was shot?"

"It's a guess," I said, trying to make lemonade. "The window was shot out. Nick's brothers were, are, physical freaks of nature. You'd have to shoot them just to slow them down. How else could the murderer have kept them inside?" Wenders wasn't lapping it up. Instead he was staring a hole through me. "It's a guess. But I'll bet money I'm right."

He ignored the chance at my personal wealth. "What else do you know that I don't?"

I snorted. "The list is endless." Then I quietly breathed a sigh of relief. The big lug's complaint was not that I knew something I shouldn't. He was annoyed that he'd learned it from a mug like me instead of being told by one of the good guys. "As far as this case goes," I told him, "I don't know anything else. That's what's so frustrating. I'm just like you, I'm not getting anywhere."

"Just like me," he sneered. "I've about had it with you."

"God, you sound like my ex-wife."

"I'm not kidding, Blake. You're interfering with a homicide investigation, withholdin' evidence, lyin' to the police. It's called Obstruction of Justice, in case your memory is as bad as your attitude. For the love of Mike, we've got enough evidence to hold you for this... for these murders."

"Damn it, Frank..."

"And, big shot, there are rumors stirring through City Hall that are very un-good as far as you're concerned. Apparently, you don't even have a client anymore. You were fired, the way we hear it. So your snooping is now unauthorized and you're rubbin' Conrad Delp's rhubarb the wrong way. He's bitchin' to the people that make the rules."

"So I'm pissing someone off, that isn't a headline. As for authorization, I have a detective's license and I'm an American citizen. I don't need Delp's permission, or yours for that matter, to look into criminal cases in the public record."

"Don't you go anywhere," Wenders snapped. "I'm going to let Stephenson County know I've talked to you and have my eye on ya'. But I want you here when I come to spring the trap."

He turned like a trick elephant in a circus ring and headed out with my photos clutched in his grubby hands. He turned back at the door. "In the meantime, you outta give serious thought to whoever it is tryin' to drop you in it. They want you drowned and you're doin' everything you can to help 'em. If you got any brains, you'll get out of this case, and stay out, or you're going to wind up suckin' your thumb on death row."

Chapter Fifteen

I'd like to tell you that sanity took over; that I did the prudent thing, took Wenders warning, and got out from under this abortion of a case. I'd like to tell you that but can't because I did the opposite. On my way out, to once again stick my nose where it wasn't wanted, I took the time to examine the Jag and found the front license plate was indeed missing. It had been ripped off the bumper, no doubt by the arsonist himself. Meaning the murderer was still there, at the Nikitin cabin, when I arrived last night. He'd gone to the trouble to vandalize my car (and apparently an innocent tree) to shove me – personally – deeper into the mess. I intended to keep that in mind.

Fresh out of clues and short on suspects to harass, I returned to the Nikitin place on Racine. Yeah, I know, two of them had just been horribly killed, so recently they didn't even know officially which two of the three were gone and which one was still up-right. It would be heartless and inappropriate to barge in on the survivor's grief. More, it would be crazy. Who did I think I was? Well, that was the point. I was the guy in it up to my neck and someone was doing their best to shove me further in, to bury me under these murders. Leaving that message, whatever it was, in the mud and my license plate beside a dented tree were sloppy attempts to involve me. Someone did it all the same and Wenders was going to use the situation to boil me in oil if he got the chance. As I had no ideas, I thought maybe the surviving Nikitin could point me in the right direction. I couldn't wait to find out.

Then again, I had to wait, at least a few minutes, because the cops (a cruiser and an unmarked unit) were there when I went past.

I found a drug store a block away and used their parking lot thinking that, if Wenders changed his mind and set the dogs on me, they wouldn't start by looking for needles in haystacks. You hide a tree in a forest; you hide a car in a parking lot. Besides, as bad as my dented brain was working, I'd gotten the brilliant idea to use the trip to – again – get rid of Willie's rattletrap of a car. I left it in the lot in its own cloud of gray smoke and put my gumshoes to work hoofing it back to the Nikitin house. I kept to the shadows as best I could, found my way back to my newest favorite alley (behind Nikitin's place), and reached the fence I'd already climbed earlier in this ridiculous adventure. I scaled it, again, and came down in the darkness of Nikitin's back yard.

I waited in the shadows between the back and side of the house, beaming with pride at how smart I was. I sneaked peeks through several windows and got a gander at the red-eyed Mike Nikitin talking with the boys in blue. That made it all but official, the bodies in the cabin belonged to Nick and John. I saw the detectives, the bovine Wenders himself and his sidekick little runny-nosed Mason, and the two patrol officers, neither of whom I knew, and I marked time until they got their fill and left. Once they did, I waited a while longer just to make sure that when I made my presence known Mike would be good and alone. Yeah, I was real smart.

I was still waiting, in the bushes, doing some late evening daydreaming about a certain too-good looking church secretary, when

I was grabbed from behind, spun around, and smacked. Thankfully, the spin and the wind-up gave me a second to react. I juked my head enough that, though I didn't avoid the fist altogether, I managed to take it as a glancing blow to my tender nose and not as the full-on schnoz buster it was meant to be. That gave me the chance to see, by the houselight spill, that my attacker was Mike Nikitin. The big guy had somehow crept up behind me and, sisters and brothers, he looked goddamned mad.

But that was *his* problem. Truth be told, there had been days when my mood was brighter. This case was going backwards at Mach 10 with its hair on fire. I'd had it with intimations that I was responsible for these killings. I'd had it with being pushed around. And I was sick and tired of getting hit in the head. Mike had the drop on me but, to my credit and his regret, this time I didn't drop easily. We proceeded to dance, to relandscape his back yard, and to redecorate the patio. I'll skip the details as long as you keep in mind that a second sucker punch, by a second Nikitin brother, in one week inspired me and that I fought a lot better when I was conscious. In short order, I handed the last surviving Nikitin his ass on a plate and, at the same time, answered the age-old question, If a big Russian falls in his backyard when there's nobody there that gives a shit, does he make a noise? The answer was Yes, a grunt when he starts to topple, an escape of air on the way over, and a dull thud when his coconut whacks the stone deck.

I opened the patio's sliding glass door, grabbed him by the back of his collar, and dragged his oversized butt through and into the kitchen. I paused at the sink to catch my breath, to tamp the blood from my nose and lips with a dishrag, and to enjoy a badly needed glass of water from the tap. I refilled the glass and threw it in Mike's face on the floor. He sputtered and ran his scales sounding like Chumley the Walrus as he returned to consciousness. Then, swear to God, he asked me if I thought I was Bruce Lee. When I finished shaking my head, I yanked him upright, propped his dripping head against the cupboard, reminded him that he'd thrown the first punch, then started the talk I'd come for.

I opened the meeting with a discussion of the cabin fire. That might seem cold but I had to erase his notion that I had something to do with it or his brothers' deaths; a notion I couldn't help but think Wenders had given him. It made no sense for me to kill the one witness I so desperately needed to talk with. As upset as he was, Mike was able to see that. He likewise got it when I explained Wenders' habit of putting me in the frame anytime it suited him. For a hunk of meat, I was delighted to discover Mike had a brain that worked. Finally, he agreed that the real killer, whoever it was, was apparently trying to set me up. Neither of us knew why. He wanted to know how his brothers got it and how I thought they went. I pleaded ignorance and made it stick by telling him nobody knew anything until the autopsy reports were finished. There are some things people are better off not knowing and, believe me, I had no interest in reliving it (and I do mean reliving it) again. That covered the cabin.

Next came the murder of the minister's wife. That would take longer. I convinced Mike that I needed to know all I could about Nick, his relationships with Katherine, the reverend, Reggie Riaz, Gina and the church. I needed Nick's side of the story, and plenty of it, if I was ever going to find any justice for his brothers (and if I was ever going to dig myself out of the hole I was in). I got him up off of the kitchen floor and onto the living room couch where we'd originally met, and I got him talking.

"John had to get him away. Not just to hide him, though that was part, but to keep him from ruining his life; to shut him up. He kept saying he was guilty, he was guilty."

"Guilty?"

"Not of murder, he did not kill the reverend's wife, Mr. Blake. He had nothing to do with it. But he said, if it had not been for him, Katherine would be alive."

"He didn't kill her?"

"No. No, of course. But he kept saying it was his fault she was dead."

"But why? Why did Nick think her murder was his fault?"

Mike shrugged. "He said he knew of what her husband was capable."

"He thought Reverend Delp murdered his wife?"

"He could not prove anything, if that is what you are asking. I asked this question. He said he could not prove it. But, yes, he thought Delp murdered her."

I shook my head, which was a mistake, and had to pause to let the marbles stop rolling and my equilibrium return. Mike used the time-out to rub his swelling jaw. "You punch like Jack Palance."

"Jack Palance?"

"He is Ukrainian. Volodymyr Jack Palahniuk. Professional boxer before he became actor."

Great. Not only was I the butt of Fates' running gag; now the jokes were coming with explanations. "Fascinating," I told him. "Can we get back to business? Delp couldn't have killed her. He has an alibi. He was in Atlanta the night his wife died. Where was Nick?"

Mike reared back as if the question burned but he recovered quickly and looked me in the eye again. "Is this another question to which you already know the answer?"

I nodded – slowly. "Yes."

"Then you know he was at Delp's house. He said he left at about 2:30 that morning. He kept repeating it; 2:30, 2:30. Then he would begin to cry once more, saying, If only he had stayed."

"Yeah, I know how he felt. Did you or your older brother ever threaten Delp?"

"What? John and I? You are being stupid. We had nothing to do with anyone there."

"What about Nick? Do you know? Did he threaten Reverend Delp?"

Mike ground his lips together and shook his head. "The way I understood it, Nick had not spoken to Delp since he left the church... and for some time before that."

"Before that. He worked for him, didn't he? You're saying he wasn't on speaking terms with Delp while he was working for him?"

"I do not know the details. Nick liked the church, he liked the people. He did not... What did he say? Speak ill, yes, that was it. He would not speak ill of the reverend."

"But he didn't like him?"

"He did not like the caste system. This Reverend Delp spent his time in his big office, away from everyone. When he wanted something done, he would dispatch his legions. When he wanted his books, uh the church finances, seen to, Nick was allowed to come among the legion. Not to be a part of them but to be among them. Then, somewhere, somehow, the reverend decided he did not like the way Nick was handling his books."

"What was his major complaint?"

"I do not know. Nickie never said. Just that the big-shot minister had relieved him of his duties. He did not fire him, officially, but he was not invited to return to his work. Not long after, Nick said, that is when the church started having financial problems."

"What sort of problems?"

"Again, I do not know. Nickie did not know. Everybody there, at this Majestic Temple, loves Reverend Delp. This translates to everyone being very close-mouthed about the church. Nick had ceased to be allowed access to its inner workings. It bothered my brother much. Soon after Nick got the boot, according to this Katherine, there arose some serious financial trouble."

"Evidenced how?" I asked.

"You ask more than I know. Nick was told little, he told us less. The staff, the church staff, most were volunteers but, of those being paid many, maybe all, were taking pay cuts. Recently, there have been these… fundraisers; constantly. The crusade teams, that is what Nick called them, these teams began staying in cheaper hotels, dispensing with room service, doubling on rooms."

"Is that why Katherine Delp wanted to skip the Atlanta crusade?"

Mike made a derisive grunt and shrugged his massive shoulders. "He… Delp, not long ago, he dismissed his personal house staff; his servants."

"Is that why he let Nick go? The financial problems? Or did Delp know about his relationship with his wife?"

"Nickie did not say. I do not think he knew. The reverend just said his bookkeeping services were no longer required."

"It's a little odd that Nick hadn't seen this financial trouble brewing?"

"Just so. That is what Nick kept saying. That there were no financial troubles. He could not imagine what might have happened to bring this on, especially so quickly. Nickie said Conrad Delp was richer than the Tsars. Perhaps he was merely trying to cut his wife off. Perhaps he had some big scam. I do not know. Nickie did not know. All he would say for sure was that this claim that the church was broke was… the farce."

"Back to my original question; did you or your brother, did Nick, threaten Delp?"

"No. I heard nothing of this before you raised the question. Nick said nothing about anyone receiving threats. Why do you ask this?"

"Because it all makes as much sense as a goose eating *foie gras*. Delp agrees with you; he's never heard of any threats. But, according to his ministry, they were coming in."

"If you ask me there is nothing new in this. The ministry of Reverend Delp claims many things."

Chapter Sixteen

You know the drill by now. After my fight with, and following the interview of, Mike Nikitin, I wasn't in the mood to deliver Willie's wreck of a car anywhere. Puking smoke, it shuttled (and shuddered) me home. I crawled up and into my apartment then teetered in place through a hot shower. With the dirt and blood washed off, I limped to my kitchen. By the flickering bar light above the sink, I rigged a bag of ice for the back of my neck, squeezed out a cool cloth for my lips and nose, and grabbed up a new bottle of gin promising myself two long fingers. After my last twenty-four hours, that didn't seem unreasonable. On second thought, and realizing I was fooling myself, I put away the glass and grabbed a tumbler. I grabbed a lime. I grabbed a knife. Then I grabbed up my Bible. Yeah, laugh sucker, laugh.

Still by the blue-white flicker, like a quiet lightning storm filtering through the kitchen shutters, I made my way carefully, painfully around to the living room. I popped one of Delp's crusade tapes into the machine and lowered myself onto the couch. This time, Lisa's mother had started recording before the crusade began, picking up a slew of commercials in the deal. Slim Whitman smiled wide beneath an Oil Can Harry mustache, strummed a left-handed guitar, and yodeled at me hawking a new TV album. He disappeared and was replaced by a sexy sweetie hinting she'd ride my baloney-pony if I'd just call her 900 number at a premium-rate. She gave way to a tarot card reader with a Jamaican accent so phoney she couldn't have pulled off ordering oxtail stew at the local jerk restaurant. I could have Fast Forwarded through it all but the remote was... way over there. Finally the show I'd been waiting for appeared (I never dreamed I'd think that) and the Temple of Majesty church chorus began to sing. I cracked the seal on the new bottle and, under the watchful eye of a smiling British beefeater, adjusted the ice on my cracked noggin and cracked open the Bible. Okay, I was cracking up; I agreed with that days ago. I eased myself uneasily back.

Sometime later, night clocked out and went home and morning took over. Enlarged photographic prints made from the crusade videos lay scattered on the coffee table. Piles of files and filled notebooks spilled onto the floor. Wadded paper decorated the carpet, cigarette butts and ashes did likewise on the table top. The tumbler, empty save for an accumulation of strangled lime slivers, sat stunned and trying to catch its breath. The near-empty gin bottle lay on its side like a corpse; like Katherine Delp, like the brothers Nikitin. A second, barely-dented bottle of Whiskey (Mr. Jack Daniels, ladies and gentlemen) stood triumphantly nearby, the night's only survivor. Another video tape was presenting another chorus of happy worshipers, all singing to shadows from the past while no one and nothing in the here and now gave a damn. Me? I was out of it. My banged up body, for what it was worth, lay left behind, passed-out on the couch with the Bible opened, to the Second Epistle of Paul to the Thessalonians, and spread on my chest like a sleeping infant. Meanwhile, for less than twenty bucks I'd bought back the 1950's and was spending the summer at Lake Sunset with the girls of my youth; one hand in Mary's pants, the other down Becky's blouse. Somewhere in the background a minister was delivering a fire and brimstone message which I was dreamily happy to ignore. Mary grabbed my wrist, her mouth insisting I stop, her wet eyes pleading with me not to. Becky, sure she could hear her father calling, grabbed the other wrist. They pulled my arms out to my sides and, while it would be stretching it to claim I was being crucified, with their soft flesh now out of reach it was its own brand of torture. The girls became one and, co-joined, took on the appearance of a certain church secretary that had been heavy on my overworked mind. "Stop." She was insistent. "Stop!" But why the sudden alarm?

It was more than an anguished cry. It was a fervent siren, an intrusion in my brain. Then the girl (the girls?) were gone but the alarm remained, demanding. Demanding again. The lake disappeared, my eyes snapped open to see my apartment had reappeared, and it finally dawned in my gin-fogged skull that – my phone was ringing. "Geez!" All right, I admit, I was startled and I jumped. My ice bag, long since melted to water, sank into the cushions. The Bible thumped to the floor (which is no way to treat a baby or the word of God). Embarrassed, despite being alone, I laughed it off and shook myself awake. The aching dizziness returned. Why did I do that! The phone was still ringing. I grabbed up the receiver and barked, "Blake."

"You were right, Mr. Blake."

"What! What?"

"You were right." The voice, even in my groggy head, was familiar. It sounded like... It was Reggie Riaz. "You were right. I wasn't telling you... I didn't tell you everything."

"Reggie? Reggie. Go ahead, I'm listening."

"It's gotten out of control. No, it's been out of control all along. It was wrong from the start. We shouldn't have been involved."

"Who's we?" I asked. The gerbil in my head was still doing laps on his wheel but my vision had cleared (as clear as it was going to get). "Involved in what? Are you talking about Katherine's murder or is there more happening here?"

"It wasn't supposed to be like this. She wasn't supposed to die. We waited for you to leave.

Then we… He just went crazy. He said God commanded it."

"Slow down, Reggie. You need to make sense. You're doing the right thing by calling. I can help, but you've got to slow down. Give me your address, I'll come right now."

"No. For all I know, they're watching us. If they find out I called you, if they even suspect."

For a second I thought the line went dead and I panicked. "Reggie!"

"I'm afraid for Rocio," he said, back again. "Before I say anything I got to get her some place safe. You got to understand she isn't responsible for any of this. I love her. Oh, God, what have I done?"

"Reggie, don't get squirrelly on me. You said, 'He said God commanded it.' Who is he?"

"I'm sorry to bring you into this. They hate you. He hates you."

"Who hates me? Are you talking about Delp?"

"I've got to get Rocio out of here. I'm taking her to her mama's in the morning. If anything happens to her… I can't live without her."

"Wait, Reggie, don't hang up."

"Meet me tomorrow… someplace… real public… I can't think."

"Daley Plaza by the Picasso."

"No, too wide open. It needs to be crowded."

Okay, he wanted a crowd. Now I had to think – and I was in no condition for it. "Navy Pier? By the submarine; the… Silversides?" I asked. He said nothing. I started a list. "Union Station? Soldier Field? The Field Museum?" I was growing frustrated. "O'Hare? Come on, Reggie, work with me."

"I know," he shouted, as if he'd struck gold. "There's a restaurant I used to work at. It's real busy at lunch. Taqueria Carmelita, on the south side, west of Comiskey Park; 35th and Normal."

"Carmelita… 35th and Normal."

"Eleven, tomorrow."

"I'll be there. Don't stand me up." I hung up and would have shook my head in irritation, if my head hadn't already been in such a tender state. Instead, I merely muttered, "He needs a crowd."

*

I'd hoped that was the last phone call of the night. But, as I couldn't have got a wish granted with a government certified magic lamp, it turned out to be only the first. My wall clock, in the dim blue flicker from the kitchen, read 3:18 am when I was again awakened by the shrill ring of the phone. I snapped it up, still groggy. "Blake."

"He's here."

That's what the caller said, just that, "He's here." A woman's voice. There may have been an accent, there must have been an accent, but I didn't hear it. "W-What?" I sputtered. "Who is this?"

"It's Rocio Riaz. Reggie told me to call you."

"Rocio? Reggie… Riaz? Mrs. Riaz."

"He's here! Reggie told me to hide. That he'd be right back. But he hasn't come back. I heard a lot of noise!"

"Tell me where you are," I told her. She was crying and I was having trouble hearing her clearly. I mean it was bad. I could have swore she answered, "I'm in the closet." The poor thing was under a lot of stress, I supposed, but that answer didn't help much. "Did you say a closet? Rocio, what closet? Where are you? What's the address? Give me your address, then hang up and dial 9-1-1."

"Reggie said not to call the police. He said we'd go to jail."

"Mrs. Riaz…"

Something cracked so loud in my ear that I ducked. Only after making myself feel like a fool did I realize the sound, splintering wood, had come to me over the phone. Rocio screamed, "My God! My God!" There was another scream and the line went dead.

"Holy shit." I hung up and rifled the files, the notebooks, the papers on the table until I found a phone number. I dialed quickly. The ringing lasted two minutes longer than eternity but, finally, Gina Bridges answered dreamily, "Hello."

"Gina, it's Blake. Gina, I need you to wake up."

"Blake, what? It's three in the morning."

"I know. Listen, I need Reggie Riaz's address. Rocio just called and I think they're in trouble. I need their home address, right now."

"Okay. Just a second. I gotta find it. I gotta put you down."

An emptiness took over the phone on the other end. Time conspired with panic to do me dirt. I was so tense, I almost screamed myself when my Call Waiting beeped. I looked to the screen on the phone and realized the number calling belonged to the Riazs'. Gina still wasn't back. I put her on hold and answered the incoming call. "Rocio?"

An icy voice crept through the line, stung my brain, and chilled my blood. "Eight, two, six," it said. "Eight, two, six on Mahr-ket Street."

"Reggie?" I asked. "Reggie, is that you?"

"For the love of Gawd, Blay-ke," the voice hissed, "hurry." Again, the line went dead.

I hung up, grabbed my coat, and ran from the apartment.

*

Finding that area of town was one thing (I'd taken my Jaguar this time, as opposed to Willie's folly, and was on Market Street in under thirty minutes). Finding the right house was something else. It was a neighborhood of faded-blue collar workers, the poor, the unemployed, and the uneducated; so run down the For Rent signs looked like ransom notes. (Come to think of it, it sounded like a subdivision for private detectives.) It was not unheard of for the residents, when they moved, to pull the numbers off their houses and take their addresses with them. Many featured no numbers at all. Still, I can count and do a little math and, through the process of elimination, I managed to locate 826. It was a small two-story sitting liked a tilted crown, above two moderate sets of cracked concrete stairs, on a dirt berm to the right. I pulled to the curb short of the house by several car lengths, on the opposite side, and climbed out. I started across the street, straining in the dim light for any sign of life behind the Riazs' windows. The place was as black as a tomb.

So intent was I on the residence, I paid no attention to the street. That indifference would, over the next five seconds, be the stage upon which I performed a one act play called Failure. I probably heard, but failed to notice, the car's engine starting. I failed to see the vehicle dart from the deep shadows down the street with its lights off. I failed to see it racing toward me. And, though the driver snapped the headlights on in the instant before the curtain came down, I failed to recognize the danger. The car hit me with the left side bumper and headlight. My feet left the road. I rolled up over the front quarter panel, hit the windshield, and I went airborne.

Chapter Seventeen

Everything went black. I have no memory of flying over the vehicle's roof but I must have. Further, I must have landed face down on the far side of the street because that's where I was when I came to. But I don't remember that either. I had no idea how long I'd lain there (I didn't know if it was still 1979). It was dark when I woke and I hoped it was still night but was half afraid I'd gone blind. I stirred, saw the blur of a street lamp, thanked the cloud-covered stars I could still see, and stood up. My head felt like a broken gourd. Blood trailed down my face and fell in black-looking splotches on the pavement. I was alone in the middle of the street and as badly used as an encyclopedia in a family of morons. The dark car was gone and I was grateful. They must have thought they'd killed me and I couldn't say yet that they hadn't. I staggered toward the curb in front of the Riaz house.

I paused unsteadily on the sidewalk, swaying there, staring up the mountain of concrete steps to the dark front porch. A pain shot through my head. I heard a muffled explosion and, above me, a torrent of blood poured through the open front door. Racing like a river it cascaded down the steps, a crimson waterfall headed my way. I stood dumb, staring, unmoving. It poured from the house, fell, and was nearly upon me. Then, as if by magic, the river was gone. The steps were dull gray concrete again and dry as a bone. Though I ached from my gumshoes all the way up to my unkempt hair the shooting pain in my head had vanished. I moved to the steps, sat to collect myself, pulled out a handkerchief and attempted to wipe the blood from my face. I might as well have tried to wipe wet from water.

The pain came again in my head. Suddenly I was indoors, in a small dark room, tinier yet, a compartment of a house. The house above me? I didn't know. Then it dawned I was in a closet. A closet, just as Rocio had said on the phone. Phone! There was a telephone receiver in my hand and I could hear a voice, my voice, on the other end of the line; my own anxious voice asking me if I was all right. I couldn't answer. I was terrified and someone outside of the closet door was banging, banging, banging to get in. I heard myself on the phone, calling to me, pleading, asking again if I was all right. Wood splintered as a panel in the door gave in. A hand shot through the jagged hole, reaching for me.

I was on the concrete steps again, outside the Riaz home, bathed in cool night air. My head was screaming in pain, vibrating with the hurt. Then something, someone, stabbed me. I was back in the closet again. The attacking hand held a razor, an old-fashioned straight razor, and was coming at me through the broken door, slashing, stabbing, slashing, and I felt it, as God is my witness, a blade being driven across my chest. Pressure, then incredible burning pain and my blood painted the flailing hand and the smashed door.

I was on the steps again, holding my chest and feeling for a wound that was not there. My head was screaming. I couldn't formulate a thought. I dropped the bloody handkerchief there, rose unsteadily, turned back to the house and climbed. I reached the porch. The door that, a moment before stood gaping wide and puking blood in my vision, was now nearly closed. Probably always had been. (Ajar, that's the word my scrambled brain finally decided upon.) The door was ajar, just a crack. Cautiously, I pushed it open and, steadying myself, peered in. Silence. Darkness.

I entered the Riaz house. I turned on a light and was momentarily blinded. My head swam so badly that all the other aches, the road rash, the bruised hips, the wrenched back seemed almost painless in comparison. My vision began to clear. I moved slowly around an old couch to the far wall and to a door within. A closet door; the closet of my most recent nightmare vision. The hinges were broken, a panel busted in at its center as in that same vision, the door thrown open. A cord ran inside where a phone lay tossed on the floor beeping miserably for help. I heard the sharp gasp of a woman in pain and spun round.

The room on this side of the couch was splashed in blood. Rocio Riaz was on her belly at the bottom of the stairs. She grabbed her chest, struggled to lift herself, looked at me and, gurgling blood and air bubbles, said, "Upstairs. He's upstairs." She struggled, fighting to climb the steps on her knees. I took two steps toward her – and she disappeared as if she'd never been. A trail of spattered blood covered the steps as evidence that she, or someone in that same condition, had been there recently and crawled the stairs to the second floor. I took a deep breath and headed unsteadily up trying not to step in the blood as I went.

I reached the second floor hallway and, dizzy again, had to collect myself. A lot of good it did me. Suddenly a new hallucination hit me and I was in another room altogether, a bedroom. I was suffering one thudding body blow after another as someone, a blur, was hitting me in the head, the chest, the stomach. Beyond the pain, I thought I'd puke. There was a rope or a chord or some such thing around my neck, biting into my throat. I couldn't catch a breath and I realized that I was being strangled. My eyes were bugging out and my vision was going again. Good God, I was literally being killed.

Then I was just as suddenly back in the hall at the head of the stairs. Christ, I was losing my marbles. But at least I could breathe again. I steadied myself, flicked on the light, and looked to the floor. The blood trail I'd followed upstairs was still there and continued on. I took one step…

...And was back in that bedroom again. No sooner did I see Reggie beside the bed, garroted, and in his death throes and recognize my surroundings for what they were – than somebody slit my throat. I felt it, sisters and brothers, as God is my witness, an icy sting of pain from my left ear to my right. Like a shot from a seltzer bottle, blood spurted in an arc in front of me, and again, and again, and it dawned with horror that it was my heart spitting my lifeblood onto the floor. I heard myself gurgle and splutter. I spit foaming blood trying to catch a breath that would not come.

I was in the hallway again, holding my throat and feeling for a gash that was not there. My head was screaming. When I could manage it, I concentrated on the blood trail on the floor, focused on it, and cautiously followed it down the hall. I opened each door along the way, terrified now but having to know, leaking gloom throughout the upstairs. The rooms were furnished but empty. The house was empty and the silence numbing. The buzzing in my head, meanwhile, went on, sawing into my nerves. I reached the end of the hall and opened the door to what once had been a bedroom, the bedroom in my vision, but now was a charnel house.

The night, which until that moment had been some sort of crazy action thriller, was now a horror show. Reggie Riaz lay beside the bed exactly as I had envisioned him, dead, his ashen face held up inches off the floor by a rope tightened about his throat and tied to the headboard post. He'd been left hanging and now I knew that I had just experienced his death. An arc of blood had spurted across the dresser, mirror and the wall. Rocio, the source of the blood, lay slashed and stabbed on the floor in a deep red pool. I stepped forward to feel her pulse. I lost my balance and dropped to a knee, staining my pants and mixing Rocio's blood with my own. Then I saw the items soaked in blood and clutched in Rocio's hand; a rosary and a Valentine's Day card. I stared, dumbfounded by the scene and shaken by my unholy experience there. Oddly, through the blurred vision and the screaming pain in my head, I caught a glimpse of a coin, a silver dollar, lying beside Rocio's head. I stood, looked the room over again, and spotted another one. Then another. There were silver dollars scattered across the floor – in and out of the pools of blood. And there was an open Bible on the bed.

A thunderous crash sounded below. "Police!" someone shouted. Soon after followed a thudding of boots on the stairs.

Grand. It was the cops; as usual, late and short. If I was going to do anything or look at anything at all, I'd have to do it fast. I spotted one of the coins not covered in blood, carefully picked it up by its edges, and slid it behind my heel and into my shoe. Then, skirting the blood on the floor, I quickly stole a look at the Bible. It was opened to the 12th chapter of the book of Romans.

Two police officers stormed the hall and, immediately thereafter, filled the bedroom doorway with their guns drawn. "Hold it," one of them (that I didn't know) shouted. He eye-balled the room and whistled. "All right, Bela Lugosi. Don't move."

Over his shoulder, the second cop, who obviously recognized me, stammered, "Blake, what the… That's Blake. He's a private dick."

"What the hell is going on here?" the first one asked.

"She called me," I said, pointing to Rocio's body. "Said there was trouble."

"She wasn't wrong," the cop said. "I'd say you got trouble, buddy."

On the surface, I couldn't disagree with him. I'd been hit by a car and felt every bit like it. My mind was a well-folded fruit salad. The images being delivered to that brain looked to be coming through lenses filled with effervesced Alka-Seltzer. I was standing in a bedroom with two still-warm bodies, whose deaths I had just experienced myself, with their blood on my hands and clothes. To a couple of dull and unimaginative cops the situation must have looked pretty rotten for me.

The first officer gawped at Rocio's body then turned to me. "You always cut their throats before you put 'em to bed?" I had no answer. Why try?

The wiseguy's notes would state that at 4:30 that morning (the start of my sixth day hunting Katherine Delp's killer) I was taken into custody on suspicion of murder. Despite his partner's assurance I was an all right guy, and because I am apparently the gods own chew toy, the same hard cop insisted on patting me down. What he found in the right pocket of my suit coat, believe it or not, made everything much worse.

Chapter Eighteen

When I carried a badge, I'd spent a lot of time on the interrogators side of the small table in police Interview Room #1 on the second floor of the 16th Precinct building. But that was a lifetime ago; so jump ahead to a miserable morning in 1979. From my arrival early on, until well-after the a.m. rush hour had done its worst to the city, I sat, my bruised and battered carcass in a slump, my throbbing head – a blood-stained patch of gauze taped to my scalp *and hair* – laying on the *other* side of that same table with one cop following another hurling questions at my face and flanks. First the patrol boys, like gnats to be shooed away, then the detectives, by which I mean, of course, Wenders in waves. He'd gone out again and I was alone, dying by inches, and not at all sure that wasn't the way it was supposed to be. I have no idea how much time passed but, too soon, the door came open again and Wenders lumbered back in like a cow into a milking parlor. His reappearance meant the break was over and round four had begun. And, yeah, if you're keeping score, little Davey Mason was there, in the hallway behind him. This time that's where he stayed. Taking a new approach, the lieutenant shut the door in Mason's face making it just the two of us. Normally I'd have given him grief, thunder to hold up my end of the storm, but not that morning (or was it already afternoon?). I felt like a log after the chipper shredder and it was all I could do to remain upright. Wenders did not let that stop him.

"Let's start again, Blake," he said, booming. "Keep in mind, I'm running out of patience."

"Would it be too much to ask that you *not* shout?"

"Well, I'm very sorry. Where are my manners? Am I hurting your ears?"

I silently mouthed, *My head.* I would have given it a shake but that would have made a mess.

"Delp's secretary sent us to the scene." He was still booming. "If everything happened the way you say it did, how come she called us and not you?"

"How come? Don't you mean *why*?"

"I don't need a grammar lesson. And stop talking in italics! Answer the question, Blake. It was your *civic duty* to call the police."

"I didn't have time to call you."

"What were you doing on the phone with Gina Bridges at three in the morning? Is she in this with you? Are you boffing her? Is that it? Some jealous little ménage ja four between you two and the Riaz couple?"

"She works for Chicago's most famous evangelist. I don't think she boffs... alone or in tag teams."

"What's going on, Blake?"

"Isn't it obvious? The animals are starting to eat their own."

"What the hell is that supposed to mean?"

I closed my eyes, not only because Wenders was ugly, but because my head was threatening to explode. "I swear," I managed to get out, "it would really be better if you didn't shout."

"You said this was all tied up with the Delp murder? And the Nikitin murders? How? What do two more killings got to do with the first three? What's it got to do with that church?"

"I don't know."

"Or you? How come every time you show your face, somebody dies?"

"I guess it's like yours, Wenders, just not much of a face."

"Laugh, bright boy. Laugh till they push the plunger."

Mason entered with something in his hands. It looked to be an evidence bag but, as I lowered my aching head to the table again, taking what respite was available, I couldn't be sure. Wenders met his junior at the door and listened to Mason's whispers.

The lieutenant returned to the table and slid the plastic bag under my nose. "You can't have that back yet. We'll need it to convict you. But you can look at it again." There seemed no way around it. I lifted my head with a grunt to see that, beneath the scribbled evidence label, the bag contained an old-fashioned straight razor. "I'm not telling you anything you don't know already," Wenders said, "but that's the razor was used to cut Rocio Riaz's throat. The same razor Officer Friendly found in your coat pocket when you were searched at the scene of your crimes." Safely folded up, newly cleaned after its priority visit to the lab, tucked neatly in its bag, the razor looked innocuous, incapable of the bloody murder of which it – read that *I* – was being accused. And it had been found in my pocket. I stared, still unable to believe it and unable to remember ever having seen the like. It was a moon rock, an extraterrestrial butt probe, a bill a Senator read before a vote. There was no damned way, my splitting head assured me, I had ever seen that blade before. Failing at his attempts to listen in on my thinking, Wenders demanded, "You want to fill me in?"

I turned my head, too quickly, from the shaving instrument to the cop. Then, while I reminded myself to exercise better judgment next time, I took a deep breath to keep from throwing up. When this (most recent) wave of nausea passed, I opened my hands in weak surrender.

"Shall we continue the verbal sparring," Wenders asked, "with all the witty banter and bullshit you're so fond of? Or should we save time and you just tell me why you had the murder weapon in your pocket?"

Wenders was as far from King Henry V as an overweight Chicago cop could get, yet *once more unto the breach, dear friends*, he seemed determined to go. Who was I to argue? I just hoped, in the meantime, that I wasn't bleeding to death internally. But I digress. "I was hit by a car," I told him (for at least the fourth time that interview). "On purpose. I was unconscious; only Christ knows how long. I told you. Obviously the killer hit me. Obviously the same person would have had no trouble putting the razor in my pocket while I was out. It doesn't take a rocket scientist, Wenders. It's as plain as the snout on your face."

"I'm not buying it."

"I'm not starting a religion. I don't need to sell *you* anything."

"Your mother wouldn't buy that story."

"No. My mother would no doubt be on your side. What of it?"

"Start over, killer. You ain't no Jimmy Cagney. Just say it and unburden your soul. I stuck the Riaz woman like a pig. I put the blade in my pocket. I got a rope... Tell me how you spent your morning."

I had half a mind to tell him. To just shout it out. I spent my morning hallucinating, bouncing from one murder to another – as the victim. It was a blast, being smacked by a car, getting my throat slashed, being punched and strangled, then getting arrested as the perp. That was my morning; a regular goddamn circus! But Wenders would have loved that. He would have insisted on sticking his knee in my back for leverage while he cinched up the straight jacket himself. Luckily, the sane part of my mind made the decision. "Not another word until I talk to my attorney."

"Screw it, Blake, and screw you too. Go ahead, lawyer up, see if I give a damn. I got your prints and the pictures you took at the first murder scene. I got your license plate, your prints again, and a bunch of permanently scarred Russians watched you take a mud bath at the second scene; a double murder. I got your bloody handkerchief, the victim's blood all over you, and the murder weapon in your pocket at the scene of murders four and five. And, if anything you've said even accidentally ends up being true, I'll have phone calls from the Riaz house to you on their luds. Hell, even a piss-poor ADA could get a capital conviction."

"You know I didn't kill anybody, Frank."

He laughed. "What? I care?" Just like that, the laughter disappeared and he bore down on me with gritted teeth. "And don't 'Frank' me, you fucker. We've never been friends, remember? This case is making me look like a putz and somebody's going to death row for it. Or to a maximum security jail cell for the rest of their whole born natural. You apparently thought I was kidding, *Nod*."

Geez, I didn't think I could hate that name more. The fat slob was using it just like my mother used to do. Next thing I knew he'd break a hair brush over my shoulder and promise to knock me into the middle of next week or remind me that he had brought me into the world and he could take me out. I really was in trouble.

Wenders was still yelling. "I'm telling you for true, Blake, give me what you got on these killings or, I swear to God, I'll pin this whole shittin' mess on you."

I opened my mouth.

"I'm not done," he screamed, cutting me off and leaving me looking like a landed carp. "Yeah, you'll probably beat the murder charges, but you'll burn through every nickel you ever squir-reled away doin' it. And I guarantee you'll lose your detective's license. What'll you have then? Your reputation? Tell me another fuckin' joke." He fell into the chair opposite as if his skeleton had collapsed under the strain. "Go ahead," he said, "smart off now."

I met his black expressionless eyes; a koala waiting for me to throw him a eucalyptus leaf so he could wrap up this case and get back to his twenty-hour nap. Like the marsupial, Wen-ders had proved he'd just as soon attack one of his own as look for a real enemy. He didn't care what I gave him as long as I gave him something that led to an end.

"There's something going on in the Delp Min-istries," I told him, exhausted. "I don't know what. Reggie Riaz was involved in the Delp mur-der; I don't know how. Someone else was in-volved as well; I don't know who. I've got a lot of questions. And I've got a bad headache."

Wenders groaned, filling the room with bad air, left me, and stepped into the hallway. Through the open door I heard him tell Mason, "His headache is catching. Now I'm gettin' it. Get me something for it, will ya?" The young suck-ass vanished. A moment later, the shift commander, Alexandra Cozzi, appeared out of nowhere and took Mason's place. I knew Captain Cozzi when she was just good ol' Alex; a decent cop and a hard worker in the old days. (If you're wondering, No, there was no love lost between Cozzi and me either.) Wenders saw me peeking and yanked the door shut. Prick.

I laid my head back down on the table knowing full-well how the conversation in the hall was going. Cozzi was asking the fat slob's opinion. Did I do it? He would answer in the negative because he knew damned well I didn't. But then he'd insist I knew a lot more than I was willing to tell. Though he'd never let on to me, he'd admit to her that he was just squeezing me. Alex would then frostily remind the big ape that squeezing me was pointless and order him to cut me loose. Not because she felt sorry for me, just to make sure I didn't die on them there.

Not long after, I guessed, a frustrated Wenders shook me awake. I was still in the interview room and struggled to a sitting position, leaning heavily on the table, in time to hear him bark, "You can go, Blake, for now."

I started to stir then stopped myself. Through the headache and the blur, I stared at the detective lieutenant. "Wait a minute," I said. "There's something you're not telling me. You know I didn't do this. But it's more than that. You have proof I didn't do this or you'd already have me locked away. And you sure as hell wouldn't be letting me go."

He scowled. "Are you too stupid to know when you're bein' handed a gift?"

"Thanks, but let's stay with this. You've got a witness, somebody who saw what happened outside Reggie's place."

"No, dumb ass," he said, "you're the one with the witness."

"*Uh-huh.* Who saw what?"

"A neighbor thought they saw a shadow, someone from the car that hit you, they think, bend over you…"

"And put something in my pocket?"

"Probably. That doesn't mean there isn't something you can tell us."

"How long were you going to keep this a secret?"

The door swung open and Mason, unknowingly (the only way he ever accomplished anything), rescued the lieutenant from any further admissions by tossing him the requested bottle of pain pills. Then, like a groundhog scurrying from dark clouds, he disappeared back through the door. Wenders looked from the bottle in his hand, the potential relief for his headache, to me, the most likely cause of it, and said, "You look like hell. Take yourself over to Cook County and get your head X-rayed. Make sure there's still nothin' there."

I wearily made my way out, thinking how lovely it would be if Wenders choked on the aspirin.

*

It was almost dawn – of the following day – when Lisa leaned me (in my Sabu-esque turban of a head bandage) against the wall outside my door. She switched the paper bag (a prescription muscle relaxer and the only pain pill my allergies allowed) to her other hand, unlocked the door with my key, and supported me into the apartment without me falling on my face. She's a good girl, Lisa.

Let me fill you in on the previous twenty-four hours. You're already aware I spent the morning, from the time of my arrest (they let me go, yeah, but when you're hauled away in cuffs, sisters and brothers, you have been arrested) until the lunch hour, being threatened by Wenders. You already got the skinny on that. The *interview* had lasted over five hours and I thought it had been an ordeal. I've been more wrong but not often. Because then I limped into the Emergency Room at Cook County Hospital and the real ordeal started. I signed in just before noon, called Lisa at the office to let her know that most of me wasn't dead (the jury was still out on my head cheese), and to warn her I'd probably need a lift once the medical staff had fixed whatever I'd broken. I warned her that, if that was the case, I'd give her a call. Then I plopped like a spilled pudding into a waiting room chair and proceeded to do just that; wait.

I waited so long that Lisa put in the best part of her day, closed the office early (just after 4 pm) and, not having heard anything, came to the ER to check on me – before I was seen by anyone. Yeah, after five hours beneath Wenders' glare, I did over five hours more in the hospital waiting room. If I *had* been bleeding internally, by then I'd have been chatting with the victims in this case on their side of eternity. I was eventually ushered into a room with a bed where my vitals were taken and the waiting allowed to start all over again. Day became evening. Lisa pitched two bitches, a small annoyed one, followed some time later by its great big furious sister, before a disinterested (but warned and wary) X-ray tech finally whisked me away to the Radiology room for my photo shoot. Evening became night, during which she took one million and six pictures, I counted; ankles, knees, hips, hands, chest, right shoulder, and my melon from every conceivable angle; so many I glowed. Then it was back to my room where night became morning. A thousand years later, a sleepy-eyed doctor rattled the films in the air, making as much noise as he was able, while he gave them twice the once-over he'd given me. His verdict: I had concussed my already-concussed head. Of that, he had no doubt. Beyond that, I was beat to hell and back but he didn't think I had any major injuries. I was apparently, for no discernible reason again, lucky to be alive. A dead relative must have put in a good word for me, though I couldn't imagine who. He, the doctor that is, warned I might have a broken bone or two. He didn't think so, but the pictures would be re-read in the light of day by someone who charged even more than he did. He wished me well and tried to cut me loose.

That's when I asked him the question; hypothetically, of course. The doctor left the room a few minutes later probably thinking I was out of my mind. He passed Lisa in the hall. She ignored him, staring in at me as if she had no doubt I was crazy. Apparently, she'd been eavesdropping.

A nurse gave me an injection, wrapped my head wound in the nifty turban already mentioned, and urged me to get plenty of rest. The advice was silly. They'd kept me up all night, given me a shot that not only knocked out the pain but was making me tired as hell and now, though I was as comfortable as I was likely to be for some time on that cot with pillow and blanket, they were ordering me up and throwing me out. Why didn't they let me rest? Not long after, Lisa shoe-horned me into the tin can she drives, stopped to fill my scripts at an all-night pharmacy, and brought me home. Confessions of a gumshoe; I probably could have taken a taxi and managed on my own, but didn't.

"Couch or bed?" Lisa asked. I did my best to stare like a hungry wolf. She wasn't feeling sheepish. "Who do you think you are, Steve Mc-Queen? Get over yourself." She led me to the couch and helped me to sit but it felt as if she'd dropped me into a car on Space Mountain. I closed my eyes and took in air not to throw up. When I was able, I groaned, "The room's spinning."

"Any pain?"

"No. No pain at all. Whatever they gave me... they ought to sell it in six packs. But my head is..." I let it go. After all, what did I expect. "Did I thank you for coming to my rescue?"

"Three times already. Can I get you anything? Are you hungry?"

"*Ugh...* The thought of food... No, thanks."

Lisa sat in the chair opposite. "Before the hospital... Before you called... Did Wenders give you a hard time?"

"Yeah," I said matter-of-factly, "Yeah, he did."

"He doesn't really think you killed anybody."

"Is that a question or a statement?"

"Well, does he?"

"Who knows what Frank Wenders thinks? He's fishing." I laughed at the thought of a whale fishing. It must have been the pain killers. Lisa was staring at me. Like she'd stared at me earlier, from the hospital hallway outside of my Emergency room, only more so. If I'd ever seen the like, she was building up to a question.

"What's going on, Blake?"

Yeah, a question. Staring back with any meaning or intensity was out of the question. I was so medicated, I could barely hold my battered head up. I tried instead for naive innocence.

"Don't bother with that look," Lisa said. "You're not sweeping this under the rug. I heard you with the doctor. I heard you tell him you're having hallucinations."

"I did *not* tell him I was having hallucinations."

"You said you were afraid you were."

"If you're going to listen to other people's conversations, the least you could do is listen. I was asking him a question about a hypothetical case."

"That's nonsense, Blake, and you know it. You were asking him about brain damage."

"I was curious," I said defensively. "I've been hit in the head a few times." I'd have pointed at my turban for emphasis but couldn't lift my arm.

"Are you having hallucinations?" Her tone was touching and terrifying. She was staring again.

"I don't know," I told her. I wanted to tell her so much more. About the things going on – in my head; the pain, the shocks, the visions or hallucinations or premonitions or whatever they were. I wanted to tell her the dead were transporting into my noggin in a blue and gold beam of light and begging for my help. I wanted to tell her that corpses say the darndest things. I wanted to tell her I wasn't merely trying to solve a series of murders, I was experiencing them. And, when she objected to all of the above, to try to convince her that, no really, I've had my head bashed in, been set on fire, had my throat slit, been hung. Why shouldn't I tell her? I trusted Lisa like I trusted nobody on earth.

The room was spinning again, or yet, and that conversation, that sharing of interesting (to say the least) experiences I'd been having, was not going to take place. Certainly not now, when I had no clue what was happening to me, when I was swimming in pain medication. It couldn't take place. If, for some unknown reason, or even a known physical reason like having my skull repeatedly smashed, I was going out of my mind, then I had no choice but to go alone. And if I was becoming some kind of psychic then, Katy, bar the door! I raised my eyes to see that Lisa was still staring with that frightening quizzical look she'd patented. "I don't know," I repeated.

Then I changed the subject. "As for Wenders, he's just fishing." Had I said that before? It didn't matter. "He's not above letting me solve a crime for him, you know that if anyone does. He's got a witness that clears me of this last performance and that probably ruins his day. As to facts in the case? I don't know. Can you imagine what Frank Wenders would do with a fact?"

"That murder scene just sounds like it was horrid."

"They've all been horrid."

"Yes," Lisa agreed. "But this time, all that blood."

It took me a minute to catch up. "The Riaz place? Yeah. It was horrid."

"You're going to think I'm a freak but it sounds kind of romantic too."

"What? What is romantic about a double murder?"

"Nothing. Not the murder. The scene. The way you described the scene."

I tried to remember, saw scattered flashes, but the meds...

Lisa was still talking, describing what she imagined the scene was like. "Rocio fought to live. Mortally wounded, she crawled up the stairs to die beside her husband. Then, with her last breath, she declared her devotion and her love by struggling to grab the rosary and the Valentine that Reggie had given her. She clutched them to her breast and died beside her mate. Don't you think it's kind of romantic?"

"I think you're right. You are kind of a freak."

"Next time you need help, call your ex-wife," Lisa snapped as she stood. "Or better yet, call that little church bitch."

"Whoa. Lisa." I grabbed her arm, nearly killing myself. Everything hurt and the room had no intention of slowing its spin. "I'm kidding. I'm just kidding. You know me... and my jaunty sense of humor. I'm grateful for everything. More, I'm completely in... in debt... I owe you."

"Does that mean you're going to teach me to be a detective?"

"Why in God's name would you want to be a detective? Don't be stupid."

"Okay. Does it at least mean you're going to start paying me with checks that don't bounce?"

"I just said, don't be stupid. Ask for something I can do."

She gave me back my hand, set it right in my lap, which was nice of her. Then she said, "I'm going to take off. I'm supposed to be at work in a couple of hours."

"What kind of tyrant do you work for?" I asked her groggily. "Why don't you take the day off?"

"Just because you stayed out and played all night doesn't mean I don't have work to do."

I barely heard her. The world was quickly fading out of existence. Still groggier, I said, "Hey, hand me that file on Riaz, would you?"

"No." She pushed me back into the couch. I had no strength or desire to fight. "Go to sleep."

"Can't sleep."

I'm pretty sure that's when Lisa headed for the door. I think I remember her opening it. I have the most vague recollection that she turned back and started to say something… Something like, "Nod, I just…" But I was gone, vanished into a drug-induced sleep. Knowing Lisa the way I do, she probably finished the truncated sentence with a sigh. It was, I'm sorry to have to admit, how most people ended their conversations with me.

She's a good girl, Lisa.

Chapter Nineteen

A splash of cold water on the face first thing in the morning is sometimes all you need to jump-start both you and your day. But there are those times, when you're dead on your feet, aching in body and spirit, where the same activity, a cold splash of water in the puss, amounts to little more than rinsing off a corpse. Jump ahead twenty-four hours, sisters and brothers, because whatever that nurse gave me in the hypo made me sleep the clock twice around. I awoke on the morning of my eighth day on that miserable case and was rinsing off a corpse all right, in spades. The big bandage was gone, replaced by a small square of gauze, but my hair was still shaped like a turban. The bruised hulk staring back at me from my drug cabinet mirror didn't need a jump, he needed a tow. But, looking the way I did, what junkyard would take me? I patted my phiz dry (the towel felt like sandpaper), used the frame on both sides of the doorway like pinball machine bumpers to escape the bathroom, and worked my way down the hall like Rich Little doing The Duke.

Always a man with a plan, I scooped up the file folder of Reggie Riaz's summarized prison and parole records on my way through the living room and into the kitchen. Even bending was a chore but, on the bright side, if I was still alive in thirty years and felt the same, I'd be having a good day by nursing home standards. I plugged in the toaster, found the instant coffee and microwaved a mug of water. (I'm probably boring you but, feeling as I was, these were heady accomplishments and I relate them with pride.) I scanned the file, an official looking thing of heavy green cardboard and bright red tabs packed with a rainbow of colored reports, until the microwave called time. I played *Fat Bottomed Girls* with a spoon on the inside the mug (I hate instant coffee), dug out two pieces of bread that didn't look to be part of the penicillin experiment, threw them into the toaster, and returned to the reports.

"Well, looky here."

I opened the counter shutters, equalizing the gloom between kitchen and living room, retrieved the phone from the coffee table, and reached through to set it on the counter. I headed back around into the kitchen, picked up the Riaz file, and started dialing. "Blake Investigations." Lisa was chewing a breakfast sandwich. Okay, I was guessing, but I thought I could hear eggs.

"What a coincidence," I told her. "That's who I called.

"Blake! You're not dead."

"Have you been worried?"

"Slept like a rock the whole two hours you left me night before last. Relished the peace and quiet yesterday. Tried to call you last night, got no answer, minded my own business and put you out of my head. Then slept like a rock again last night."

"You are a rock."

"Ye-ah," she agreed. "And well rested. You ought to get yourself nearly-killed once a week."

"And here I called specifically to tell you you were the best."

"I'm completely charmed. How are you feeling? What's up? And why am I the best?"

"I'm feeling awful. So what else is new? As to what's up; I just opened the Riaz file." I was about to elaborate when something caught my eye; black smoke rolling from my toaster. My breakfast was going up in flames. "Damn it!" I dropped the phone, yanked out the plug, and attempted a rescue. I couldn't manipulate the butter knife, the only utensil at hand, into either slot as my fingers weren't cooperating (even my hair hurt). I turned the toaster over, shook it, and watched my toast and six months of charred crumbs bounce on the counter top. I picked the phone back up. "Sorry."

"What happened?"

"Nothing." Suddenly Lisa's breakfast sounded good. I returned to rescuing mine. "Where was I?" I scraped the char away then buttered my briquettes.

"You were saying how important I am to you."

"The prison report, right." I crunched a bite of toast (that's not an exaggeration) and picked the file back up. "Guess who appeared as a character witness at Reggie's parole hearing?"

She didn't give it much thought. "Mother Teresa."

"You're closer than you know. The Reverend Conrad Delp."

"Blake," Lisa groaned, "get off this case or my mother is going to end up hating me."

"You? Don't you mean me?"

"No, I mean me. She already hates you."

"*Uh huh.*"

"Wait, that's your hang-up sound. Was that it? Was that all you wanted?"

"It's the only interesting fact I've learned. I wanted to share it."

"Thanks for sharing."

"*Uh huh.*"

"Hey," she asked, still chewing, "are you coming in today?"

I took another bite, giving her a little of her own medicine, crunching toast, nearly breaking teeth, as I assured her, "I'm not even getting dressed today."

It wasn't a whole lot later, I admit, that I was dressed and walking around the apartment. I'd returned the phone to the coffee table and was doing laps around the couch, trying to keep my limbs from stiffening up, while I dug deeper into the Riaz prison record. It hurt to sit for very long and, even if it hadn't, that report was interesting reading and hope was keeping me on my toes. I'd been flipping the pages casually, without coming upon any more bombshells, when I came across a list of Reggie's former cell mates. I read down the page, stopped at a name that rang a bell, and let it ring until the explosion went off in my brain. "Son of a bitch."

For once the mental explosion didn't hurt, or feature a cast of ghosts making guest appearances in my noggin, it was just an idea, a notion, a question. But it was a hell of a question. I tossed the file down and dialed the phone. "Blake Investigations."

"Lisa, I need you to call… Stop eating for a second. Call Brian Scully over at the 16th precinct. Tell him I need to get my hands on a photograph of a convict…" I paused to give it a thought and made myself shiver. "…or, heaven forbid, an ex-con named Eddie Love."

"Eddie Love?"

"That's the one. I was responsible for his last trip to prison back when you were still trying on your prom dress."

"I didn't go to prom, Blake. I wasn't asked. Thanks for picking that scab open."

"Eddie Love," I repeated with a sigh. "He was a transplanted Montanan, or Idahoan, or something like that. I worked overtime to forget him. No, wait, he was from Wyoming. Doesn't matter. He was a country boy brought himself to the city like some kind of Midnight Cowboy. I sent him up ten years ago; some nasty business involving prostitutes and a knife. He's a major head case and I need to know if he's out and about. And, if he is, where. Have Brian send the picture to you. I'll be in."

"You're coming in? After the other night? Who do you think you are, Audie Murphy?"

"Never mind; I don't have time. Just make that call and tell Brian I need that picture a.s.a.p. We'll pay for the courier. *Uh huh*."

Before I could hang up, she shouted, "Wait!"

"What? What?"

"Your car is still on Market Street. Do you want me to come get you?"

"In your car? Get out of here."

"It served you well yesterday."

"Yes. And I already thanked you sincerely. But the next time I'm in a container that small there'll be handles on the sides and you'll be fruitlessly searching for six guys willing to carry it. I'll get a cab." I looked down at the list again and, moving to hang up, complained out loud, "Damn it. I should have paid attention."

I heard Lisa's shout just as I was about to cradle the phone. Exasperated, I brought the receiver back up. "Are you still talking to me? What?"

"To what?"

"To what, what?"

"Geez, Blake! You just swore. Then you said you should have paid attention. You should have paid attention to what?"

"I should have paid attention to the bloody scene of eternal romance you were yakking about this morning."

"That was yesterday morning, Rip Van Winkle."

"Whatever," I told her. "While we're in the category of Famous Literary Characters I Have Been, Art Fleming, I hate to break it to you but, when you were doing your Dr. Watson yesterday, you read the murder scene wrong."

"I did?" she asked, sounding deflated.

"Don't get down on yourself," I told her, "at least you gave it a shot. I'm the dummy. I didn't read it at all. Rocio Riaz didn't struggle romantically, dragging herself through a pool of her own blood, to declare her love for Reggie. She was trying to leave a message. She was telling me who killed them."

*

The rest of the morning and well into the afternoon I was tied up with the nonsense of merely getting back on my feet – before I could chase the one clue that Rocio Riaz, that anybody up to that point, had been able to supply. I cabbed it to my office, argued with Lisa over whether or not (we both agreed not, but so what?) I should have been on my feet, and took a gander at the photo of Eddie Love that Brian had sent over from the precinct. It was a beaut; one of our old mugs, with two side-by-side portrait and profile images with a Chicago PD custody number on a placard in front of him. He looked half-naked without his usually-present weather-worn black Stetson (I think I mentioned he was some kind of cowboy) which had been forcibly removed for his booking and, I assumed, incarceration. (Do they let you wear a cowboy hat in prison?) Otherwise, though I really had tried to forget that creep long ago, Love looked every bit the hungry demon I remembered. I couldn't help but stare. A county-issued button-down shirt covered the hellish tattoos I knew decorated his upper body, but his long brown hair, hanging to his chest and the middle of his back, and manicured Jesus beard and mustache were on display. He looked like your standard hippie trouble-maker until you got to his eyes. His piercing blue-gray eyes always sent a shiver through me (and did again then in spite of myself).

Picture in hand, I intended to cab it to AC's (I think I mentioned my photographer friend before too) where I would have a negative and a handful of copy prints made. But Lisa threw a fit. I'd made the mistake of comparing her to Dr. Watson on the phone and the result now was she was certain she could help. She insisted she make the photo run while I rest in my office. She knew what I wanted, she spoke the same English I did, and she knew where AC lived, on what grounds could I argue? Lisa turned the phones off when she left. I behaved myself while she was gone. I didn't turn them back on, or open the fridge (or any of the bottles in the mini bar). How's that for control? I got a few more winks of well-needed sleep and, when she returned, I got immediately back into the ballgame.

I left Lisa behind and cabbed it over to see Large. I questioned him in detail about the prison report he'd secured and got all he had and knew about Eddie Love, the evil cowboy, that human nightmare from my past that I was very much afraid had again raised his 10-gallon hat (on his one pint head) and was peering over the eight ball at me.

*

This case was a ball-buster; I don't have to tell you that. I don't remember a time I was ever so deep into something while at the same time being so physically – and more importantly, mentally – out of it. I was down and out, struggling for my skin, and not a little afraid for my sanity. With that in mind, here I'll digress for a moment. Understand, I wasn't there and I don't know all, or even most of what happened for certain. I don't even know these events should be told at this juncture in the story. But it needs to be mentioned somewhere and this seems as good a place as any.

Like I said, I left Lisa behind in the office. But she wasn't just Lisa Solomon, my secretary, the efficient and loyal dogsbody and sometime annoyance that had (just between you and me, and I'll deny I said it) gotten me into this deep do-do. She was also my friend. She was horribly worried over what was happening to me and had a gnawing feeling she had to do something to help. Worse, she wanted to be a detective and, I had no idea then, she'd already taken another step in that direction.

I told you she'd made the run for me to AC and secured the prints of Love's mug. At the same time, without my knowledge, I learned much later, she'd had print work of her own done. Had I known, I would have killed her. But I didn't. When I took off to do my thing with my photos, she tended to her office duties, answered calls, transferred old paper reports onto new computer files, and ran the office until she couldn't stand it any longer. Then she closed up shop and, with her own packet of photos, did her own thing. She climbed into her lightning-yellow roller skate and pulled from our lot into traffic on the world's longest continuous street, Chicago's Western Avenue, headed in the opposite direction from the one I'd gone. From that point on, to tell it the way Lisa finally told me, when she wasn't in the office slumming as my secretary, she was doing what she could to help solve this mystery and to earn her stripes as a detective.

Her first stop? She never did tell me. My best guess would be the Thai restaurant one block over.

Chapter Twenty

I cabbed it back to Market Street to get my car. The Jag was, unbelievably, where I left it over thirty-six hours before, with all of its tires, windows, and engine parts in place. How would Boston say it, *Feelin' Satisfied*! It did have a parking ticket on the windshield but those wad up effortlessly and fit through any storm sewer grid. I took two long strides and proved it. I climbed behind the wheel (too quickly) and had to pause for a breath. I decided that I'd better accept the fact I was crippled, at least temporarily, and adjust my movements accordingly if I hoped to remain up-right long enough to get out from under this case. The Riaz house, wrapped in yellow police tape, stared down at me, cursing me for not knowing more than I knew sooner than I knew it.

I fired up the Jag and hit the streets feeling like death warmed over but well aware I had no time to lose. If I was completely off the track, I was burning fuel for nothing. If I was right, someone out there was homiciding his way through the membership of the Temple of Majesty, dragging me through the blood behind like a prospector pulling a stubborn mule, but never letting me catch up.

I cruised for a long time with purpose but without luck. Then, finally, I spotted what I'd been looking for, my adopted wayward waif, Connie, at the far end of a gas station parking lot near the intersection of Cicero and Division. She was doing what she had to do to get by, which boiled my blood. She was talking to some scumbag that was haggling to get the price down, which made that boiling blood want to shoot out of my eyes. It wasn't bad enough those girls sold their bodies and their souls, they were supposed to do so at a discount. I cut across traffic, partially blocked the drive near the air hose (it probably didn't work anyway), and jumped out, calling, "Hey, school girl."

The would-be john took exception to the interruption and told me to fuck off. He found the pussy, he said, and he was going to tap it. That was his first mistake. I tapped him instead, right across the bridge of his nose. Somehow he stayed on his feet, which was both admirable and his second mistake. I issued an immediate correction and he laid down on the blacktop where he belonged.

"Blake," Connie screamed. She looked terrible and I'm not exaggerating. Her eyes were dark pools, she was twitching as if she were being given electric shocks, and she was getting mad on top of it. "Who do you think you are, Edward G. Robinson?"

I ignored her, bent down, and slapped the john's cheeks until he came to. Then I helped him back to his feet, threatened him politely, and set him adrift. Thoroughly adjusted in attitude, he followed his red and swelling nose down the street.

"What are you doing?" she demanded.

What was I doing? I didn't really know and wasn't in the mood to think about it. "Get over here," I told her. I grabbed Connie and jerked her toward my car. "Get in." She did though, shaking as she was, she had trouble with the door handle.

"How bad is it?" I asked.

Her arms and legs were still fidgeting but her lips were a tight line. "I'm fine. You have no right to interfere with my life."

"Right. Okay. But I need your help."

She studied something on the carpet that wasn't there and nodded.

"Take a look." I showed her Eddie Love's mug shot. "Do you know this scumbag?"

She looked like a leaf in a wind storm and had a time holding the picture still enough to focus on it. For the first time I realized just had badly she was hurting.

"No," she said with surprising certainty. "He's got crazy eyes. I'd have remembered him."

I gave her a copy; wrapped her twitching fingers around it. "Do me a favor, huh? Check and see if any of the girls have done business with this mook."

"Is he bad?" Connie asked.

"He's definitely bad. Stay clear of him. Do you hear me; stay away from this guy. But, if he's around, I need to know about it."

She nodded her understanding while all but swallowing her knuckles.

"Jesus, Connie, how long since you had a hit."

She shrugged and mumbled, "Too long. Obviously."

"Have you been eating?"

"I get along."

I gave her a twenty. "Don't shoot or smoke it. Buy food. I know you're hurting but you need to eat. Promise... and don't lie."

"Okay. I will. I promise," she lied.

I hated myself for knowing it. "About that guy in the picture," I told her. "He's got a western drawl when he talks and might be wearing a cowboy hat, vest, boots, or any of the above."

"In Chicago?"

I shrugged. "It's a big world."

"Don't I know it," she said with a twitch.

"Let me know. And be careful."

She pecked me on the cheek and said, "Love ya" absently. I didn't take offense; the poor thing was running on automatic. She jumped out of the car and vanished around a sign at the corner. Eighty-six cents for a gallon of Regular, eighty-nine for Unleaded, smokes forty-five cents a pack; robbery. The world was going to hell.

*

I hit the bars, the bowling alleys, the strip clubs, every one I came to, down every street I drove, showing off Love's ugly puss and asking questions about a tattooed cowboy. I did that, without any luck, until I couldn't move anymore. Then I dragged myself into my apartment with my head pounding, my body aching and, thanks to my comic book heroics in front of Connie, my hand throbbing as if it had been whacked by a cartoon hammer. I belonged in a museum (or maybe an asylum). I worked my coat off, threw it down, and opened a bottle of booze. It was green, the bottle, so it must have been gin. I poured some and drank. Yeah, gin. The phone rang. "Blake."

"I've been calling and calling." It was Lisa. The late afternoon had slipped into early evening. She'd closed the office (I knew), and ceased her extracurricular snooping (I didn't know) for the night and was calling, I assumed, from her apartment. She was smacking her lips and talking through food. For some reason it sounded like lasagna though, to think of it now, that made no sense. What did lasagna sound like? "There was no answer."

"What are you eating?"

"Lasagna." I didn't take a bow; who'd have cared. She was still talking. "Where have you been?"

"Next question."

"How come what I'm eating is your business but where you've been is not my business?"

"Because you called me while you were eating and you're doing it in my ear."

"Okay. Never mind," she said. "Did you have any luck?"

"Do I have any luck?"

"That answers that one," she said. "Sorry." Then she brightened. "I was just going to up-date you if you cared what happened today."

I waited for what seemed a significant while. "Well?"

"I was waiting for you to say whether or not you cared."

I wasted a sigh then asked, "What happened today?"

"Not much."

"Lisa, you could drive a man to drink."

"You're not drinking while you're taking those pain killers are you?"

"I know better than that," I said. I moved the receiver away as I quietly sipped my gin. Lovely juniper heaven. Bringing it back, I told the phone, "I'm hanging up now."

"Wait."

"What?"

"I didn't tell you what happened today."

"Oh, fer Christ's sake…"

"Mrs. Banks stopped by. She said Willie would be getting out tomorrow and would come for his car. I told her he'd better because you'd already taken it over to their place twice and that nobody had been around. I made sure she knew you were ticked."

"Good."

"Then she tried to pay her bill with a check. I told her you'd kill her and dance on her grave."

"Good."

"Some rich old bag, who's missing a painting, called to check on your fees. I told her you charge on a sliding scale, but that I didn't think she'd be coming down the slide."

"Good."

"Then some chickie-babe named, 'Fidel' called. She didn't leave a number."

"Fidel? Like in Castro?"

"Not Fuh-del," she said. "F-eye-del. Like Fido the dog, plus an L."

"Fidel. Okay."

"Who's she," Lisa asked.

"I haven't the foggiest," I lied. "Anything else?"

She hesitated. "No." She hesitated again. "It was a quiet day... at the office."

Something was biting her. I considered asking her what, but decided against it. She'd tell when and if it bit hard enough. "Okay," I said. "That all?"

"Yes," she said. "But I'm not doing anything, if you just feel like talking."

"About anything in particular?"

"No," she said. "Just if you feel like talking."

"I'm hanging up now."

"You know, it wouldn't kill you to *just once* say, Good bye."

"*Uh huh.*" I hung up. I couldn't help it; the moment was simply too irresistible. I took a sip of my gin and the phone rang again. "Blake."

"Blake!" she repeated.

Speak of the devil. I could hear the traffic and knew she was on a pay phone near the street. "Let me guess," I said. "Fidel?"

"Pretty cool, isn't it!" she said. She was fighting to be herself, the self at least that she'd always shown me, but she was struggling. She sounded awful, really shaky, and it didn't take a genius to realize that she was still hurting for a fix. The up-side was maybe, maybe, she used the money I'd given her to actually eat something. She was going on. "Fidel was a mythical sea nymph. I found it in that library book I had. What do you think?"

"I think it's better than Charisma. But I'm still calling you Connie."

"Yeah," she said, sounding distracted. "Hey, listen, I found someone who knows that guy in the picture."

"Eddie Love? That didn't take long."

"No. I showed him to Peaches and she went ape shit."

"Peaches? What's with you guys and the names?"

"What do you want, Blake? If we were writers we wouldn't be doing what we're doing."

"I can't argue with that. Okay. Where do I find Peaches and how will I know her?" She told me, her voice shaking all the while. "Thanks, Connie. Stay safe. Do you hear me?"

The line was dead and she was gone.

Chapter Twenty-one

I could not believe my luck (there was that nasty word again), in a town of three million people, latching on that quickly to somebody that had seen Eddie Love and would admit it. Despite the battle with her horrible addiction, and the fact that anyone unfortunate enough to meet Love knew what it meant to be scared, Connie had come through. She'd found a working girl, Peaches, no less, that had spent a recent evening with the mad cowboy and lived to tell the tale. Now I needed her to tell me. What I didn't envision was the chore it would be finding Peaches.

I guess I never thought about it, and certainly didn't realize, between pounding the pavement on their own and hitching rides with pimps, friends, and johns, how many miles those ladies could put behind them in one night. I spent the whole evening searching, putting those same miles behind me, through relentless traffic from the near north to the south side and back again, with two dozen stops and twice as many short interviews along the way, using a full tank of gas and then some without finding anyone who had seen her. I finally spotted her myself not a stone's throw from where I'd started looking. She was hovering all by her lonesome at what Connie had mentioned was one of her haunts; a bus stop kiosk on the far east end of North Avenue just south of the Lincoln Park Zoo. In the late 1800's, at the same time gumshoes were making their appearance, the zoo got it's first bear cub. He became adept, so legend says, at escaping his cage and roaming the park. (Wouldn't that bruin your night?) Okay, I'm no comedian but with the night getting on and the street light an amber nimbus casting long shadows on the bus shack I couldn't help but hope the zoo had solved their security problem. Peaches, to hear Connie tell it, and getting back to the story at hand, liked this spot because it was near the kids' petting farm (cows, pigs, goats, and ponies). It was no surprise to me. A lot of hookers are street-hardened creatures with lost little girls inside. I pulled up nearby. Her eyes locked onto the Jag. I climbed out and stepped to the sidewalk, calling out, "*Mmmm.* Look at those peaches."

"Baby, you got that right."

I would describe her to you, sisters and brothers, but it turns out I already have. I didn't remember it then but she was the same girl in the zebra-striped spandex that had been with Connie, displaying their wares to passing would-be customers, near the mouth of the alley in which I'd taken that painful and – it seemed, fateful – header on the morning I got into this mess. It was a small disgusting world.

"Want to play Show and Tell?" I asked her.

"Sounds yummy," Peaches said. She dropped her voice as I reached her. "You got a place?"

"Oh, we can start right here." I produced Love's photograph. "You know this piece of work?"

She took one look at the picture, even in the dim light, and glared at me. "Fidel put you on to me, didn't she, that bitch? I knew I seen you before."

"Yeah, yeah." I tapped the photo. "Have you seen him before? Do you know him?"

"Yeah. He's a freak. If you're a friend of his, you must be a freak too."

"I'm not a friend. I've got a problem with him."

"Who are you, Fred Williamson? You a cop?"

"No, obviously, and no. Now, how do you know him?"

She stared daggers, twisted her lips, then decided not to fight city hall. "How would I know him? We did business once; once."

"Tell me about him."

"You are a freak."

I pulled out a couple of twenties and waved them in the air in front of her. "Let's get out of the woods, angel," I told her, then repeated, "Tell me about him."

Peaches considered the cash, took it, and slid it into her bra. "He talks funny. He looks funny. He wears a stupid hat. And he's whacked," she said. "He's a hot mess. What else you want to know?"

I lit two cigarettes and gave her one. "Whatever there is to tell."

She took a hit, sighed a cloud, and sagged in place. "He's a small time white boy set to country music; some sort of religious freak. He wanted me to read from the Bible *while* we did it. The motherfucker's nuts. And he ain't no lonely pillow biter. He's scary crazy."

A hearse rattled past, dodging a pot-hole, followed by a Spaceman ice cream truck. Freud might have had a field day with the symbolism but I was neither superstitious nor nostalgic. One meant the same to me as the other; noise on the street. When they were gone I returned to Peaches. "So what'd you do?"

"Exactly what I was told." She looked around as if she was embarrassed, though there was nobody there but the two of us, and I sincerely doubted she embarrassed that easily. Still, she lowered her voice. "He had me on my hands an' knees; made me read out loud about Sodom an' G'morrah. An' the whole time he's wearin' that damn cowboy hat."

Sheesh. That was going to replace the whale in my nightmares. I disappeared into my thoughts, considering the situation without making any effort to picture the scene. Peaches apparently read my silence as indifference and, annoyed, snapped, "You want more details?"

I stirred, frowning. "No."

"Why? Don't you want your money's worth?"

Now she was bugging me. I had gotten an idea and was trying to firm it up. "Where did he take you the night you went with him? Do you re-member?"

"No way to forget. A pig sty motel on the south side called the Flyin' Saucer. He was al-ready checked in; had a key on him. We went straight to the room."

I pointed to the Jag. "Get in. You're going to show me."

"Not for free."

Now it was my turn to sigh heavily. "Get in."

Traffic remained heavy and it took the bet-ter part of an hour to get where we were go-ing. Despite my objections, Peaches played non-stop with the radio, switching stations every few seconds the whole way. She started with *Rox-anne* but said she wasn't listening to nothin' by no-body called The Police. She rotated the dial, found Cheap Trick's *The Dream Police*, and swore. Then, complaining that white radios played nothing but shit, she went to Rio with Pablo Cruise. That kept her entertained for darn near a full-grown minute. It was turning into a long evening. We eventually got there and I parked on a dark side street in view of the Flying Saucer. Without cussing, low-rent shabby was the only way to describe the motel and, for that matter, that section of town. A perfect place for Eddie Love.

I turned to Peaches in the passenger's seat. "Which room was it?"

"That's it on the far end," she said, pointing. "The last one; number twel'e."

"I'm going to take a look," I told her, getting out. I poked my head back in the window. "Don't even think about leaving." Peaches huffed, crossed her arms, and slid down in the seat.

I skipped the office, heading straight for the room. I did not expect Love to be there, not that early, but I needed to be sure. I stood to the side of the door to room 12, out of the line of fire, and listened but heard nothing. I rapped sharply, got no reply and heard nothing still. I rapped again and got more of the same. Wherever Love was, he wasn't there.

I returned to the car to squeeze Peaches (that's a figure of speech) for more information. "Where did you meet Love?" I asked her. "The time you dated him."

"I don't know, I..."

"Don't give me that. You're sharp as a tack. You know all too well. Now where was it?"

"A bar down on Broadway; the Four Aces."

"That where Love hangs since he got out?"

"We hooked up for one date. I'm not his fuckin' parole officer."

"Knock it off," I told her. "You think you're here because I love spending time with working girls? You ladies see and hear everything on the street. You know what's happening. If you wanted to hook up with Love again, would you go back to the Four Aces or would it be a waste of time?"

"Yeah. If I wanted to find him, I'd go there. He drinks there; I seen him there before we dated and after. But when I see him now I disappear because who in the hell is goin' to date him a second time?"

"You are," I told her. I fired up the Jag and pulled away from the curb.

With The Grateful Dead's *Shakedown Street* backing her up, Peaches was still arguing when we pulled up a half-block away from the fashionably decrepit Four Aces. It wasn't so much a drinking establishment as it was a fire trap with bar stools. But it had a bottle opener up front and a raincoat dispenser in the john; what more could your average alchy or wastrel ask for? "Now remember," I barked, shutting her up. "No matter who approaches you, or what they offer, you're busy. You're waiting on a date. And you don't move. Nobody is to pick you up but Eddie Love, got it?"

"I don't know. You askin' a lot of a poor workin' girl."

"What am I asking? I'm paying for your night; drinks, food, what you would have made if I hadn't come along. A whole night without having to do anything with any of these eh gentlemen."

"This cowboy must be worth a lot."

"He isn't worth a damn. It's my health and freedom I'm concerned about. They're worth everything to me and I need to talk to this Black Bart wanna-be. Now, do you understand the gig? All you've got to do is get picked up by him and let him bring you back to his room at the Flying Saucer."

"Oh, is that all?"

"I'll be waiting. Just bring him to me. There's no danger to you until he gets you into the room.

And you're not coming into the room. Just get him there and, when he opens the door, stand back."

I held out a wad of bills. She hesitated, then took and counted them. "You said three hundred. This is only a buck and a half."

"You'll get the other hundred and fifty when I've got Love wrapped up."

"I didn't agree to that."

"I didn't ask for your agreement. I'm buying your help and making it worth your while. That doesn't mean I'm stupid. The minute I drive away you're free to do what you like with one hundred, fifty of my dollars. That's risk enough. Help me out and you get the easiest working night of your life and the rest when it's done."

She twisted her lips then added the bills to the forty already inside her shirt. "Room twel'e. You be there," she said, climbing out. "See ya'." She didn't look back, just vanished into the Four Aces.

Peter Frampton laid down the first few bars of *I Can't Stand It No More*. In total agreement, I turned the radio off and returned to the Flying Saucer in blissful, thoughtful silence. I parked in the shadows a block away, and made my way through the back of their lot to Love's room, according to Peaches, doing my best not to be noticed. Unlike the others, this room had a new dead bolt in the door. It could have been a problem but, on a second peek, didn't look as if it was thrown. I slipped a plastic card into the jamb and found for once I was right, the bolt was undone. I loided the standard lock below and entered.

Once inside, I closed the door, turned the light on, and gave the room a once over. It looked and smelled like you'd expect for a sleazy motel that rented to crib babies by the hour. A closer inspection showed a couple of interesting modifications. Beneath the corners of the stained coverlet a short rope had been attached to each leg of the frame and left to trail on the floor under the corners of the queen-sized bed. It didn't take a genius to see that someone was meant to be tied there. Extra towels, a roll of duct tape and, I'm disturbed to report, a shiny new bedpan sat on the overhead rack in the tight closet. I looked back to the bed and amended my earlier thought. Someone, apparently, was meant to be tied there for an extended period of time. The windows, beneath the tatty curtains, under the bent metal blinds, were covered with thick black plastic and the sill nailed shut. No light, no looking in or out, no escape save the door. Most interesting of all, the new dead bolt had been installed so that it could only be locked and unlocked from the outside. It wasn't a motel room; it was a homemade prison cell.

I turned the light off, felt my way to a chair at the small beat-up desk near the bathroom, and took a seat. Then I settled back for what I imagined was going to be a long wait.

*

A good long while later there was a knock at the door, which made as much sense as a pig in a beauty salon. Eddie wouldn't knock on his own door and the sick bastard couldn't have a friend in the world, let alone Chicago, to come visiting. I quickly thought up a lie to explain my presence in case it was the motel management, put on a rock hard face in case it was anyone else, and yanked the door open. There stood a startled, at first, and then dejected looking Peaches. She was alone. I jerked her inside and shut the door.

"Where's Love?" I barked, turning the light on.

"I don't know. I haven't seen him."

"Then what are you doing here? We had a deal."

"I been there all night. He didn't show."

"How did you get here?"

"I walked."

I looked at my watch. The glowing dial said it was just nearing two am. "The bar isn't even closed. You didn't even stay until closing?"

"I couldn't drink no more. I'da been drunk an' not able to bring him if he did show. What was I supposed to do? Stay there an' be bored?"

"Heavens no," I said. "I wouldn't want you to be bored."

"That's what I'm sayin'," she agreed. Sarcasm, apparently, was wasted on her. She moved into the room. "How come a straight guy like you knows this creep in the first place?"

"I sent him to jail," I told her reluctantly. "Ten years ago." I didn't want to go into it then.

"You lied. You're a cop!"

That's why I didn't want to go into it. "Take it easy. I already told you, I'm not a cop. I was once; not anymore."

"But you still lookin' for this guy? Well, at least you ain't crazy. At first, I thought maybe you was one of his church brothers."

"He wasn't into religion when I knew him. He was just an ordinary wacko. He must have…" I stopped as, suddenly, an idea occurred. "He must have… found God… in prison."

"Wanna get it on?"

"What?" I asked, my concentration completely broken.

"Wanna get it on?" I looked over to see that Peaches had found the bed, was on it on her knees, and was peeling her shirt up. She was a streetwalker, and a drug addict, but she was still a woman. Her pert breasts, a lovely dark chocolate brown with erect purple nipples, were demanding attention. She pulled the top over her head. "I'd still like to earn that other hundred an' fifty. Besides, I'm bored as hell. Wanna pass the time?"

Chapter Twenty-two

Don't lose your heads, sisters and brothers. I said her breasts were demanding attention. I didn't say I gave them any. I didn't agree to pass the time either. I had something other than peaches on my mind, like stopping a murderer, and keeping myself out of the death house while I was at it. I told her in no uncertain terms to put her top back on.

"What about my money," Peaches whined. "You owe me a hundred an' fifty."

"You didn't follow directions. You quit the game early. You blew it. It's my money and you haven't earned the loot I already gave you. Don't push your luck."

I heard a car pull up. It seemed an appropriate moment to swear, and I did. I hit the light switch, throwing the room into darkness. Peaches squawked and I told her to shut up. I went to the window, parted the curtains, lifted the blinds, made a small hole in the black plastic, and peered out. It was a car, but it was on the other side of the lot. Two other poor slobs making arrangements to use each other, then rip each other off. Sing it, Satchmo.

I checked my watch and frowned. "It's after 2:00," I told Peaches. "He must have found a different rock to crawl under for the night. Go ahead. Go home."

Amazingly, she seemed disappointed. "You don't need me to set the little prick up? I thought you needed me to set the little prick up?"

"I'm changing my plans."

"But I wanna earn…"

"You've earned my appreciation. Take a lesson in the true value of things."

"My ass. I can't buy shit with your 'preciation."

Against my better judgment, I pushed a couple more twenties into her hand. "There's forty more that you did not earn; a down payment on the next time I need your help. And you're not going to forget it." I took her by the elbow and lifted her from the bed. "Now, while the coast is clear and the getting is good; get. Go home."

"You goin' too?"

"No. I'm waiting for Love."

"You waitin' for love but you throwin' pussy out the door?"

Everybody was a comedian. I opened the door to shove Peaches out.

"Can you give me a ride?"

"No."

She grumbled but she went. I watched her disappear into the darkness beyond the streetlight at the corner of the motel parking lot.

No sooner did I shut the door and lock it when another car pulled into the lot. The light was still out, so I was good to go. I moved to the window to take a peek – but never got there. The engine was turned off very near by, two doors opened and closed almost on top of me, and a gravelly male voice, slurred with drink and a western drawl, growled just outside the door. "Home, sweet home, dahrlin'." The closet wouldn't hide me and I had no time to get to the bathroom. I flattened myself against the wall in the corner so the door would conceal me. A key turned in the lower lock. The door came open.

Amber fingers of light reached in from the lot throwing the shadows of two figures across the floor. It was no surprise to me that the tallest of the two was wearing a Stetson. It had been years, but when Love said, "Step on into my pahr-ler, honey," I recognized the same gutter twang that had threatened me in court as if his sentencing hearing were only yesterday. The girl giggled as he pushed her in. I was trapped, so I took the only jump on him I was going to get. I slammed the door behind them, snapped the switch, and said, "Eddie, long time no see."

The good news was I'd surprised the living hell out of him. Love and his rented street meat were caught like roaches; completely off-guard. The bad news was I was as momentarily blinded by the light as he was. The hooker screamed.

I ignored it, squinting as my eyes adjusted for a look. She kept screaming. My pupils caught up and I took the pair in. Love was absolutely everything I'd expected, no more and no less, from the hat down to the boots. But the girl; you could have knocked me down with a feather. It was Connie. Not Charisma, not Fidel, or any other name out of a borrowed library book. Just plain ol' Connie, twenty-six going on sixty, unhinged, shaking like a freezing Chihuahua and Jonesing like a fiend for a fix. Excuse my horrendous language but my only thought was, What the fuck was she doing with this murdering piece of shit?

I forgot myself for a second. No more than that, just a second. But with Love in the room it was a second too long. He shoved Connie hard at me. I caught her and, stumbling, went over backwards with her on top of me. Lucky me, I hit my head on the wall. Worse, in the time it took us to fall, Eddie opened the door and bolted.

Connie was still screaming as I fought my way to my feet. "Shut up!" I yelled. I don't know when I've ever been so angry. I started out the door, turned back and, from just outside, shouted, "Get out of here, Connie."

She was still in a ball on the floor, crying, "Help me, Blake!"

In over two years of trying I'd made no dent in fixing any of Connie's problems. For all I knew, I'd made them worse by telling myself I was feeding her while all the time knowing I was just feeding her habit. I sure as hell didn't have time to do anything about any of it then. All I could do was repeat the frantic order. "Get out of here, Connie. Get the hell out of here." With my square head once more throbbing, I ran into the lot, then into the dark, after Eddie Love.

*

This was exactly the situation I did NOT want to be in. Love was no Adonis or Kratos, but he was muscled and mean; not to mention ten years younger and crazier than hell. Back in the good old days, the night I'd busted him for his last long prison stint, he'd bitten off – and swallowed – the finger of one of the jail attendants placing him in his cell. Physically, I guess, it wasn't that big a trick, less than an ounce of raw meat plus the index distal phalanx (the fingertip bone to the first knuckle). But hell! It still gave me the willies.

Now I chased Eddie into what, at first, looked to be a poorly lit junk yard but, going in after him, turned out to be the back forty of a tile and brick stoneworks. I slowed down because I'd lost sight of him in a labyrinth of shadowed hiding places. Brick, any color you want to name, but heavy on reds, browns, and whites, in stack after stack of varying heights, all along the fence row and projecting in, five yards there, ten yards there, twenty there, back to the street to the right and for as far as the eye could see into the lot to the left. Not that you could see far; I've been in vaginas that were better lit (pardon my French). I paused trying to let my eyes adjust again to their new surroundings and, (okay, I admit it), trying to summon a little courage. Don't get me wrong. I wasn't afraid of the wayward cowboy. I'd whipped him before and enjoyed it. I was afraid of the creepy murdering rat-bastard, with no inkling of right or wrong, using the dark as cover. There were a million hiding places, un-counted tons of brick weapons, and a hundred places I'd have rather been just then. I moved into the yard and the stacked brick fence line be-hind me became an expansive miniature skyline.

I passed a collection of concrete cisterns, look-ing like sepulchers, stacked atop each other on pallets and slipped into the shadows of a group of trees growing like an oasis just off-center in the lot. In the distance, the lights of a few stray cars glinted as they made their way through the neighborhood, then quickly disappeared. The brick yard was as quiet as a tomb and, though

I'd slowed to a crawl, my heart was racing and I could feel the blood thundering at my temples.

The yard's interior was more of the same, stacks of bricks, tiles, shingles, bags of mortar, concrete, sand, and gravel, a city of building material, all stacked in imposing squares, rounded heaps, or rising in mini towers into the dark night. All were segregated again by use, color, and design, separated by gravel lanes wide enough for semi tractors to maneuver their flatbeds. Leaving the Greek myths and nodding to the Romans, the place seemed a shopping mall for Hercules. The feeling was heightened by an empty flatbed with a rounded red cab sitting immobile as a sleeping monster in the shadows to my distant right. Another, with a yellow cab, lurked nearby to my left waiting for the motion that morning would bring. Somewhere beyond, behind, beside them, Love was hiding with murderous intent and hunting for him in that maze was like looking for a pool cue with one end.

Ignoring the notion he might be hunting me, I stealthily made my way. I entered a section of the grounds roughly fashioned into thinner mini-streets fronted by stone hills, masonry mountains, and endless walls of displayed designer brick. I should have paid more attention to the bricks because, when I passed, they were full of people. One of them, Love I'm guessing, came out playing magician and doing a trick; he tried to pass a metal bar through my head. It was probably a crowd pleaser but I was too busy falling to be sure.

The whole world had Chicago confused with Las Vegas and my head confused with a one-armed bandit; every player in town was hitting it. Which brought to mind (for the ump-teenth time during that caper), the stereotype of seeing stars when you're hit on the bean. The question was, do you? The answer, sisters and brothers, is: the universe belongs to you. As I fell I saw millions of them glistening brilliantly, and their orbiting planets, moons, and hurtling comets, salting the air (I'd never have seen pepper in that night sky) above, and reflected on the glassy surface of the deep black lake into which I was falling. Then came a crash like the shatter of glass and all the stars fell with me.

Chapter Twenty-three

I woke to muted rock and roll, the Stones playing *Shattered* somewhere in the distance. I was still in the brick yard, surprised to be alive, and alarmed to look down and see my face fractured. Not to feel it, to see it, busted into a hundred pieces. That blew my mind. I lifted my head, amazed it came up in one piece, and stared down to see I'd been laying on a broken mirror. Dizzy, I stood, staggered like a sot and, finding my balance, limped to the street fence line. I saw the red and blue lights of squad cars away but closing in. In on what? Me? If so, why? Who'd called them? They had to pass the yard to get to the gate. I ducked out of sight with a bad feeling building. Something told me to get out of there *without* meeting the boys in blue. The Stones faded and, as distantly, AC/DC came on warning me I was on the *Highway To Hell*. Like I didn't know.

Once the cops had passed, I scaled the fence and used the shadows to get away from the brick yard. I tried to think along the way. I assumed of course that it had been Love who brained me. Likewise, I assumed (though I didn't know) it was Love that had called the police on me. Putting me in the barrel was starting to become somebody's habit and just then Eddie was heavy on my mind and suspected of everything. Mind you, I had no clue if any of my thinking involved facts, made sense, or was merely part of the brain damage I feared I'd suffered, and added to, as a result of my clumsy snooping.

Disoriented, my noggin thumping, I hugged the shadows until an opportunity presented itself to stumble in front of a cab. The poor startled driver managed not to hit me. I wrestled the door open, fell into the back, and returned the favor by trying not to bleed on the seat. You'd think he might have appreciated the effort, but no. He called me a number of names implying doubt in my heritage, sexual orientation, and sanity, then bitched me out for running into his path. He had a valid complaint so I let him rant, ignoring him until his lips stopped moving. Then I told him to take me to a pay phone.

"Stupid son of a bitch," he said, winding up. "You're lucky you're not dead."

"Yeah," I agreed, "aren't we all that way."

Through clenched teeth, quashing my own crappy disposition and rewording it into a polite request, I repeated my need for a phone. He didn't seem all that willing, mad as he still was, but once I dropped a couple of dead presidents onto the seat beside him he put the cab into motion. He even waited while I made the call. While I dialed, slowly, the numbers going in and out of focus, two more squads raced by. I showed them my back and listened to the phone ring.

Finally, it picked up. "Gina. It's Blake." The church secretary asked a groggy question, then an excited one, while I caught my breath. "No," I told her. "I'm not. I need your help. I need to see you. No, I can get there. Give me the address."

*

The cab made a circle at the end of a long, ill-lit, and all but deserted culvert and stopped. I tipped the driver to ensure all was forgiven and we were life-long pals then oozed out in front of the address Gina had given me; surprisingly, just a stone's throw from Market Street and the home of the late Riaz family, the scene of my most recent arrest, most recent mental freak-out and, excluding tonight's club to the brain, most recent brush with death. In other words, too close for comfort. It was a large apartment house of red brick, painted gray when Pocahontas was a papoose and now all-but faded back to red. It rose six stories while the rest of the places on the dead end block, small mom and pop businesses and a scant few residences, had either been abandoned or leveled. Having begun a misguided attempt at renewal, the city had lost interest it appeared and moved on without a backward glance. It stood like the last grave marker in an ancient cemetery. I tried to picture the sexy secretary, and her long legs, in this moldering red-gray tombstone but she wouldn't feature. But what did I know? How much did a church staffer make anyway? In the distance behind the apartment building, beyond a wide and overgrown empty lot, stood a foreboding conglomeration of connected square buildings with a tower at its center black against the cloudy night sky. If memory served they made up what once had been an old brewery long since closed down. A recycling company had moved into portions and, to the best of my knowledge, the rats had claimed the rest. The eerie set-piece behind seemed a fitting backdrop for the lonely apartments.

With a last admonition that I, "Watch where the hell you're goin' next time," the driver revved his cab's engine and left me. Aching beyond my ability to describe it, particularly between my ears, I limped toward the apartment building. I passed between two concrete planters decorated with flowers and garden rocks on either side of the entryway steps. I would never have noticed before but lately rocks interested me. Each contained pea gravel, six large gray and black stones arranged in what, if my head hadn't hurt so badly, would have been an aesthetically pleasing configuration around red flowers. No, I don't know what kind of flowers they were.

The lobby was wider than it needed to be with two used tables, three comfy-looking easy chairs, lots of scattered old newspapers and magazines, and a mop of gray hair atop a front desk clerk who batted an eye, just one, as I passed then returned to whatever it was he was reading without any indication of having been moved in any way. A door on the right claimed there were stairs beyond. I took its word for it but continued by. Stairs were out of the question. Beyond stood an elevator, open and waiting. I didn't like elevators. As a rule they left my stomach on the ground floor. But, all things considered, I was grateful for this one. I sank against the inside wall, took a second to make out the fuzzy fourth floor button, and gave it a push. I expected a quick trip in the direction of the angels. Instead the lift growled like an angry demon and, slowly, began an upward trudge. I cursed my luck, finally reached the fourth floor with my life, and escaped the trap elevator swearing 'never again'.

Hunched in pain, I sagged against the frame when Gina opened her apartment door. My suit was trashed and I could feel the skin tighten as the blood coagulated and dried on the side of my face.

"Heavens, Blake!" she gasped. "What happened to you?"

"Ran into an old grudge."

"Come in. You look terrible." She looked lovely in a soft blue robe with a show of pink jammies at collar and cuffs and mere hints at what lay beneath. I know, disgusting of me to have noticed but, really, I wasn't dead. Then again forget my noticing. There was nothing I was going to do about it because, let's face it, I was almost dead. She gave me her shoulder and, with it, a shock of static electricity that dilated my eyes. Touching Gina, touching anybody, was quickly moving down on the list of things I wanted to do. She didn't seem to notice the jolt as she ushered me into her living room and helped me to the couch. "What were you doing, trying to convince someone you were Sylvester Stallone? Let's sit you down," she said, "before you fall down."

Barely had my bruised butt dented the cushion than she told me the police were looking for someone of my description. She'd turned her scanner on after I'd called. My brain was too scrambled to even wonder at a devotee of Reverend Delp having a police scanner. It had no time to unscramble because immediately after she asked if it was me. Then, swear to God, she asked if I killed Katherine Delp? It was quite a leap but that wasn't the end, in fact it was only the beginning. From there she quickly ran the gamut. I could hardly keep up. Did I kill the Ri-azs? Nick Nikitin? Nick's brother? She worked herself up to near hysterics and it took almost more effort than I had to follow. It's no fun de-fending yourself against unfounded charges. Try it when your head is playing snow globe.

I denied all, of course, and eventually, shakily, managed to calm Gina enough that she could put two and two together. With some simple math under her belt (even her soft velour belt) Gina could see it was all nonsense and accepted my side of the story. Trust me, with all I'd been through that night, that week, it was nice to be believed even if only grudgingly. She relaxed.

I needed to. "Do you have anything to drink?"

"Apple juice. Milk. Hot chocolate?"

To look at her from the outside you'd have sworn she was an adult. "It's quicker," I told her, "if you just say, No."

"Is that your hair," Gina asked, reaching, "or is there a lump under there?" She touched the back of my head.

Katherine Delp screamed. No, not from the grave, and not out loud. Gina touched me and, in that instant, Katherine screamed in my head. She screamed, then went silent as death, her scream replaced, overwhelmed by those of Nicholas and John Nikitin as they too died horribly – all over again. I saw nothing while this was happening, nothing but a blinding flash of blue-white light as if I'd been struck by lightning. Then my vision, my extra vision, my psycho-vision cleared. I was standing on the dimly lit street... outside of the Riaz house. I heard an engine rev. An engine? The engine. Geez, not again! This time I screamed.

"Don't be a sissy."

I winced, groaning at the real pain in my head and, as the vibrations of the imagined pains ebbed, opened my eyes and turned to glower at Gina. It seemed that it had been her touch that had sent me away... away to Market Street or wherever my cross-wired mind had gone. It was her voice that had called me back to her apartment. Her voice that had... called me a sissy.

"I'll get some ice." She disappeared, rattled things, slammed things, shook things in another room and returned with a bag of ice. She started for my head but I threw up a hand to stop her. In no hurry to repeat the performance of Traumatic Murder Theater on the stage inside my skull, I smiled my appreciation, thanked her, and applied the ice to my head on my own.

"Let's get this off of you," she said, then helped me remove my jacket; a painful operation that took longer than you'd think. As she chucked the ruined coat away, out of the blue, she asked, "You don't carry a gun?"

I spend a lot of time in left field by myself but that question caught even me off guard. When I recovered, I told her, "You sound disappointed."

"Of course not," she said, looking slightly embarrassed and blushing rose. "It's just with your being a policeman..."

"I *was* a cop," I told her. "I used to be a baby. I don't carry a bottle anymore either."

"There are some subjects," she said, "you're a little touchy about, aren't there? Come on. Let's get you cleaned up before you bleed all over my couch. Can you make it to the bathroom or...?"

"I'm fine to walk."

Gina's bathroom was as light and filled with fragrance as you could possibly imagine. A lug like me had no business there. I stood facing a brilliantly lit mirror with Gina behind helping

300

me off with my shirt. Amid the many bruises she saw, and unexpectedly touched, was an old raised circular scar on the upper right of my back. Electricity shot through me again. This time, it was not the fast boat I'd been taking (too frequently) across the river Styx and into hell. It was merely the jolt that springs when the time, the touch, is right between a man and a woman. My reaction, for the first time since I'd entered her apartment, was not one of pain. I took a breath. "What's that?" she asked.

I stared into the mirror and stiffly answered, "It was a bullet hole."

"You were shot? You don't like to talk about it?"

"There's nothing to talk about," I told her. "It was a bullet hole. Now it's just another scar." I was having trouble concentrating. My head was spinning, for several different reasons, and she was not helping the situation. "Do you have any acetaminophen?"

Gina slipped around me, her left breast brushing my arm, and searched the medicine cabinet. She extracted a bottle and, holding it up, apologetically asked, "Ibuprofen?"

I carefully, sadly, shook my head. "I'm aller-gic."

Chapter Twenty-four

"Do you know Eddie Love?" I asked.

The early morning had moved on and, cleaned and bandaged, I had moved with Gina into her living room. Like her, it was too attractive for the neighborhood it was in. Dehydrated, thirsty, and without palatable options, I settled on black coffee and we settled into her couch. "I've never heard the name," she said, pouring me a topper. "Who's he?"

"Doesn't matter. I'm just knocking down the cobwebs." She didn't know it, but not knowing Love was the best thing that had ever happened to her.

"Does he have something to do with the condition you arrived in?"

"Forget it," I told her. I didn't know for certain why I was there. It had seemed the place to go when I was injured. Once there, I'd started thinking of this blonde creature in a heavily social way, if you get my drift. But, now I was a welcomed guest, I felt like a private dick again with a thousand questions racing through my brain and the desire (like the need for food and water) to interrogate an important witness, no matter how luscious, at my fingertips. Feeling it, I also felt a corresponding mood change. When I'm in that mood, I don't answer questions, I ask them. And the first rule of detecting is don't loiter in the asking. Time and pace are tools, like chisels and wrenches, for prying lids and tightening down thumbscrews. For free I'll warn you, sisters and brothers, beware of detectives making polite conversation. No such beast exists. Suddenly, without meaning to, I was pressing Gina. "Let's switch to Reggie Riaz. He told me he'd never missed a crusade."

She smiled like she was doing a toothpaste commercial. "He was old faithful, all right."

"Gina, Reggie and Rocio were *not* with the crusade the night Katherine was killed."

She looked a question, then turned her gaze inward, giving it some thought. Finally she nodded in agreement. "That's right, they weren't. Rocio was sick. I remember thinking how sweet it was, Reggie staying behind to take care of her."

"Riaz lied to me."

"I'm sure he didn't."

"Gina, let me back up and try this again," I said. "I just told you what Reggie said; that he had never missed a crusade. You confirmed it."

Her face reddened. It was apparent she'd caught the bus the second time around. But her shock had nothing to do with Reggie's actions. "Are you calling me a liar?"

"No. I'm asking you what's going on. Riaz made a statement diametrically opposed to the facts. You confirmed what he said. When the truth was brought to your attention, you just smiled."

"Fact and truth are not the same things."

I picked my coffee up. She set hers down. She needed her hands to talk. "People say, welcome to sunny Florida. But it isn't always sunny in Florida. Are they liars? Florida is sunny, when it's not raining. I'm not a liar, Blake. And, while we're at it, I didn't know this was an interrogation."

"I wasn't interrogating you."

"Was that a lie?"

Okay, so it was; that was none of her business. We stared, each searching the features of the other for – what? Something significant?

A gambler's tell? I silently wished Gina luck. Many had tried before to examine my imagined depths, found nothing but unending layers of rotten onion and had eventually given up peeling. I was having no better luck. I saw a beautiful, innocent-looking, hurt young woman, nothing more. But I could have been mistaken. A round hole in my back, now *just another scar*, was evidence I'd been fooled before. So much for reading books by their covers.

"I thought you and I were talking," Gina said. "I answered your question about Reggie; about the type of person he was. I thought that's what you wanted to know. I assure you, Blake, I'm not trying to keep any facts from you."

"I've been keeping some from you," I told her. "Reggie *was* involved with Katherine's death."

She shook her head and, to keep her hands busy, pushed her cup back from the edge of the table – spilling coffee. She tamped at the mess. "I won't believe that."

"I don't believe he killed her," I said, trying to soften the blow (though I wasn't sure why). "I don't know that Katherine was meant to be killed. But Reggie was involved. He told me that himself."

She clenched the napkin and stiffened. "He did?" The bottom had dropped out of her voice.

"We were supposed to meet. He was going to tell me everything, but he never got the chance."

"Everything?" She cleared her throat. "What did he say? I mean, what did he say when you arranged the meeting?"

"Just that he was involved. He was killed before he could elaborate on anything."

She sagged. Oddly, it looked for an instant like relief but must surely have been emotional exhaustion. She verified that thought when she said, "I don't want to believe it."

"Tell me something, Gina, did Reverend Delp know about Reggie's record?"

"Of course he knew. He met Reggie in… Whichever prison he was in?"

"Stateville."

"Right," Gina said. "That was it, Stateville; through his evangelism program. When Reggie was paroled Reverend Delp hired him. That's when Reggie met Rocio; through the church."

Something about our conversation was cock-eyed but I couldn't put my finger on it. I soldiered on. "Has the church been having money problems?"

"Blake, you're all over the map."

"Yes. Has the church been having money problems?"

"How did you even know about that?"

"I don't know."

"You're just asking questions?"

"Yes. Now, for the third time..."

"Yes. All right, yes. But I don't know any details. I don't know how bad it was. Reverend Delp asked me to take a salary cut. But I didn't mind. That's what you need to understand. I'd work for a man like Reverend Delp for free. Besides, those problems are over. With all he's been through, people around the country have been donating like crazy to help."

"You mean that the money's been pouring in?" She frowned at the way I'd put that but I wanted to scream, 'Bingo. On the friggin' nosy. Don't you get it?' She stared, wearing a smile that made her look like the Grinch's dog. For a smart woman, she seemed clueless as to where we'd arrived. We had arrived, hadn't we, at another motive? That's what it was another motive, on top of a possible jealousy, for murder. Gina didn't see it; didn't see a thing. Was she willfully blind or was I completely wrong? Was there nothing to see? Delp had something to gain, riches. He had something he might have wanted to lose, a cheating wife. No, it wasn't in and of itself proof the reverend had done anything, but... Couldn't she see the motives? Gina blinked and smiled the Temple of Majesty smile; Max the pooch on a sled on Mount Crumpet.

"You're devoted to him?" I made it a question at the end but it had been a statement all the way. She answered without hesitation.

"I'm devoted to God. I believe in Reverend Delp."

"What if he isn't what he seems?"

"I won't listen to this, Blake."

"Gina, everything isn't as it seems."

"Apparently not," she said. She didn't exactly spit the words but nobody could have lived on the difference. She gave a look that, no matter how much I loved myself, made me not like myself very much. But she wasn't finished. "Why do you disdain reverence?"

"I don't. I disdain reverence for things that don't deserve it."

"Who decides, Blake? Reverend Delp has a book he goes by when he makes moral judgments. You can agree with him or disagree, but there it is. What have you? Your objectivity? Heaven forbid, your subjectivity? Your feelings for your fellow men? Who and what, in your world, deserve reverence? How do you decide? Who are you to decide?"

"You're under the impression this personal nonsense matters," I told her. "I'm not writing Delp's biography, I'm trying to solve his wife's murder, and all the killings that have resulted. You don't make friends when you're trying to solve murders."

"You could."

"I could what?"

The anger had left Gina's eyes and she was staring intently. For the first time I recognized how closely we were sitting. I could feel the heat from her body and, something else, something magnetic. I'd felt it in the bathroom when she'd touched my back and now, again, a twitching of the nerve endings I hadn't felt in a long time. It was nuts. What about our conversation had led us, led me, there, with thoughts of body heat dancing in my head? My throat had gone dry. I tried to clear it and wondered how, at the same time, I might clear my head. "I better go," I managed to say, and licked my lips. "I've imposed on you enough."

"You can't go like this." She leaned in to me. Her hand found mine. More electricity. The natural human kind, thank God, but electricity all the same. "You're half dead," she said. "You need…" Her moist red lips could have turned a desert to a wooded glade. "You need some sleep." Her eyes were lakes. I was dying for a swim. She was still talking. "It would probably be better… if you just stayed… if you wanted."

I'm not a romantic. At least I don't think I am. I'm a dinosaur, a creature out of time. But I was pretty certain about what was happening. I could feel her hot breath on my bruised lips. Her long, intense stare, our stare, was threatening… to become a kiss.

But it didn't. Not then.

Gina broke away, rose, and headed for the hall. I followed her like a mutt chasing a plush play toy. She opened a cupboard built into the wall, pulled out a pillow and blanket, and pushed them into my chest. She pointed back to the living room and, by proxy, to the couch. "That's your bed, Blake," she said. I didn't whine but I wanted to. "You're a train wreck," she added. "You're half-dead. If you were in good working order... Forget that." She closed her eyes. When she opened them again, she said, "You are probably, make that definitely, very bad for me. Right now, I'm bad for myself." She pointed again and shook her arm for emphasis.

I turned, pillow and blanket in hand, tail between my legs, and started back to the couch. I slept uncomfortably, in pain, with occasional moments of bliss. Gina visited me in those moments, and Mary and Becky from high school, and (I'm sorry Mrs. Solomon) Lisa too, in their turns. Brain damage. There was absolutely no doubt.

Chapter Twenty-five

A few hours later, what the calendar laughingly called *the next morning*, I tip-toed out before the sun came up. Okay, I couldn't have tip-toed if my life had depended upon it, but I did leave quietly doing my best not to wake Gina in her bedroom a few feet away. I vetoed a cab thinking a walk might be good for me. It turned into more of a limp as I headed back to the Flying Saucer, taking the long way around the brick yard, and keeping my mind off the aches by day dreaming about the pain medication I didn't have with me. I reclaimed my car and, when I reached my office, called Wenders and gave him what I had (omitting, for reasons of brevity, any mention of chats with the dear departed, psychic visions, or criminal trespass in a certain brick yard). He wasn't impressed. In fact he had difficulty making it sound as if he cared at all. No surprise there.

The surprise came later that afternoon when I was sitting at my desk, gingerly as I was one big bruise, with that self-same Lieutenant Wenders sunk into the chair across from me. He was frowning above his row of chins and hating himself because, and this was the unbelievable part, he was trying to be helpful. Not that he was; he was useless as tits on a boar but he was trying. That was phenomenal. Of course it was also very short-lived. Within minutes of assuming our usual positions, our tempers worked themselves into their usual positions as well.

"Eddie Love?" Wenders asked with a sneer. "I don't get it. Make the connection for me."

I sighed deeply. "He was an old cell mate of Reggie Riaz. I've already told you. Either through Reggie, or because of him, Delp got a hold of Love and conspired with him to do in Delp's wife."

"And you have evidence of this?"

"No." I moved (and shouldn't have), then tried to move back (and shouldn't have done that either). "No," I repeated, "I don't have evidence."

Wenders swore. "I know it's been a while since you were a cop, Blake, but see, the real police, we still need to collect evidence against people we suspect of committin' crimes. They don't put people in jail on your word that they're naughty. If you could prove he was in the city…"

"I was in his motel room. How many times have I got to tell you?"

"Keep tellin' me, Blake, only stick in a fact or two for flavor. If you did get in his room, the way you say you did, it's breakin' and entering. I admit, that's a minor felony for you, so I'd overlook it. But it isn't the way you say."

"The Flying Saucer Motel; room 12. Get off the dime, Frank. Check."

"We checked, smart guy. There's nobody in room 12 at the Flyin' Saucer. The manager says there hasn't been. Been closed for repairs; no carpet, unplumbed. But it does have a nice new door – that does *not* feature a deadbolt."

"And none of that seems at all convenient to you?"

"Yeah, it does. But here comes that nagging word again, Blake; evidence. There's no evidence the room hasn't been closed for repairs. There's no Love in the room. There's no Love on their books. There's no evidence he's in the city. He's skipped on his parole officer."

"I know," I said. "I've talked to his parole officer."

"Then you also know, since he's chosen to violate his parole, he'd be a numb nuts to still be hangin' around Chicago. He's gone, Blake. Probably back to the wild west. He 'got along little doggie' and he's someone else's problem."

"I'm telling you, he's here."

"Great. He's here." Wenders sighed a ton. "When we find him we'll smack him with a ruler. Meanwhile, there's no evidence he's a murderer and you're still missin' a motive. If you could at least suggest a reason for Love to go on a killing spree, I might buy it."

"He's a psycho."

"So are you!" Wenders growled. Then he made a noise that I won't try to recreate. When he got himself under control, he started again. "I know he's a psycho. I read his jacket. But he's never shut off anybody that we know of. The trouble, Blake, is that the world's full of psychos. What I need to know is, is he a psycho I got to worry about? If we find him, if we can nail down a motive, if we can collect something like evidence, I'll buy Love. But so far we haven't done any of those things. That makes it look like you pulled his name out of your square hat. As for Delp, forget him. You ain't Clint Eastwood. You got dick on him and I'm not buyin' Delp."

"His wife was playing hide the corn dog with Nick Nikitin."

"You have zero evidence Delp knew anything about it. And even if he did, and he had nothing but black bubbling murder in his heart, he had no means because he had no opportunity. He was on television, from a different state, bein' stared at and cried over by his voluminous flock."

My mouth fell open. "Where'd you learn that word?"

"What?"

"Vo-lum-in-ous?"

"That's what I said. I said it right."

This from a mug who signed his name with an X. If only I could have shook my head.

"Do you mind?" he barked. "Nobody is goin' to buy Delp, until you come up with something that will impress someone other than your mother."

"If I could impress my mother, they'd give Delp the chair." Staring at Wender's pig eyes staring at me was helping to turn my already queasy stomach. I got up, like a bag of broken bones, and limped to the window to get a look at all the air outside that didn't have his breath in it.

"Your old lady has all my sympathies," Wenders continued behind me. "But I ain't your analyst, Blake, so you can just put away the couch. Now, leavin' your family problems and getting back to Delp, I repeat, you got nothin'."

"Then I'll have to get something."

"Forget it. On Delp, you're out of room to push. I'm not asking you, Blake, I'm tellin' you. For once in your life you'd better listen. Delp is an important man; he isn't to be screwed with." He was watching me stare out the window and, apparently, didn't like it. "Are you listenin' to me?"

I couldn't help it, I was sighing too. "I hear you."

"I'm trying to do you a favor, whether or not you're too stupid to realize it." He was rising from his chair. It sounded like a farmer pulling a trapped boot from a mound of bullshit. I watched the street, looking at nothing, avoiding the sight of Wenders foundering. He drew a loud breath when he finally reached his feet, then started back in on me. "The Reverend Conrad Delp has made it plain he is going to file harassment charges against you if you don't stay the hell away from him."

"Yes, I heard."

"You heard? But it didn't sink in, you dumb bastard. This man is the biggest thing in the God department Chicago has ever seen. He has friends that make you look like an ant."

"Yeah," I told the window pane. "I've seen his photo collection. I was uber impressed. I'd worship him myself, if he hadn't killed his wife, Nick and John Nikitin, and Reggie and Rocio Riaz."

"A minute ago, Eddie Love killed them."

I turned slowly. "Follow the bouncing ball. He hired Love."

"This is America. You need to prove that."

"I'll prove it when I find Love."

"You're not a cop anymore," Wenders said, plodding for the door. "We'll find him."

"Yeah, you'll look under your plate at lunch. And if you accidentally fall into a hole full of evidence against him, and he calls up and tells you which bench he's sitting on in Grant Park, you'll walk right past him. Or, worse, you'll shoot the bastard. Love won't go to prison again; he'll make you kill him."

"So where's the downside?"

"I need him alive to prove Delp was behind this. If he dies, Delp goes free."

At the door, Wenders tossed his hands into the air and let them fall – resigned. "I give up. You're like a crazy person."

"How many silver dollars were found around the Riazs' bodies?"

"What difference does that make?"

"I'm just curious, Frank."

"You're just curious? Twenty-nine. *Ding. Ding. Ding.* Twenty-nine silver dollars. Does that solve it for you, Sherlock? Is that the last piece of the puzzle?"

"No."

Wenders opened the door to the outer office, startling Lisa into spilling her *mocha poop-a-chino* all over the papers on her desk. She glared like an angry owl. The lieutenant ignored her and turned back to me. "Do not bother Reverend Delp again, under any circumstances, Blake. Do you understand?"

"Yeah. I got it."

Chapter Twenty-six

Of course I ignored Wenders. I didn't have a choice, my case was burning out for lack of fuel. When that happened, the first, the only rule of detecting was: relight the fire, no matter the cost.

I can't really describe much of what I saw when I entered the radio station. I'm okay, now, to tell it. Trouble was I wasn't all that okay then to take it in. Between the original concussion, the subsequent head injuries, the head-to-foot pummelings, the headaches, the ghostly visions (call them hallucinations if you want), the special pain-killer, and the most recent shouting match with a certain block-headed lieutenant, my brain had taken on a life of its own and pretty much included me out of everything. Anyway, I saw what I expected as I walked into the lobby of WKNG, friendly business-like colors, waiting room chairs that (like those in the fast food joints) looked comfortably inviting but were molded in hard plastic telling your butt to be on its way. The station's call letters, in splashes of pink, white, and blue (pastel patriotic?), and a golden 'crown' logo filled the wall backing the high reception counter top. A conservatively frocked blonde stood on duty behind it. Once upon a time, she would have been my type. Of course, once upon a time, my type was eighteen to eighty, blind, crippled, or crazy. Now they were all too good for me.

"Hi," she said, delighted I'd finally come into her life. "Can I help you?"

"Hi." I saw her delight with a warm smile, then raised it with a phoney business card. "Onslow Stevens," I lied. "I'm with Reverend Delp's ministry team."

"Oh, you must be new." Her smile didn't actually disappear it just went to *parade rest*. She waved the card away, certain I was who I claimed to be, and waved me toward a pale wooden door on the far side of the room. "They're in Studio One."

"Of course." The big clock on the wall said the Temple of Majesty's Power Hour would be on air live in twenty minutes. Well, partially live. The living and breathing minister was somewhere within preparing his sermon for the listening faithful. His secretary would be with him. His announcer would be at their side hawking the reverend's newest book, church tote bag, coffee mugs, and T-shirts, and ever-ready to verbally trumpet Delp in and out of the commercials. The rest of the show, from theme song, to chorus, to guest speakers, to transitional music, came out of a can or, more accurately, off of tapes. Gina had filled me in on the mechanics of it all and, even with my faulty memory and my recently scrambled brain, I remembered that. I offered the blonde a friendly wave, told her, "God bless you," and, with the click of the door latch behind me, headed down the long hall to the studio.

I know what you're probably thinking and you're right. I had no business there. Had Wenders known I was there, he'd have shot (or at least arrested) me. I didn't care. Delp was my man; he had to be. That meant I needed to go into the lion's den and give him a poke.

The hall door to Studio One was closed. Through a window I saw the reverend, Gina, and their announcer rehearsing before music stands and microphones. On the other side, through another window, the show's director and sound engineer were going about their business, making last minute preparations to go On Air. The studio door to the control room was closed as well. I didn't know the announcer, and I was willing to excuse Gina for reasons that probably shouldn't have existed but did, but for my money, Delp looked like what he was; a rat in a box.

Delp and Gina looked up at the same time and saw me standing there. It was a coin toss which of the two grew the grimmest expression quickest. Delp stepped from the studio into the hall with Gina following. "Well," the reverend said, sounding either frustrated or tired. (I didn't know which but hoped it was both.) "If it isn't the man who can't take a hint. Mr. Blake, what can I do for you?"

"Well," I said, aping his creepy smile. "If I can have anything I want for Christmas, you'll confess to five murders and take your ass to prison where it belongs." Had I punched him between the eyes I don't think I could have produced a better reaction. I almost felt sorry for him; almost.

Then he got rude and stifled all my compassion. "You need to see someone, Blake. You are mentally ill."

"Nah." I waved it away as if he'd offered me a hard candy covered in pocket lint. "You just think I'm nuts. Truth be told, it's a common misconception; given the lie back in the first grade."

I expected Gina's jaw to drop like Jonathan Winters' pants but, to my surprise, she pinched her lips and hung in there studying the two of us as if she were watching a tennis match. Her boss, meanwhile, (and I give him credit for the act) looked a trifle confused. "What," he asked, "are you talking about?"

"My first grade teacher wanted me seen by a psychiatrist," I confessed. "Every time the class colored, no matter what the project, I always used a black crayon. She was very concerned. But my mother is a miserable old bitch who makes it a point never to agree with anyone. So, rather than take the teacher's advice, she demanded I explain myself. I told her that when we lined up for crayons I did as I was taught and let the others go first. By the time I got to the box, black was the only color left. You see, I didn't need my head candled at all. I just needed to go first once in a while."

My effort to clear the minister's confusion had failed. The poor man's eyes were all-but crossed. "I'm certain that is fascinating," Delp said. (I noted with amusement he didn't sound fascinated.) "I congratulate you. Now, if you don't mind, we have a show to prepare and I have no time to listen to any more of your idiotic ranting." As an afterthought he added, "or your accusations."

"I don't mind," I assured him. "Actually, Reverend, I came to apologize. In hiring me, you threw good money after bad and it's my fault. This case, it turns out, was so simple, I should have been able to solve it from bed. Instead, I've been running down blind alleys, balancing ice packs on my nose, and stiff-arming the cops for nothing. So, I apologize." He stared warily. I tried not to be hurt. "I also came to congratulate you on the impressive operation you manage. I'll lay odds there aren't any two members of your organization with a damned clue what the other is doing."

That made him mad. "You, Blake, are a vile little man."

"I have my moments," I agreed. "But, enough about me, let's talk about you. You discovered your wife was sharpening the bookkeeper's pencil." I paused, struck by a notion, and pointed at Delp. "I'll bet you thought Nick Nikitin was a vile little man as well?"

"Yes," the minister said in a monotone, "I suspect he was."

"You stood to lose everything because your wife had hot pants for a vile little man."

"What are you implying now?" Between sentences, you couldn't have slipped a sheet of paper past his pinched lips. "You're saying I killed Katherine?"

"No. Heavens, no. You didn't have the guts to kill her. You just wanted her dead. And regardless of how little your religion means to you..." I ignored Gina's gasp. "You have surrounded yourself with actual believers, so they weren't going to do it for you. You needed a killer. Luckily, you had an ex-con to find one for you. All you had to do was pull the wool over his eyes."

Delp glared. From the corner of my eye I noted that Gina finally wore the look of shock that went with her earlier intake of air. It was about

327

time. I'd been around cigar store Indians easier to annoy. I soldiered on. "Poor Reggie Riaz actually believed all that bullshit you fed him about the church having money problems." I turned to look at Gina, "They all did," then back to Delp. "You needed Reggie to believe that God's work would come to a screeching halt if you didn't find a way to shake everyone in the congregation up; something dramatic to bring in donations." Delp's glare had, surprisingly, turned to one of utter confusion. I didn't know what that was all about, but I wasn't buying it and chose to ignore it. "Reggie gave it away with a Freudian slip. When I asked if Katherine had any enemies, he said 'I don't know anyone who would *take* her.' That's what it was in the beginning. You convinced Reggie to take your wife; to kidnap her."

"Nonsense!"

"Show a little faith." The muscles in Delp's jaw tightened as he stared holes through me. On the bright side, I had his attention. "When Reggie said he couldn't do it alone, you agreed. You told him the sort of individual that might help. You suggested, or got him to suggest, an old cell mate; Eddie Love. Reggie had turned the wayward cowboy on to the Lord in prison. You met both through your evangelism work. You appeared for both at their parole hearings. What Reggie never considered, what he never imagined you were counting on, was that a maniac, even a religious one, especially a religious one, is still a maniac. Eddie rented a motel room, telling Reggie it would be a safe place to keep Katherine out of sight until the church was saved. The poor slob had no clue you'd met with Eddie alone and made arrangements for that kidnapping to become a murder."

Delp's lower lip trembled and he started to sputter. I plowed on.

"Reggie didn't know you altered the plan. He went to his grave thinking the maniac cowboy just *lost control* that night. He had no idea Eddie was filling an order for you. Trouble was, you didn't know Eddie had a plan of his own. While he was handling your business, he was getting revenge for himself on a broken down private detective that, ages ago, had put him away."

"I watched Katherine and Nick from a tree limb outside your wife's bedroom window. Which, come to think of it, could prove that I am nuts. Anyway, they were too busy undressing each other to worry about a peeping Tom. What I didn't know then was I had a couple of peepers of my own; Eddie and Reggie watching me from the bushes. Thinking back, I heard them rustling around below but, when I studied the yard, I saw only shadows and heard only the breeze. It's what everyone tells themselves in horror stories and murder mysteries, isn't it, it's only the wind."

I'd given up trying to guess what my listeners were thinking. They were attentive, so I continued.

"Your wife did not accompany Nick to the front door. They said their good-nights upstairs. Young Nikitin drove away and I watched Katherine turn out the bedroom light and go to sleep; her head filled with the stuff that dreams are made of. Then I descended, hopped the fence, and took my leave confident I had done the job for which you'd hired me. Whether or not the evening had turned out as you imagined was not in my power to guess. I hate to admit it, but Nikitin was only one of the myriad complications of which I was ignorant that night. The others concerned the presence, the intentions, the actions of Eddie Love and Reggie Riaz. They were there the whole time, saw me on stakeout, saw me pop the lock on Nick's car, watched me watch the lovers. They waited for Nick and me to leave."

"With their intended victim, your wife, alone in bed, and now that the coast was clear, Eddie and Reggie emerged from the bushes headed for the house. They forced a withdrawing room window located, significantly and unfortunately, above the rock garden at the side of your house and entered. Reggie went first. Behind him and, I believe, without his knowledge, Eddie grabbed up a hefty rock and followed. They were headed upstairs, Reggie thought, to *kidnap* your wife. But Love had something else in mind."

Chapter Twenty-seven

It felt as if the temperature had dropped twenty degrees in that radio station hallway. I ignored the chill and cold stares coming from Delp and, it hurt to say, Gina. But I wasn't sorry. I was determined to unravel the web of deceit we'd all been caught in and, to that end, I had a story to tell. "As your right-hand man, and your rented psycho, climbed your stairs that night headed for Katherine's room," I said. "I don't think Reggie had any idea they were bringing on her doom."

"You're not only delirious, you're fanciful as well."

"But you digress. No. It's far more likely that Reggie freaked out when Eddie stole past him into that bedroom, rock held high, and bashed in your wife's skull. He thought he'd just snapped; thought the idea of Katherine and Nick fornicating right there in front of them in your house made Eddie so righteously indignant that he went ballistic. You were most likely shocked yourself when you heard about it. When you heard what Eddie had done."

Delp shook his head. "I know Eddie Love, of course," he said. "Through the prison service. I did appear on his behalf, as I do for many, at their hearings. But this conspiracy… Blake, you're ranting. I *was* shocked by Katherine's murder. Of course I was shocked," he added acidly. "She was my wife."

I wanted to laugh in his face or at least blow a raspberry. Instead, I merely smiled (Delp wasn't the only one that could muster quiet dignity from whole cloth) and moved on. "My guess is he wasn't supposed to kill her until he had her alone at the Flying Saucer Motel. But we'll come back to that. The real question the night of the murder was, what the hell was Eddie doing? His rage made no sense. He knew your wife was an adulteress, that's how you convinced him to kill her in the first place."

Gina finally made her presence known. "The whole thing is ridiculous, Blake," she said. "If this were true, if any of it were true, why would the Reverend have hired you?"

I gawped at Gina (and couldn't help but notice that Delp did too).

"The answer of the week," I told Delp, "is that I come highly recommended." Gina frowned. "But the fact is, the reverend didn't hire me." The ping pong was killing me but I turned back to Delp. "If my scorecard's accurate, Eddie hired me, through Reggie and Gina, in your name." I said it all nice and slow, then added, "Gina knew nothing about your plot with Eddie, and you knew nothing about me. In fact I'm going to guess that, not only did you not order my hire but that, if it was even suggested, you specifically told Eddie *not* to do it."

The minister and his secretary traded unreadable, but what to them might have been meaningful, looks. I took is as a sign I was right and, with my confidence bolstered, continued.

"Eddie suggests hiring me to strengthen your alibi," I said. "You're not only out of town but your lovely wife was being guarded by what was purported to be a professional private detective. How could you know I was a screw up? You tell him you're Reverend Delp and you don't need an alibi. As far as you're concerned that ended the matter. But Love had a hard-on for me of which none of you were aware. I sent him to prison. Eddie was going to get me back; he promised that at his sentencing. He used the occasion of killing your wife as an opportunity to set me up. It makes little difference really, either without your orders or against your orders, he got me there, to your house and, after killing your wife, anonymously reported my presence to the police."

The reverend had run the gamut of facial expressions and, for the moment, had returned to giving me the stink eye. Oddly, it looked good on him. Gina, I confess, remained unreadable. "Yes, Reverend, you conduct your business in many directions at once. You fight on many fronts."

"I fight the great enemy of mankind," the pompous bastard said. Then he stared right at me and got insulting. "And his minions."

If I'd known what a minion was I'd have been hurt. But, not knowing anything at all, I continued unmoved. "Yes, and I'm sure the world appreciates it. But we keep getting off track. As great a team captain as you are, you're not all that perceptive. Certainly not as perceptive as your followers give you credit for." I hadn't entered the studio with my name on anybody's Christmas card list and there was no point in pulling punches then. Gina was either going to follow me toward the light or stick with her boss but she was a big girl and the choice would be hers. The way I saw it, there was a truth that needed to be told. "You had plenty of balls in the air. But it never occurred to you that Eddie did too. You thought him just a killer. But he had his own game to play. Like I said, after killing your wife, he turned me in to the cops. That could have been bad. The police need little incentive to give me a hard time. But they aren't stupid. They thought I knew something about what was going on but they never, for a minute, believed I had anything to do with Katherine's murder."

Delp was glowering. I didn't know if it was because I kept bringing up his dead wife or because the Alpha wolf in him had learned something about one of his pack he hadn't known. Not my problem.

"Long story, short," I continued, "Where Katherine died was inconvenient but, ultimately, it didn't matter. She was dead and as anticipated your followers were amazed and inspired by your ability to carry on. The donations to your stale dog and pony show, which had begun to dry up, once again began flowing like wine. But Nick Nikitin was out there, somewhere. It wouldn't have made the slightest difference had your wife died during a botched kidnapping. But she'd died at home. Nick could be tied in, if you happened to get an investigator on the case that was worth a damn. And Nick knew things about the church and about you. You put me on Nikitin's trail. You did the same with Eddie. He found him first, hiding away in a lakeside cabin with his brother, and he killed them both. All justified as far as you were concerned because he was tying up loose ends for the glory of God's chosen one."

"It's ridiculous," Delp insisted. "The whole thing is outlandish."

How the minister still managed to hold his nose up was beyond me. But there it was. You could have flown a flag off of it. To hell with it, and him. Where was I? "Did Eddie give you the details? How he shot the big one, John, blocked the cabin doors, then set the place on fire?"

Gina gasped and, if it wasn't the crappy lighting in the studio, grew pale. Delp was stoic but I thought I detected a bob of his Adam's apple. A gulp was the least he could do.

"Those two extra murders might have been the end of it; were the end as far as you were concerned. But little did you know, there was that goddamned crazy cowboy, Love, still trying to stick it in my keister; trying to set me up as a killer. Again, he left evidence of my presence at the scene, just as he had at your house. But this time it was a major blunder. Like a kindergartner in a sandbox, he left a message in the mud by the lake bank where I'd slipped and fell. Then he wrenched the license plate from my car, beat it against an innocent tree, and left it to be found. It was not only less convincing than before, it was cartoonishly embarrassing. It called attention to itself. I've already said I'm no friend of the cops but they're not complete morons. For no apparent reason, suddenly, an unrelated fire in a cabin in the woods a hundred miles from Chicago was connected to the murder of a prominent minister's wife. Instead of floating away on your resurgent river of money, with your cheating wife out of your thinning hair, you're hearing your name pop up in another investigation."

"Only from you, Blake."

I wanted to take a bow but settled for a smile. "Love was quickly becoming a liability." Delp stared, as icy as Capone's corpse. "You discovered Love wasn't your only trouble. Reggie Riaz and his wife, and their collective consciences, were threatening to further bitch things up."

Gina had gone from pale to gray and, standing still, looked like a statue. "You were at your desk," I told her, "most likely staring at his office door with a mask of concern while your boss and Reggie had it out." She opened her mouth but didn't speak. I felt for her and turned it back on Delp where I was certain it belonged. "You'd used Reggie, Reverend. He saw his whole life collapsing around his ears. Rocio had nothing to do with any of it. Reggie wouldn't have if he'd even suspected murder. It doesn't matter what finally fueled him, his love for Rocio, fear of a return to the joint, guilt. Whatever it was, Reggie wanted out. That's what you had words about the morning he went on sabbatical."

Delp was shaking his head as if he just could not grasp anything I was saying. "Now you're going to tell me... that I killed Reggie and his wife?"

"There was no need. Regardless of how much trouble he'd been, you still had Eddie. Not that it takes you off the hook. As far as I'm concerned, you can take a fall for everything he did."

"So," Delp said with plenty of elegant snottiness. (If he was wounded he was doing a good job of hiding it.) "This Eddie Love killed the Riazs?"

"Yes, brutally. But save the 'this Eddie' crap. You hired him, you set him motion. He isn't a stranger. The cops found twenty-nine silver dollars scattered around the Riazs' bodies." I pulled a coin from my pocket; the one I'd swiped from the murder scene as the cops barged in. I held it up glinting in the studio light. "They missed this one," I said. "The thirtieth piece of silver, paid to Judas for his betrayal of the Lord." I flipped the coin, caught it, and pushed it back into my pocket.

"The only thing I wondered about was the Bible reference. Eddie had been leaving me biblical love notes at the scenes of each murder; Deuteronomy, 'stone that person to death,' when he killed your wife, 2nd Thessalonians, 'In flaming fire, inflicting vengeance on those who do not know God and on those who do not obey the gospel of our Lord Jesus,' scratched into the mud when he murdered the Nikitin brothers. So I wasn't surprised when I saw the Bible near Reggie. But Judas' treachery was in the first four books of the New Testament; Matthew, Mark, Luke and John. I expected any one of those four. But he left me with the end of Chapter 12 in the book of Romans." I shrugged. "Oh, well, I can't know everything."

Delp was studying the inside of his head; giving the question, it seemed, serious thought. Then a light went on in his eyes. It suddenly occurred to me that, though I hadn't meant to, I'd issued a challenge. "Could it have been the beginning of Chapter 13?" he asked, rising to it. Oddly, he didn't appear to do so with any glee or sense of triumph. He was merely questioning a fact.

I shrugged again. "It may have been."

He nodded. "If some of what you have suggested were true, Blake, if Eddie Love, or anyone for that matter, thought he was righteous in what he was doing, then perhaps I can assist you. Romans, Chapter 13, verses 3 and 4, 'For rulers hold no terror for those who do right, but for those who do wrong. Do you want to be free from fear of the one in authority? Then do what is right and he will commend you. For he is God's servant to do you good. But if you do wrong, be afraid, for he does not bear the sword for nothing. He is God's servant, an agent of wrath to bring punishment on the wrongdoer.'" He cleared his throat. Then he tried to stare right through me. "Regardless of who killed my wife, *Mister* Blake, or the Nikitins, or the Riaz couple, their deaths, though horrible, I'm sorry to say must ultimately be laid at their own feet. By your own account, *Mister* Blake, my wife was a harlot and died a harlot's death. The Nikitins, the Riazs, were wrong-headed betrayers."

"You make me want to puke," I said. It may have sounded like drama but, sisters and brothers, I swear, it was a plain fact. "Five murders, including your wife's. They are all on your head."

"I assure you, Blake, they are not on my head. This story of yours is fanciful at the very least. But you've got it wrong." The reverend rose to his full height. Now my indictment was over, seemingly unphased, from his towering position of power, he continued, "But, even if you were right, you might keep this in mind. Had the ram not appeared to Abraham by the grace of Almighty God, he would most assuredly have killed his beloved son, Isaac. Abraham was a great man of God. You can't prove this fantasy of yours because it didn't happen that way. Now, if you will excuse me, and even if you won't, I have people to minister to."

"I will prove it," I told him, "the whole ball of wax, when I find Eddie Love."

Something flashed in Gina's eyes, concern, fear maybe, but it was gone as quickly as it came. She laid a hand on Delp's arm. He smiled his patented smile, the one I'd seen on a dozen crusade tapes. "Why don't you stay?" the reverend said. "Listen to the show, Blake. I'm presenting a message on the subject of humility. It might do you good."

Delp turned and disappeared behind the door back into the studio recording booth. I stared after him, then turned to Gina. We locked eyes for a moment in a stare very different from that of the night before. Then, without a word, she turned and followed Delp. There was nothing left for me to say. The hallway seemed longer on my way out.

Chapter Twenty-eight

You'll remember that, the last time he and I talked, Detective Wenders had made it crystal clear that I'd better never pester Reverend Delp again. You also know I'd ignored him with relish. My goal, if you can call it that, had been to get something going, to aggravate Delp and his minions (two could play at that game) into doing, well, anything really, as long as it was ill-considered and hasty. Well, sisters and brothers, I missed it by that much. Instead, and you won't be surprised, I opened a can of whip-ass all over myself. (That was not a figure of speech.)

The scene was reminiscent of one of the floggings you see in the old pirate movies; at least it felt that way. I leaned against my office wall, arms extended to each side of the window, while an irate mountain of a police lieutenant stood behind lashing me with his acid tongue. Don't get me wrong, it didn't hurt all that bad. I was used up, worn out, and didn't care enough to feel any pain. But with his halitosis, I would just as soon he'd used a cat-o-nine tails. So, while Wenders hurled legal threats (peppered with verbal abuse), I took it without reply, watching out the glass as evening came on.

Willie Banks, *finally* out of the can on bail, was in my parking lot with the hood of his beat-up Mustang raised. He was trying with all of his might, his heart, and what little bit of brain he had, to get the thing started. (So far his luck had been about equal with mine.) The show he was putting on wasn't ready for the Goodman Theatre, but it was more entertaining than the badge-carrying banshee screaming behind me. Then, because even God likes special effects, the Mustang's engine fired. Willie raced from under the hood, leapt into the front seat like a crazed Nadia Comăneci, and mashed the parked car's accelerator. His engine growled while I thanked the heavens under my breath. He would finally get that piece of shit away from my building. The tremendous cloud of gray-black smoke filling my parking lot almost, but not quite, matched the smoke coming from Wenders' ears and filling my office. "You're not even listening to me!"

I turned from the window and Willie's parking lot performance to the show the police detective was putting on on the other side of my desk. "What did you say?"

"Are you kiddin' me? Do you think I'm talkin' to myself?" Wenders was red as a beet. "I said, I specifically told you to leave Delp and his people alone. Did you listen? NO. You raced right out and accused the man of murder; libeled him right to his face."

"Slandered," I said. "Libel is written. You mean slandered."

"It ain't fuckin' funny anymore, Blake. The police department, city hall, all the heavens from God on down are ready to fall on you at once and you're crackin' wise like we're at a stag party. You just can't see it. Blind people got better sight than you. There is more concrete evidence says you committed these murders than there is pointing to Delp. And no matter how many times I warn you to lay off, you won't lay off. Why?"

Completely fed up and out of things to say, I told him. I mean, I really told him. Why not? Nothing else had made a dent. So I just said it, right out, "I'll tell you, Frank. It's because of the visions I've been having."

Wenders looked at me like I'd whacked him on the forehead with a two-by-four. "What?" That was it; the best question he could come up with. He was dumb-stunned.

For myself, I had no reason to stop there. So I gave it to him, the whole silly-assed truth. "Ever since this caper started," I said. "I've been experiencing visions, full color, 4-D, interactive movies in my head." Wenders started to wave it away, but I wouldn't let him. "Honest to God visions," I insisted, "of each of the deaths in this case. In those visions, I've not only seen, I've experienced each of the murders from the point of view of the victim. I've been bashed over the head, burned alive, shot, had my throat slit, been hung, just as if I'd been there. And that isn't all. Sometimes they talk to me, the victims. I haven't figured out how to talk back, they don't seem to hear me and we don't carry on a conversation, but they look at me and ask me for help. Rocio Riaz even directed me to the scene of her murder, eh after she was dead. Each time it's more real, each time it's clearer than it was the time before. Something…" Like an anxious Sicilian mother, my hands flew from my temples to God. "Something out there is sending messages to me. I don't know what it is. It can't be clairvoyance," I told him. "That's French for clear vision, I looked it up. But it can't be that because I can't even spell clairvoyance; which, I don't mind telling you, made looking it up a bitch. It could be ESP. I've never had ESP, but I can at least spell that."

"What the fuck are you doing?"

"Certain persons and things," I went on, as if he hadn't spoken, "lend power to this. When I touch them I get… whatever it is I'm getting. I'm not saying these things, these people (and there have been several) are causing it, but they're somehow connected. So what can I do but follow the connections? I'm the first to admit this seems a little *out there* but it all started with me sitting in a tree so where could it go but *out there*? Believe me, I know how much you love facts, and I know there isn't much here that's concrete. But each vision, I think, leads me closer to the identity of the killer and…"

"Fine!" Wenders hollered, shutting me off. (You should have been there. The tone and volume could have closed the valve on the Hoover Dam.) "I warned you," he said, still yelling, "you stupid son of a bitch. Clown. Laugh yourself silly while they strap you onto that gurney with a priest reading the Last Rites. I don't give a fuck anymore. You buttered your bread, now you can just lay in it!"

Wenders stormed out the door past Lisa, standing behind her desk, and out of the office. I guess the truth wasn't really what he was after. I trailed slowly behind him, as the lieutenant slammed the outer door, motor-boating my lips in resignation. I turned from where Wenders had been to where Lisa was. There I got two surprises; one, she wasn't eating anything and, two, she looked painfully puzzled as she turned off her answering machine.

"What's that look for," I asked. "You're not letting Wenders bother you after all this time?"

"Huh, no," she said, strangely deep in thought. "Blake."

"Yeah?"

"I just came back from the bathroom…"

"I don't need to know that," I told her. "I've got an idiotic small-robber using his junk car to asphyxiate mosquitoes in my parking lot. I've got a cement-headed cop mixing his metaphors right here in my office. I've got God's very own messenger on earth trying to kill…"

"Damn it, Blake, will you listen!"

Again, yelling? And swearing? And from my secretary? I stared a question and, for once, Lisa appeared completely in earnest.

"I just came back from the bathroom," she repeated, "and this was on the answering machine."

She pressed the Play button. The machine clicked. The tape began to turn.

"Blay-ke," it hissed in a whisper; evil, oily, and leaving a slick in its wake as it slithered from the machine. "Blay-ke," it said again. Lisa shivered and, I admit, I did too. "This is…" The caller interrupted himself with a breathy cackle right out of hell, then finished, "This is Rev'rend Delp."

I shook my head, not even entertaining the idea. "That isn't Delp."

The voice came again. "So much dam-mage have ya done to the kangdom of Gawd, Blay-ke, and the foundations of mah ministry." He laughed again with less energy but more cruelty. "So much needed to be cleansed." The caller wasn't fooling anyone, and didn't sound as if he was even trying. His western drawl was unmistakable and recognition hit like a hammer.

"That's Eddie Love."

The tape continued to turn. "There is," Love said, "but one har-let left in the fam'ly. Yer har-let. Once she's paid for her inick-qui-teez, and you have paid for yers, all shall be ri-aght." The phone was cradled and the connection broken. The tape stopped and went into reverse as the machine reset itself. There had been no evil laugh at the end but perhaps there should have been. Whatever his cryptic message had meant, it didn't sound like Love was kidding.

"What is that supposed to mean?" Lisa asked. "There is one harlot left? Your harlot? What's that supposed to mean?"

The machine clicked off. The reels in my head were just beginning to spin. "Come on," I told Lisa. "You're coming with me."

She hesitated. That was something I wasn't used to and it caught me by surprise. Then it dawned, Love's creepy message had scared the hell out of her. Worse, it had made her angry. Confession of an aging private detective, it hadn't done much to boost my spirits either.

"Come on," I repeated, just as forcefully but a tad more supportively. "I need you." We were, after all, in this together. I already had my suit coat on. She grabbed a jacket and we headed out the door.

Willie was still screwing the pooch outside, his Mustang running in its own special way. A cloud of blue-black smoke billowed through the parking lot and we had no choice but to run through it to get to my car. "Hey, Blake," he shouted through his nose.

I ignored him and told Lisa to get in the Jag.

"Willie's calling you."

I ignored that too.

We took off at a scream out of the lot. I saw Willie watching after us in the rear view mirror, then the cloud enveloped him and he disappeared from sight.

*

We were breaking every inner-city traffic law on the books, forcing pedestrians to eat our dust, and were still less than a third of the way from my office to our destination when the last thing in the world that I needed or wanted to happen happened. We had just passed between the concrete pillars and under the rusted girders of a section of El track when the shooting pain in my brain returned. There was a flash of light inside my eyes. I stomped for the brakes, hit the gas instead, and we did a loop de loop south of The Loop. We didn't flip taking the corner too fast but did go up on two wheels. The centrifugal force threw Lisa sideways in her seat and knocked her head against her window. It wasn't on purpose and it wasn't my fault, really, for the trouble I was having with my head too. See, while I was still physically behind the steering wheel of my Jag, I was also, suddenly and simultaneously, back in Katherine Delp's bedroom – in the middle of her murder.

I was lying face down on her pillow and, again, it was my head being smashed by the decorative garden rock. I screamed in the bedroom while, back in the real world, I let go of the wheel. I know I did because Lisa told me a few minutes later. Then she yelled for me to stop the car (I don't remember that either). She grabbed the steering wheel from me, slid over and half-under the dash to hit the brakes, and brought the racing car to an eventual stand-still. Sometime during the next few seconds Katherine's bedchamber disappeared. I can't describe any of it other than to say that the beating stopped and, though it felt shattered as a divorcee's heart, my head was intact and working.

My next genuine memory found me standing beside the parked Jaguar, my driver's door open and sticking out to the street like the tongue on a schoolyard brat. It was in no danger of being hit by passing traffic however, as the car was parked cock-eyed up on the sidewalk. Driving in the real world while riding a psychotic roller coaster in the murder world in my head, I had just missed taking out a parking meter. And I'd taken Lisa with me for the ride.

She was still in the car. While I collected my marbles, she caught her breath, released the wheel, slid back over, and jumped from the passenger's side to the grass hollering, demanding to know if I was 'All right!'. After all that, that was her question, was I all right? What a pair to draw to. The only good thing about the situation was no one was paying us any attention; it was still Chicago.

"What's going on?" Lisa shouted. She was holding her head as she came round to my side of the car and only then did I remember she'd smacked it on the window of her door.

"I don't know what's going on," I replied, holding my head too (for reasons of which you're aware). We were like two mystic monkeys creating our own pictorial maxim but, in our case, 'Everything we saw, heard, and spoke was evil.'

"We've got to get you to a doctor," she said.

"I don't need a doctor," I insisted. "There's nothing wrong with me. Not that we have time to fix now. We've got to get to Gina Bridges apartment."

"Gina!" Lisa was indignant. "Is she the 'one harlot' Eddie Love was talking about? Your harlot? Is that where we're going with our tires on fire?" There was acid in her voice and it wasn't coming from an upset stomach. It came straight from a surprisingly enraged heart.

"There's something I've been waiting to tell you about Gina." she said.

"Not now," I barked. "We've got to go."

"I'm not going another inch with you at the wheel."

I couldn't blame her for that sentiment. I couldn't wait either. "All right. Then you drive."

"Really," Lisa asked, brightening instantly. "You're really going to let me drive your car?"

"Yes, really," I said. "Let's go." It had to have been beautiful; both of us holding our respective noggins, circling the car on the sidewalk like two idiots in orbit, me limping and unbalanced, she suddenly jubilant.

Now, picture it, me in the passenger's seat of my own dear Jaguar with Lisa behind the steering wheel. (That ought to give you some idea of how scrambled my brain was.) The sun was setting as we took off again, a brilliant red bleeding through the clouds above the city. Lisa described it to me later. I didn't see it myself because the pain had come again.

I was surrounded by the equally brilliant but flickering reds, oranges, and yellows created by, in, or for my mind. But I couldn't appreciate it. I was back in the Nikitin brothers' burning cabin. While my body was safe and sound, bucking in the bucket seat of my car, while Lisa raced through the Windy City traffic, my skin was blistering, my eyes stinging from the burn of imagined-but-real smoke. Then somewhere in the burning and popping lumber, I heard the brothers' screams followed by, yeah, the gunshot. A searing pain tore through my chest. By now you know the score and so did I, I'd been shot. I fell backwards, saw the heavy wooden beam above me give way and, as I was about to be crushed, found myself back in the passenger's seat of my car.

Lisa was trading worried glances between me and the street. Gasping for breath, I looked out to see the end of the block housing Gina's apartment building and realized I'd been gone into the vision for some little while. I rolled my window down, gulping for fresh air, and staring across the dark open lot to the foreboding old brewery in the distance.

Lisa raced the car down the drive into the cul-de-sac and pulled up to Gina's building. She didn't bother to park in a marked stall but rolled to a stop in front. I all but fell out of the car. By then, sisters and brothers, you've probably guessed that I was gone again. I had somehow been projected back into the Riaz house and, as with the previous murders, was being given the full bloody treatment. It's an experience, let me tell you, suffering others peoples' violent deaths, being stabbed and bludgeoned, being strangled and hung, having your throat slit, all in quick succession. I was living the life of Riley. All I can say is, you try taking it without a peep.

The cool evening air hit me and I was back in the present, on my knees on the walk outside of Gina's apartment, with Lisa at my side. My poor secretary looked horrified as she helped me up off the ground. I felt for her but couldn't help her. I felt for me, but I couldn't help me either. Just then, if I'd guessed right, Gina needed help more. "Come on," I said and ran for the building.

Lisa was a trooper. I hadn't taken the time in the office to explain why we were taking off like a shot. Despite that, after dealing with the shock of Love's creepy phone call, she'd come not only willingly but energetically. She'd suffered my psychic (or, if your prefer psychotic) antics en route, learned our destination only when it became necessary for her to take over the driving chores, and had gotten us both across town in short order and alive. Now, though she knew nothing about our mission, she was running with me stride for stride.

On our way inside the building, we passed the decorative planter I mentioned to you some time ago. I didn't recognize it then, being too rattled by my recent mental adventures and my aching physical condition and too intent on getting upstairs on the hop now that we'd arrived, but I certainly should have. The artsy-fartsy six-pointed design that once existed in the garden planter had been spoiled. Only five large rocks remained. Somebody had taken one of them.

Chapter Twenty-nine

Lisa and I entered the lobby at a run. Well, she was running. I was limping but giving it all I had. Aside from the whacks I'd taken all along, beyond that first fall in the alley chasing Willie, being beat by John Nikitin, ambushed in the dark by Love, smacked by Mike Nikitin, and being hit by a car, beyond the hallucinations that made Charles Manson's visions look like cartoons, on the trip there I'd again gone through (don't ask me how, but you saw it yourself) the violence of all five murders in this case. Not seen them, experienced them in place of the victims. Not to complain but, other than that, Mrs. Lincoln, how'd you like the play? Lisa started for the elevator but, remembering my oath, I hooked a finger in her belt to catch her from behind. "The elevator hates me." I pointed to a door. "The stairs. Fourth floor. It'll be faster." The front desk clerk, the same fellow as on my last visit, ignored us entirely. Apparently he really had seen it all.

Lisa took the lead on the stairs again as, desperately sore, I fell behind. She beat me up the zig-zag of steps, through the fourth floor fire door, stretched her lead in the hall, and was the first to arrive at Gina's door. She found it locked of course and started rapping and shouting Gina's name. Thudding down the hall behind her, I shouted, "Move!"

Lisa jumped to the side as I slammed my shoulder into the door. Thank God the jamb busted and the lock gave way. The wood splintered, the lock plate flew. I stumbled face-first to the floor and rolled into the room like a hundred-eighty pound wad of chewed Bazooka Joe. When the building quit spinning, and it took a second, I stood painfully to see that I'd guessed right.

Eddie Love was there in all his miserable and creepy glory, black cowboy boots, leather vest over a chiseled chest with no shirt between them, hellish tattoos (heavy in dull blues and bright crimsons), cascading straight brown locks, trimmed beard, ear rings, and that big black Stetson. God, I wanted to knock him out from underneath that hat. On the bright side, for once I'd actually guessed in time and maybe, finally, had gotten my chance to do just that. He had Gina on the floor and was straddling her stomach, but she was still alive. The way this case had been going, that was a monumental victory for the good guys. Best I could see, Love had her hair with one hand pinning her down and held the stone, from the planter out front (obviously), in the other. Gina let loose with a scream. Who could blame her? He'd been about to bust her face in when we'd made our chaotic entrance.

I took more credit than we deserved with that last remark. Love had the chaos well started before we got there. He was about to prove he was fine with letting it continue. Seeing us he stood, towering above Gina, then turned on me. He held the stone above his head and the glint in his evil eye showed he had every intention of hurling it. I leapt before he had the chance, over the couch, tackling him. We struggled and I don't think it's whining to say that, due to my earlier injuries, though I had the drop on him I was still at a severe disadvantage. Lisa tried to help and got slapped back for her trouble. If I wasn't already mad, and I was, that did it for me. But I was prevented from going to her by Love repeatedly punching me in the throat and chest.

I lost track of the next few minutes. No, it wasn't owing to brain pangs or hallucinations. I had nothing but the excuse that the good old-fashioned throttling had interrupted my ability to breathe and see. In the interim, both from what I pieced together myself and from the things Lisa told me, Love got to his feet, grabbed Gina by the front of her coat, dragged her to the window, and with zero hesitation shoved her out.

That was a freaker.

I caught my breath until I saw Gina's head pop back up on the other side of the window sill and realized there was a fire escape outside. (I couldn't say for sure that I was entirely convinced Eddie knew it was there when he pushed her.) Anyway, Love said something pithy as if he were a Bond villain making his escape in the new *Moonraker* and slipped through the frame after her. On the other side, he grabbed Gina and they disappeared. The orange curtains flapped in the breeze like Bozo's wild hair while the empty window, the clown's mouth, laughed at me like the muck I was.

I tried to get up but fell twice. Feeling the way I was, I'd have had as much chance climbing to the top of the Sears Tower on a pogo stick. I tried again – because I had to – and finally, clutching my throat and gasping for a breath of air, struggled to my feet. I stumbled to help Lisa up. She said she was all right and I took her at her word. I told her to call Wenders. She hurried to the phone, dialed a number she knew only too well, and asked for the lieutenant.

I looked out to see that Love had dragged his kidnap victim down four flights of fire escape, had yanked her up off the ground at the bottom, and was running, pushing Gina toward the open field behind the apartment building. The scene was like something out of one of the old television westerns from when I was a kid. I got a leg out the same window.

"Blake," Lisa shouted, "they're getting the lieutenant now."

"I can't wait," I told her. "I've got to stop him before he finishes her."

"But Wenders is coming to the phone. The police are on their way and the lieutenant will be any minute."

"That doesn't solve my problem. They'll kill him, he'll force it. Then I'm really screwed. Without Love, I have no evidence."

"Blake, wait," Lisa insisted. "There's something else. Something I've been trying to tell you. Gina..."

Gina, Gina, Gina. I couldn't believe it. At a different time and place her catty jealousy might have been adorable but this was the absolute worst possible moment for it. She was being such a girl and I didn't have the time. "Not now." I slipped the rest of the way out.

The fire escape rattled and shook like a bag of rib cages as I descended two steps at a time. I knew Lisa and could just imagine her, behind me, harrumph-ing in anger at my cutting her off, then returning to the phone to try to explain to that pig-headed Wenders what was happening. After she hung up, she'd poke her out-sized glasses back on her nose and stare at the empty window in annoyance, wondering after me. She was a good girl, Lisa.

*

The full moon was partially hidden by clouds making Eddie and Gina little more than two black smudges moving through the untended field. He was screaming at her and shoving her along, she looked to be fighting him and arguing back. I couldn't make out what either was saying. They made it to the other side, left the high grass and crossed a series of long-unused railroad tracks, a branch line of the old Milwaukee Railroad, with Gina alternately dragged and driven by Love, and entered the lot beyond. This fronted (backed) what once had been one of the city's premiere breweries.

Though Chicago was never the beer mecca that Milwaukee, Wisconsin was, there were still plenty of breweries through most of the last century. The industry was at its height here in the 1890's and, soon after, was destroyed – like everything else – by the government sticking its nose in. Three acts of Congress, the temporary Wartime Prohibition Act (known as the 'Thirsty-First' and intended to save grain for the war), the 18th Amendment (making the production, transportation and sale of alcohol illegal), and the Volstead Act (defining *alcohol* and enforcement), initiated a nation-wide fourteen year ban on booze from which Chicago never recovered. This *Law of the Land*, this hat-trick from hell known to the world as Prohibition, forced the brewery in front of me to close in 1918. Many of the others in town suffering the same fate were abandoned, given over to the rats, or demolished without a trace. This one had been lucky. Though it never reopened as a brewery, two years later a meat packing company moved in – until the Great Depression. The complex traded hands in '34 and again in 1940 when another packing company took it over to warehouse hams. Small businesses came and went in the night while the buildings aged and crumbled. In the late 60's, the facility was put on the National Register of Historic Places. When the designation prevented the owners altering their property, they had a cow and the buildings were erased from the register. So much for honorable history. Now it was a dilapidated shell; the lower floors in the hands of the recyclers, with the vast unused majority of the plant little more than a warehouse for memories and ghosts.

Yeah, Prohibition was a pip. It created the murderous gangs of Chicago but did nothing to curb alcohol consumption. Everyone that wanted a barley pop got one, Al Capone saw to that. Legend had it that when this brewery closed, Capone took the facility over, ran it himself, and shipped beer out in milk cans. I could just picture the city's most infamous gangster in his white coat scaling the ladders and walkways inside with a copper ladle in his hand; the city's own crime master a happy Braumeister breaking Federal law. No matter how bad Chicago had been, as I chased the cowpoke kidnapper and his victim I couldn't help but think how sad and pathetic we'd become. Under that hat, Eddie Love was just another twisted murderer; no style at all. He wouldn't have been a pimple on Capone's ample ass. Then again, who was I kidding? I was no Elliot Ness. Still, as low rent as we were, I was the good guy and he was the bad. I intended to get him.

A good distance behind, I heard thumps and thuds and could just make out Eddie kicking open one of the doors of what looked to have been the old brewery's rail shipping dock. Gina screamed as Eddie shoved her inside.

I made it across the field, hurting like crazy, and came to a stop in the rail yard staring, first at the black hole of a door they'd vanished into, then up at the whole dark edifice; a collection of antique buildings like crazily stacked boxes stepping up at roof levels of varying heights with a tower rising over five stories near its center. I'd seen it the way it had been meant to be seen, in the daylight, from the front, a few times over the years; a complex of buildings, crowned with castle-like cornices, with old-world limestone tablets over each entrance telling of the specific function once carried out inside. From the back, none of what remained of the Germanic touches, sculpted design, windows, or face brick could be seen. It was a shadow of what once had been; a lot like me

I drew nearer to see that I'd guessed right, these were the loading docks on the rail side of the rear-most building. The washed-out brick and weathered, in some places rotting, wood of the exterior wall gave it the look of an abandoned prison rather than a recycling center. A sign beside the door, beneath a broken light, barely visible in the cloud-covered moonlight, featured three blood red R's (almost black in the dimness) and, under those, the words Reduce, Reuse, Recycle. Nothing else, not even their company name. It didn't matter what it looked like now; storage facility for miserable criminals or a staging place for trash to meet its end, either way it was the perfect hiding place for Love.

I took a deep breath and followed them into the dark.

Chapter Thirty

I don't know why westerns were on my mind, but another entered my head just then. The ailing John Wayne, handed his death sentence by Dr. Jimmy Stewart, approaching the saloon, the villains' lair, for the final shootout. But The Duke had a gun. I stopped myself. I had a gun too, locked in the safe in my office. There was no one to blame for my being unarmed but me. I'm no hypocrite, I didn't completely regret it, I do hate guns. It was just that… John Wayne had a gun. Anyway, my villain's lair was the old brewery. I followed Love and the kidnapped Gina in slowly with ears pricked, taking baby steps Wayne would have been proud of, aching in every muscle, and gulping my spit to deal with the unease of the eerie dark unknown; at least trying to. My mouth was so dry it made the streets of Tucson look like Venice in the spring.

Just inside the Love-battered wooden door, I strained to examine the old loading dock. It was creepy, as all old buildings are, but I can't say I saw Capone's cigar-smoking spirit or any ghosts of beer shipments past. Neither did I see Eddie or Gina. I moved off the dock and into the first floor of the rear building. At its booming height, the place had nearly 225,000 square feet of floor space, a half-million dollars' worth of brewing equipment and ice machinery, water from an artesian well on the premises (long dried up I assumed), and an annual production capacity of 300,000 barrels of beer. (Being a curious gumshoe, I looked it up.) Now it had been taken over by the recyclers. The resource-saving statistics were impressive too, if that was your bag. Ten-thousand pounds of material shredded every working hour, a half-million pounds of paper a day, a hundred and fifty million pounds recycled every year or, as they liked to remind us, kept out of the landfill. To the birds, squirrels, and greenie tree-huggers, that was 4,250 trees a day. And that was just the paper. They also melted, shredded, pulped, then renewed nearly every product imaginable from polyester bowling balls to vinyl LPs. But that was in the daytime, when the resource-savers were out and about. In the nighttime there was nobody out but the users and no one and nothing in the plant except the rats, including one with a black cowboy hat. Plus yours truly, of course, one banged-up rat catcher. And, somewhere in the dark, Gina, his captive, whose time I imagined would soon be running out.

To my right was a large windowed office, all closed and locked. Posters covered the warehouse side of its particle-board walls like cheap wallpaper. Group posters, green posters, proclamations about their city-wide "Anything That Tears Program," and endless repeats of the "Reduce, Reuse, Recycle" mantra. To my left, partially lit by leaking moonlight, partially in gloom, but mostly in shadow and pitch darkness across the expansive first floor was a maze of crushing, tearing, shredding, and sorting machines, and stacks, walls, mountainous piles, and wheeled bins of both plastic and canvas filled to the brim with product, before, during, and after crushing. With the exception of the scratching and the occasional high-pitched squeak of the facility's afore-mentioned furry residents, all else seemed quiet. Where on this expansive first floor, or worse, deeper within this monstrous five-story labyrinth, had Love taken Gina?

Despite my anxiety and sense of urgency, I sighed heavily and slowly started my search doing my best to move from one shadow to another as I went. I wanted to catch up to them quickly, obviously, but it wouldn't do anyone any good for me to take another surprise shot to the head. I passed a tower of trashed computer monitors and, once I'd recognized them for what they were, paused in amazement. They'd just perfected the things for home and office. Ours had only just been installed. Lisa hadn't even spilled any food on one yet. How, I wondered, could something that new already be junk? I was brought back to the mission at hand when, somewhere in the distance, I heard Gina cry out. It was a cross, if you asked me, between pain and terror and it not only alerted me but made me angry. Then I heard Eddie's demonic hiss. I'll leave out the colorful bells and whistles, you can imagine what he said, as he ordered her to shut her mouth. I quickened my pace as I headed that way.

I could describe it for you, step by step, inch by inch, chill by chill racing up my spine as I hunted them over the next interminable minutes. But what would be the point? It all ended in the same way. Somewhere deep in the first floor, while I scanned the dark straining for a glimpse of anything, my ears pricked desperately searching for a sound, walking a tightrope of pins and needles, Love somehow got behind me and jumped out of the shadows, screaming.

Okay, I assumed it was Eddie. I couldn't see his face, it was all in shadow, but the shadow was wearing a Stetson and Eddie was the creepy transplanted cow-puncher I'd chased into the building. I could claim I recognized the scream but it was just a scream with a terrifying echo but no discernible Wyoming twang. What I knew for certain was he had the drop on me and was holding some sort of club. I ducked, backed up and ducked again, hearing too clearly for my tastes the repeated *swoosh* of whatever he was swinging. I wanted to save Gina, to save the day, to save the city from this maniac, just like in the comics; truth, justice, and the American way. Somewhere inside I wanted all of that. But as he attacked and I ducked the blows, as he came on and I retreated, the only real thought in my mind was to avoid, at all costs, letting him whack me in the coconut. My head had had all it could take.

Still screaming, Eddie swung the bat again (Dave 'Kong' Kingman going for a storefront window in Wrigleyville) with all his might. I dodged, tripped backwards, and fell. I landed gracelessly, jarringly atop an air hockey table. Yeah, air hockey; one of those home versions of the game and, if I was seeing right in the dim moonlight, champion Jesse Douty signed, now just garbage in a recycling center. I stole a glance to the side to see that the table, with me on top, was lying flat on a conveyor belt.

The moonlight brushed him and I saw Love grinning like a circus monkey just beyond my up-raised shoes. Suddenly the floor, the walls, the building shuddered and vibrated, accompanied by the shriek of hell's demons making a jail break. Machinery growled to life. Metal rattled, leather joined in, making enough noise to raise Katherine Delp, rile the brothers Nikitin, and disturb the resting Riaz couple. The conveyor belt rumbled and started to move. It groaned as the rollers turned cruelly beneath the belt, beneath the table, beneath my back. You could forget my escaping. Already winded, I was struggling merely to breathe. In that condition, I was carried up, watching the shadows in the high ceiling bend and stretch as I was lifted. I felt like a Baby Ruth bar, lumpy with nuts, on the way to wrapping. On the way to... It dawned that the last conveyor I'd seen was placed to feed material to a shredder. That thought was followed by the realization I could do nothing about it. Well, at least I'd escaped Love's pummeling. At least he hadn't hit my head.

But cool air did; bathed my hair. I felt a great punch in the middle of my spine. I realized suddenly that the table had crested the top of the conveyor and I was going over. I shouted (how could I not?). I fell. I landed unceremoniously in a great canvas bin atop a pile of chipped wallboard, under the air hockey table – on my head.

I couldn't see them for the cloud of dust I'd raised, or hear them for the still-growling conveyor above, but I knew they were there – cartoon bluebirds swooping circles. *Zip-a-Dee-Doo-Dah*. I should have been grateful, I know, that

I hadn't broken my neck. But truth be told I was fresh out of gratitude. I shoved the table off, sputtered, rolled painfully to my knees, spitting chalky wallboard and looking like the ghost of a washed-up detective. I grabbed the bin rail for balance but, before extricating myself, looked over the portions of the factory I could see. In the scant moonlight, with plaster dust stinging my eyes, I managed to make out the stacks, piles, and other bins on the wide floor, the lanes between, and the pitch black voids connecting them, but no Love. He'd vanished into the shadows; escaped it seemed with Gina into the depths, no, worse, into the heights.

I gained the floor, found a metal stairway, and started up only to discover I was still making mistakes. On the third step a shot rang out. I barely heard it, with that conveyor still running in the background, but I saw it as it ricocheted off the railing near my hand. There was an impressive spark in the gloom and the echo sounded louder than the shot had. I had been right, they were above me, and I was a sitting duck. I bit my lower lip and raced for the landing above. I vacated the stairs for cover in the shadows.

Everything hurt but I ignored it, sucking wind and scanning the second floor. Other than a few bins and stacked boxes, it looked empty. There was certainly no shooter, meaning the bullet had come from higher still. I called out Eddie's name, good and loud, hoping to find him by drawing his fire, then hurriedly moved to another spot in the dark, hoping to avoid it when it came.

It didn't come. Outside of the rumbling conveyor, now just a white noise below, the place was a tomb again. I waited, unmoving, hating myself for it but unsure what was next. Then I heard Gina cry out again. I felt like a kid's pull-toy being led around on a string but there was no choice, I had to follow the voices up. This time I raced the stairs, as best I could, from the start. No sense, limping as I was, giving Eddie more time than necessary to find the target. On the third floor, I hit the shadows again and strained to see that it was one big gaping space; empty as my reserve of courage, empty as Wenders' head. I could see little of the fourth floor and nothing of the fifth floor tower but knew they were there, harboring a killer and, if I didn't put it in gear, the soon-to-be-killed. Originally a gravity brewery, the place had been expanded and retooled over the years, the high tanks removed as other means of production took over. There was something else, something lethal, in the dark tower now. Gina screamed again and then, if I understood what I was hearing, was violently made to stop. I heard movement, running feet on the old tile above, and then the scuttling too came to a halt.

I reached the fourth floor, hit the shadows, sidled up against an outside wall, and repeated the routine of scanning the expanse for any sign of who, what, why, where, and how. It was a big facility with a lot of buildings holding lots of junk but, if I was right, Love and his captive were there, on that floor. They had to be. Moonlight intruded in a stream between stacks of refuse guarding an open door in the north wall, the same outside wall against which I was hiding, and, of course, I was curious where a door over forty feet in the air led. I moved quickly and quietly to a window some distance short and, like the bear going over the mountain, looked out to see what I could see.

What I saw was space and, four stories below, surrounded by the buildings that made up the complex, an open courtyard. Long bench tables dotted the flagstone floor between stacked totems of dirty cardboard and great snowy mountains for shredded office paper. It looked like a picnic area on a bizarre planet of papier mache. Near one of the towering mounds sat a giant sorting machine, while beside another stood an immense paper baler with yet one more conveyor belt poised to carry debris up to its gaping mouth. A huge magnet, to snag metal scraps before the plunge, dangled like a lifeless chandelier from the top of the rig. On the far side of the open area a faded-yellow front end loader sat quietly at bay; the junkyard's sleeping dog. It seemed a dire venue for the employees' brown bag lunch breaks. Then again, perhaps I was unaware of the entertainment value in watching old things become new again. I caught my breath as the events of the evening, the last week and a half for that matter, caught up with me. My whole being shook with pain. If only they could recycle old detectives.

The clouds parted and the moon, which had been playing peek-a-boo all night, shown full. I looked below again taking in the courtyard that was all aglow. The area was accessible from ground floor doors in each of the buildings and from all four floors at one spot or another by an outside set of metal stairs that started in the courtyard's northeastern corner and zig-zagged up to an iron walkway and balcony level with the floor I was on. The door in the wall I reported a moment ago opened onto this balcony. Now that the moon shone on it, I could see to its far end over-hanging the courtyard. When I did, I got a stunner. There lay Gina, half in moonlight, half in the shadow cast down by the old brewery's tower, curled up on the walkway floor.

But where was Eddie?

I'll let the history writers decide how it went from there. Some will say I made the next decision with my heart, some will say I used my little head, and others will say I used no head at all. I admit I was careless and probably foolish. But Gina was out there, unmoving, alone. I moved down the moonlit aisle, between the short shadowy gauntlet of bins and rubbish bookending the door, as quietly but as quickly as my limp allowed, and peered out at the church secretary face down at the far end. She was as still as death and I can't describe the bottomless feeling that overwhelmed me. With no further thought, I started out after her.

The beauty of some mistakes is you find out so quickly that you've made them. I was still a good ten feet away from her when I discovered mine. From behind, there came a scream that would have gone swell with a monster movie. I turned and what I saw was right out of a horror flick too; a half-assed cowboy, big black hat, leather shit-kickers, a vest over top of evil-looking wall-to-wall tats and a meat-eating snarl as Eddie Love burst from the shadows of the doorway coming hard at me. He'd been hiding behind one of the stacks and I had, obviously, walked right past him. I deserved whatever the crazy bastard was about to deliver and, if I survived that night, I promised myself a swift kick in my own hind-end. Eddie bulldogged me with a shoulder to my gut and his Stetson in my face. I yelled, grabbed instinctively back at him, and left my feet as we slammed into the rail. If you're worried for Eddie, don't bother; I took the blow with the square of my back. He wasn't hurt a bit.

I was just thanking the spinning stars that I'd shouted, expelling my wind and leaving him nothing to knock out of me, when I noticed the maniac was trying to bite me. You might think that made me mad but you're wrong. While he'd grown up in the wilds of the Rockies, I'd earned my stripes scraping in Chicago sandlots and, if the psycho jackwagon wanted to forget the Queensberry rules in favor of a good old-fashioned rumble, it was okay by me. I grabbed his ears, leaned right, and drove his face as hard as I could into the balcony rail to my left. Twice. I can't describe my elation as his big cowboy hat came off and kited away.

Eddie reared back. Spitting blood, with gleaming eyes, he cried, "Be af-raid, for he does nawt bear the sword fer nothin'."

"Yeah," I said. "I heard it already." I slammed a fist into his jaw.

We fought for what seemed a long time, but must really have been only a scant few seconds, trading blows to the rising sound of approaching sirens. I thought our dance would continue until the cavalry arrived – but it wasn't to be. I tripped over my own feet and fell backwards. Love looked startled, as if he couldn't believe his luck, then made a quick motion to the small of his back. Again, I found myself staring down a cold steel barrel. The homicidal lunatic had pulled a gun.

He laughed the same laugh that had played earlier from Lisa's answering machine, a cackle straight out of hell. A chill raced up my pain-wracked spine. This was it. The crazy bastard had managed to fulfill the promise he'd made the day of his last sentencing. He was going to kill me then and there. God, it was embarrassing.

"Freeze, scumbag!"

It seemed a stupid thing for him to shout with the situation being what it was. He had me dead to rights. Hell, he had me dead. Where was I going? What was I going to do? Then I realized, at the same time Eddie did, that Eddie wasn't the one that had shouted. It had come from behind, from the door to the fourth floor, in a high-pitched, nasally voice. Then, in a near-panic, it came again.

"I said, Freeze!"

Eddie turned, and I looked past him, to see a silhouette in the door opening. It was a man in a military crouch, arms extended, hands cupped, presumably around a gun though there was something wrong with the picture. Details were lost in the shadows. He took a half-step forward and moonlight glinted off his chest; a badge. He was pointing at the convict and, by extension, at me. I was both grateful for his arrival and hopeful he was a good shot. I never found out. With no hesitation, Love spun around and fired at him. The cop howled like a kicked dog, grabbed his shoulder, and went down in the dark. So much for the cavalry.

Still, as I wasn't ready to be dead, I didn't let the interruption go to waste. I was up in that same beat and moving as Eddie spun back. He took a second to bring his gun around. That was enough. I kicked him in the groin as hard as I was able, screaming, "No more fucking guns!"

His weapon flew into the air. I couldn't believe my luck. A second later, I couldn't believe my bad luck. Doubled-over, clutching himself, Love fell – right between the middle and top bars of the balcony rail.

I hated Eddie Love. I wanted him dead as much as I'd wanted anything ever. He was a murderer and a psycho and, on top of that, he wanted me dead. But I needed him. He was Delp's hit man. Without him I had nothing but a story to tell at bedtime; no proof of anything. My heart went into my big mouth when he fell because I was watching my case take a header.

Then I gulped it down. To my amazement, he caught the edge of the catwalk and stopped his fall. Love was dangling by his fingertips forty feet above the courtyard. I saw the ground below, I saw Love, I saw his whitening fingers. Suddenly, in one of those instances that takes you outside of yourself, with Love hanging over eternity, my attention was captured, riveted to the strangest, most inconsequential thing. I saw Love's fingers, only his fingers, and the tattoos he had obviously given himself during the ten years he'd stewed in prison. He'd inked my name, Blake, in blue, from the thumb running across his left hand, one letter on each digit. I couldn't believe it. Without knowing it, I'd gone to prison with him and had been living rent-free in his melon since the minute they slammed the cage on him.

I shook myself out of it. The tats were fascinating but I also couldn't believe the situation we were in. After I kicked him, I thought Love was a goner. But there he was, there it was, my case against Delp hanging by its fingertips. "Son of a bitch," I said, under my breath. I had no choice but to pull him back onto the catwalk, so I grabbed his wrists.

That was all it took. The pain hit like an explosion in my head and the vision followed. I was standing in the middle of Market Street outside of the Riaz house. From the dark a car engine fired and growled. A vehicle, the vehicle, raced from the shadows as it had on that morning. It veered from the curb, across the center of the road, and came straight at me hell-bent for leather. Unlike the real event where everything was just a blur, I now saw all the details with crystal clarity, in a bizarre slow motion as if the scene was an action sequence in a Peckinpah film. I saw Love as I'd seen him in the murkier real-time version of the same mental movie, grinning maniacally through the windshield of the vehicle's… passenger side. The racing car hit me… again.

I was back on the balcony, shaking myself out of it. I shouted and fought to get my bearings while the marbles rolled to a stop in my skull. In so doing, I turned and saw with delight that Gina was not dead. On the metal walk just out of reach, she'd risen to an elbow and was cringing against the railing bars, crying. I still had a hold of Love. I realized that when he reversed his hands and snatched me, grabbing my wrists. I could have kicked myself. Instead he started the kicking, below me, to get his legs moving and his body swinging. Great, I could barely breathe and he was doing a trapeze act. The motion yanked me forward where I hit the rails and, it dawned, he was trying to pull me off of the balcony. Apparently he didn't mind going if he could take me with.

Then, somehow, Gina was at my side, reaching down through the rails toward our conjoined hands. I assumed she was trying to help me but, truth be told, I didn't know. I didn't know anything. She grabbed my wrists and – BOOM – I was hit with another mental flash as a new searing pain passed through my head.

I was on Market Street again. Above it, as I flew up and over the racing black car. My feet cartwheeled over the hood, the roof; my chest brushed the windshield as I went past. I saw Love in the passenger's seat and, turning, I saw the driver.

I was instantly back on the catwalk, teetering on the edge. Gina had my wrists above, Love below; both were making a wish. All the emotions of that incredible, heartrending case welled up from the pit of my soul, from the pits of despair. "Son of a bitch!" I cried. To hell with the case. To hell with the murdering cowboy trying to pull me to my death.

Distantly, as if in a dream, Gina was yelling my name. I ignored her. I ignored everything but our connected hands just outside and below the balcony. I strained mightily to put distance between me and the rail. I threw my gumshoes against the lowest crossbar for leverage. I sucked in a load of air. I can't say I actually heard the Atlanta Rhythm Section playing *Do It Or Die* but should have. I shouted and, with everything I had left, yanked my hands free. Gina fell back on the balcony, screaming. Love groped, grabbed nothing but air, then fell, screaming.

Nothing could have muted my cry either, and didn't. "SON OF A BITCH!"

The cowboy landed with a dull thud. I caught the rail on the still-vibrating catwalk and pulled myself to safety. Gina was still screaming. I looked past her with unfocused eyes then turned below, found the ground and, half on the flag-stones of the courtyard, half in the high grass below the balcony, spotted Love's broken body. He'd reached the end of his trail but wasn't much of a cowboy anymore. I'd gotten my wish and knocked him out from under his hat and, after, he'd only managed to die with one boot on. A cloud sashayed past the moon and Love disap-peared in shadow.

"Blake. Blake!"

It was Gina. I ignored her and turned instead to the gloomy doorway where the balcony met the fourth floor. I called into the dark, to the crumpled cop lying in a heap, "Willie! What the hell are you doing here?" Holding his wounded shoulder, Willie Banks stirred then struggled to his feet and, smiling weakly through obvious pain, stepped from the old brewery into the moonlight.

From below, from a thin alley leading from the courtyard to the side of the property between two of the buildings, came the sounds of sirens, the screech of tires, and the red-blue flicker of lights. Then came the sound of shouting voices and the clamor of running boots.

Chapter Thirty-one

"You been good to ma and me, Blake," Willie said, through his nose, as he tried to explain his *nick-of-time* appearance. "I wanted to make it up to you somehow. When I saw you and your sec-r-tary run out, I thought maybe ya'd need some help, so I followed ya."

We were a sight, three-abreast, me support-ing the wounded Willie with my left arm and holding the traumatized Gina in my right, slowly zig-zagging from one landing to the next, mak-ing our way down the four flights of vibrating metal stairs from the balcony to the courtyard; the Spirit of '76 without the fife and drums. I have no clue what was holding me up.

"You were lucky he only winged you," I told Willie. "You could have been killed, you know?"

"I guess. I didn't really think about it."

"You're even dumber than I thought." Yeah, I said it and I meant it. Then I smiled through the pain and thanked him. I meant that too.

"Hey, Blake," he said, "how'd ya know it was me up there in the dark and not a real cop?"

"Real cops point real guns. They don't hold up their finger like a six year-old."

"The cops wouldn't give my gun back when they let me out."

"Remind me to thank them for small favors. Oh and for future reference, real cops also do not yell 'Freeze, scumbag' through their nose."

"I got a deviated septum. Besides, I'm shot."

"You weren't shot then."

"No. But I'm shot now."

"New night, same old whine. Blake, I'm shot, be nice to me. You damned baby."

The courtyard, once bruised black with shadow and blue with moonlight, had suddenly come to life with bright white search beams and the red-blue strobe of emergency lights stealing down the alley between the buildings from squads baha'ed through the grass on the side of the dilapidated complex. Two real patrol cops, guns drawn, had arrived on the hustle and were waiting for us at the bottom of the stairs. I don't know who they planned to shoot; the three of us, using every ounce of energy to remain up-right, were certainly no threat. My gun, as you know, was in my safe waiting for a war to make me drag it out. Willie was wearing an empty holster and, outside of his fantasies, his finger wasn't loaded. It finally dawned they were safe because the patrol boys lowered their shooting irons and were tucking them and their flashlights away as we reached the flagstone floor of the courtyard.

Because I'm a crap magnet, the flatfeet weren't alone; the detectives were there too. Dave Mason, near the uniformed cops, was staring at us like a starving wolf ogling three crippled rabbits. Wenders, out of breath from moving fast (he never ran), not tucking in his gut as usual, was leaning on one of the rusted metal balcony pillars, staring down at the twisted body of our murdering maniac. "It is a small world of villains," the lieutenant said. He slipped in a stick of gum and looked up chomping. "Eddie Love. What's he doin' dead?"

I have to tell you, sisters and brothers, after what I'd just been through I was not ready for another accusation. I opened my mouth to explode. Wenders waved it away. "Forget it," he said. He took another look at Love. "I gotta admit he looks like a killer. Guess you were right, Blake."

I'd lived long enough to hear that, but closed my mouth in a frown because I knew it wasn't true; not entirely. I shook my head, oh so gently, let go of Willie while keeping hold of Gina, and started what felt like a confession. "No," I told Wenders. "I was wrong."

"Huh?"

"Well, not so much wrong as not completely right."

The lieutenant left Eddie and waddled over to us. "As I am so often forced to ask, Blake," he said, "what are you ramblin' about now?"

"I'm telling you I've been giving Love too much credit all along," I said. "He was the mechanic, no doubt, but he wasn't running the shop."

Wenders sighed, then said, "If you say Reverend Delp again, I swear, Blake, I'll kick your ass."

"Save the shoe leather and keep your balance." I let loose of Gina, still folded into my chest sobbing and sup-supping, took hold of her arm, and pushed her toward the lieutenant. Her look of shock was priceless as I told him, "Sorry she's not tied in a bow. You'll have to take her as is."

"Take her?" Wenders asked stupidly. "Take her for what?"

"Murder and arson for a start. Oh and conspiracy to kidnap, of course." The waterworks stopped as if I'd turned off Gina's tap. She stood straight as a honeymoon hard-on. Her mouth fell open in a round O. She looked like an inflated vinyl blow-up doll (not that I'd know). "You can pile it on later," I said, "with the help of one of those brilliant assistant DAs." I turned to Gina. "Go ahead, sweetheart, tell the nice policeman all the naughty things you've been up to."

She sputtered wordlessly for a second, cried "Blake," then stopped herself. You could see the toys turning in her head. A change came over her face and, like that, she was as innocent as a nursery rhyme heroine. "I don't know what you're talking about," she said.

"Yeah, me too, Blake," Wenders shoved in, "what are you talkin' about?"

"I'm talking," I said, "about a case where nothing added up the way it should have. There were clues all over the place. But every one shined a light in the wrong direction." I jerked my head toward Love's body and was immediately sorry (not for Love, for the pain it caused me). When the acute ache ebbed and I knew my gourd was going to stay in place, I continued. "From the beginning, thanks to that prick cow-puncher, God rest his soul, most of what you boys were finding pointed at me. But you knew I didn't kill Katherine Delp. At the same time, what I was digging up put the cross-hairs on her husband, and you weren't having any of that. Because, in your world, rich people don't do bad things."

"You're talkin', smart guy," Wenders said. "Are you gonna say anything?"

"I've already said most of it, when I laid the case out for Delp…"

"You mean last night, when you accused him of multiple murders?"

"Yeah, Frank, then. Everything I told him, and you, was dead on. It was no surprise he innocently denied everything. I mean, what prison isn't full to the rafters with convicts that didn't do it? But it seemed strange that even a professional liar like Delp could seem so sincere. When he told me I was out of my mind, he genuinely appeared to mean it. Weird, huh?"

Wenders smacked his lips.

"My point is, if I hadn't known he was guilty, I might have thought him innocent. It took me a long time, too long, to wrap my brain around the notion that those same facts…" I turned to Gina. "Fit you, Miss Bridges, very nicely."

She stared icy daggers but didn't say a word.

"You worshiped the ground Reverend Delp walked on. And you wouldn't have minded a bit owning some of it. You would have been happy to replace Katherine and, to that end, you made plans to get rid of her, for good. You met Reggie and Eddie in the prison outreach program. You convinced Delp to hire Reggie, a faithful servant. Meanwhile, you cultivated a relationship with Love because you knew that a maniac, under certain circumstances, might come in handy. I don't know if Delp had any part in the plan to kidnap his wife. If he did, I can't prove it now. But I know that you came up with it and you saw it through."

"Wait," Wenders barked. "What? That's the second time you've said that. What kidnap?"

"We've been over it, Lieutenant. That's how this started. The first intended criminal act; a kidnapping. But it actually started before... with rumors."

"You mean like... at a church picnic?"

"No," I said. "The opposite. Rumors at a church picnic are part true and spread like wildfire. These were calculated lies; nasty, un-Christian, but effective. Whispered secrets shared between the devout, secrets that to an amazing degree were kept. Different, contradictory secrets told to specific individuals for specific results with oaths sworn in the name of the Almighty. Conceived and initiated by the reverend's real right-hand, his secretary. Gina fired Nick Nikitin in Delp's name, then spread the word to the right people that the church was in financial trouble. As the sole remaining bookkeeper, handling everything from crusade reservations to ordering paper clips, she had no difficulty convincing those necessary. She conned Reggie into believing the ministry had to be saved and got Eddie to propose a drastic, dramatic plan. They would kidnap Katherine to spur donations and public interest. She would be hidden someplace safe and, when the church was saved, triumphantly returned unharmed to the glory of God. What Delp knew, I don't know. But what nobody knew, other than Gina and Eddie, was that Katherine would not be coming back."

"How's she do all this," Wenders asked, "without showing her hand?"

"Oh, you gotta spend some time around her, Frank. Gina could sell matches to Satan and convince him he's getting a bargain. She knows how to move people. It's quite a trick."

"So she's Svengali's sister," Wenders griped. "A perfect wonder. How's that make her a killer?"

"It doesn't. And she's not perfect; she made mistakes. Her biggest one came in the early innings when she let Love talk her into hiring me. Then she convinced Reggie it was his idea."

"Blake," Gina piped in. "This is all –"

"You were good, sister," I said, cutting her off. "But you had no way of understanding my..." I stopped myself. I'd entered a mine field and was going to have to watch my step. "Let's put it this way," I said. "You had no way of gauging my memory."

It had come to me, in that last startling psychic flash I'd gotten on the balcony, the moment that Gina locked hands with Eddie and me. In that instant, I'd been transported back to Market Street, back in the path of the racing black car. I saw Love grinning like a chimp in the passenger's seat. I saw his chauffeur as they escaped the scene of multiple murder. But it was more than an escape; it was a trap, conceived on the spur of the moment, to murder a used-up detective that was getting too nosy. I'd never given her a critical suspicious thought because, beyond the personal feelings I'd allowed to creep in and destroy my thinking, I'd also taken certain aspects of the case at face value. That night, I'd just called her myself, awakened her to get the Riazs' address. It never occurred to me that, while she was sleeping soundly, she was acutely aware but blissfully indifferent to the murders taking place at that moment. That, at my call, she had gotten an idea, left her bed, hurried the short distance to the Riaz home, and collected her killer. That, with Love beside her, she then laid in wait for the ignorant gumshoe. I was a putz. I'd seen it in the vision as clear as a bell, Love's organ grinder, the steering wheel gripped tightly in her two white hands, glaring through the windshield at me as I flipped over the roof; Gina gritting her teeth as she tried to wipe me off the face of the earth. I couldn't tell any of that to Wenders of course. He wasn't a fan of my visions. I merely said, "I remember it now, clearly. Miss Bridges was driving the car that ran me down."

"You can't prove that, Blake," Gina said.

"And what," Wenders growled, "will a defense attorney make of your returning memory?"

"Not as much," I said, "as the DA can make of this." I jammed my hand into Gina's coat pocket and, before she could react, like magic, pulled out a gun. The cops were as startled as she was and the patrol boys proved it by jerking for their weapons. I gave them the frown they deserved, then handed the little Raven .25-caliber Saturday night special to Wenders. "Like I said, just a few slip-ups that would have been easy to miss; odd things that didn't add, like inventing threats against Delp, nervously spilling her coffee when she thought Reggie had spilled the beans, distancing herself by pretending not to know the prison Reggie was in. And why does a church secretary have a police scanner? Hang on, Frank. They were meaningless threads that couldn't be tied, but there's more. Just now," I told Gina. "Inside. It was cock-eyed that I could be laying on my back on that conveyor, watching Love grin like a hungry lion at my feet, when the machine fired up and took me for a tumble. Who started the belt? Not Eddie. And imagine my displeasure, upstairs a few minutes ago, when I checked Love's gun and found he'd fired only one round." I pointed at Willie. "He has temporary possession of that bullet."

The lieutenant offered a fleeting glance at Willie, who was leaking liquid red from the wound in his left shoulder, staining his newest stolen cop's uniform.

"A few minutes before Willie collected that," I said, "someone fired at me inside. The shot ricocheted off a railing." I turned to Gina. "That meant there was another gun; which meant that you weren't being very nice, angel. You played me for a country boy and I went right along with it. And all because I forgot the first rule of detecting: the worst trouble always looks good from the outside."

For the first time I realized how blind I'd been about her, how blinded I'd been by everything. It had all happened exactly as I thought but I'd gone too high with the blame. Conrad Delp was a pompous ass but not a murderer. The wrath had never been his. It was possible he might still have had a hand but I doubted it, and knew I'd never prove it. No, Gina and Eddie had engineered the entire affair.

"How long did you lay there, Gina, on your apartment floor? How long was Love on top of you, holding that rock, waiting for me to get there? You were never in any danger, were you? It was all about Eddie setting me up one more time. The rock was meant for me."

"You're wrong, Blake," she said, refusing to give up and sounding as convincing as ever. Her eyes misted over. "It was Love. He was crazy. He wanted to kill me!"

"What's so crazy about that?" I asked. The mist turned to acid and Gina stared daggers. I returned them, sharpened. "Just now," I said, "I'd like to kill you myself."

"Blake, please."

I wiped the blood from the corner of my mouth with the back of my hand, gave the gorgeous church secretary the last smile she'd ever see from me, and told her, "Shut up."

She stopped the crying. She was a cold, hard baby that had had me completely snowed but the heat was on and the icy mask was melting. Her wide green eyes shrank to mean slits as surprise was replaced by something dark. I saw the change as clearly as I'd just seen her behind the wheel of the hit and run car. Evil took over her face; her lips peeled back from fierce white teeth, fire glinted in her eyes. "I should have taken my time," Gina said. "I should've killed you when I had the chance."

"Don't worry about it, honey," Wenders told her sympathetically. "Everyone Blake meets comes away with that same thought."

"He can't prove any of this," she hissed. "Neither can you."

"Yeah, well, we'll have to talk about that. Tracks get left in lots of places hard to cover up." He turned to one of the uniformed officers. "Escort the lady out. Read her her rights." The cop snapped the bracelets on Gina and, taking her by the arm, started down the alley out of the court-yard.

Though I'd participated in her downfall, I still couldn't believe it. How could anyone with those legs be so damned evil? It just wouldn't add. My head was starting to swim again and it must have shown because, somewhere outside of it, I heard Wenders bleating, "Blake. Hey! You all right?"

Before I could answer, Willie jumped in. "Forget Blake," he demanded. "What about me?"

"Yeah what about you?" Wenders asked with disinterest. "Are you just sweatin' blood like usual? Or are you shot a little?"

"I'm shot!" Willie whined through his nose.

"That's just the start of your troubles," Wenders growled. "You're under arrest for impersonating a police officer... again." Mason and the remaining boy in authentic blue grabbed Willie and hauled him away. As they neared the mouth of the alley, Mrs. Banks' weasel of a son shouted back over his shoulder, "Blake, take care of my car, will ya?"

"Oh, Christ." He was gone before I could refuse or call him a name.

"You know, Blake," Wenders said, pointing in Willie's wake, "he ain't the only one's gotta quit acting like a cop." It wasn't an argument I was ready to have. I grabbed my aching head, turned uneasily and started away. "Blake."

I turned back to Wenders. The lieutenant pulled a plastic bottle from his pocket, the pain pills Mason had dug up for him the other morning, and tossed them to me. I was genuinely touched. Then I looked at the label, sighed all the way down to my toes, and tossed the bottle back. What could I say but, "I'm allergic."

Wenders shrugged, pocketed the bottle, and turned his attention to Love. I followed his stare to the cowboy's mortal remains and thought a thought I never imagined I could. I hoped that though Eddie had refused to go gentle into that good night, anything but, he might at least go quietly. Yeah, I silently prayed that this corpse had nothing more to say. I limped slowly and alone from the courtyard, through the alley between the buildings, and into the flickering lights on the forgotten lawn – now a staging area for Chicago's finest.

Willie was being shoved into the back seat of a prowl car. Not far away, Gina sat in another, staring straight ahead with unmoving eyes. Mason was jawing with a couple of the patrol boys and, by the chevrons on his sleeves, the shift supervisor. Though we were in an area of the city too remote for the gathering of a large crowd, it was still Chicago, and there were still a few rubberneckers in attendance. From among those, behind one of the empty squads, I heard a familiar shout and saw a familiar silhouette running my way. "Nod! Nod!"

The name alone was more than enough to identify the clamorer. It was either my secretary or my mother. And, as there was no way on earth my mom would miss one of her shows just to see if I was alive, I knew it had to be Lisa. One of the cops tried to stop her but she wasn't having any of it. She was by him in a flash and by the time she reached my side he no longer cared. Lisa grabbed me, hugged me, almost knocking me down. "Are you okay, Nod?

I was almost embarrassed by the anxious look on her face; almost.

"Eddie Love?"

I started to shake my head, regretted the vibration, and instead said, "No."

"I see you got her," Lisa said, indicating the squad holding Gina. Though I detected relish, there wasn't a hint of surprise in her voice. "I knew that you knew," she added with pride. "For a while I thought you couldn't see it. Then I was afraid you refused to see it. But, in the end, I knew you'd figured it out; that Gina Bridges was behind the murders."

Believe me, I was staring. If Lisa noticed, she didn't show it. She merely continued. "I should have had more faith in you, Blake. You're the greatest detective in the world."

"You... knew... about Gina?"

"Well, yeah," she sputtered. "I hit all the restaurants, coffee houses, bars like you were doing. I took Love's photograph everywhere and paired it with Delp's. Outside of those who knew the reverend from television, nobody placed them together anywhere. I showed Gina's picture with them and yesterday I found the restaurant where she met Love, several times. I knew then that she brought him aboard and assumed that's when they planned the murders, together. That's what

I wanted to tell you in the office. It's what I was trying to tell you on the way over here. I should have known that you already knew. And I went to the trouble of putting together a list of witnesses. I should have known you wouldn't need them."

"Oh," I said, grinning like the idiot I was, "we'll need them. We'll definitely need them." I had no problem adding, "You did a good job."

Lisa was beaming. "You don't still think Reverend Delp had anything to do with the murders?"

"I don't know," I said, letting a sigh get away. "I tend to doubt it. If he did I can't prove it. He's not about to confess and Love is dead."

"Any chance, if he did, of flipping Gina?"

"Not a ghost. She may or may not have an inside scoop on God, but she worships Delp and will quietly spend the rest of her life in jail."

"For him?" Lisa asked. "Or because of him?"

I shrugged. "I don't think he was involved. But if he was, he gets away with murder." I offered her a look of resignation and she shared it. What were we going to do? On the bright side, I wouldn't need to apologize to the esteemed minister. With his secretary and help-meet responsible for the killings, the both of us would best let by-gones be.

Delp had already moved on. Across town in the sprawling Temple of Majesty, unheard by us but no doubt heard by the heavens, applause gave way to one of Chicago's most revered theme songs, which gave way to the sturdy baritone of The Windy City's most famous televangelist. "Join me, brothers, sisters," the Reverend Delp asked (politely commanded), turning to the 5th chapter of the book of Galatians. From it, he proclaimed that "the fruit of the Spirit is love, joy, peace, patience, kindness, goodness, faithfulness, gentleness and self-control. Against such things there is no law." His flock, minus several once high-ranking members, nodded its beaming collective head in agreement. But that was across town, on the other side of the tracks.

At the old brewery, on the near south side, Lisa wrapped her arm around me and supported my aching everything as we walked away from the flickering lights. "You know, Blake," she said quietly, "it's been really sweet of you not mentioning even one time that I got you into this mess."

I smiled, though it hurt to smile, leaned on her, and asked, "What good would it do to place blame?"

"All the same," she said, pushing up her glasses, "thanks."

"You're welcome." I wanted to be nice to Lisa. The two of us were going to need to have a long talk about what had happened to me on this case; what was apparently still happening. I didn't know if suddenly I was a psychic, or some kind of bizarre fortune teller, or a budding psychopath. I didn't know why I'd repeatedly visited with the dead; why they'd spoken to me. All I knew was something strange and powerful inside my head, maybe deeper, had altered the way I perceived the world. If I ended up surviving it, undoubtedly, it would affect how I went about my business. That meant it would affect Lisa. As we walked away, I knew we needed to have that talk... soon.

"Placing blame would be a waste of time," I assured her. "Of course, now the case is over..."

She looked me warily in the eye. "Well, you're not going to blame me now, are you?"

"Yeah." I started walking again. "Oh, yeah."

"Don't just walk away. Who do you think you are, Richard Burton?" She caught up and took her place, again, as my crutch. "What's the first rule of detecting? It isn't fair to place blame."

"That's crap. There's no such thing as the first rule of detecting. And what's fair got to do with it?"

"I can't believe you're saying this."

"Why? It's true. This was entirely your fault. I told you I was turning down this case. That's what I said, I am turning down this case. You might not have heard me, you were probably chewing. But I could not have been more clear."

The dark closed in around us. But, have no fear, we were still there.

Dear reader,

We hope you enjoyed reading *Corpses Say The Darndest Things*. Please take a moment to leave a review, even if it's a short one. Your opinion is important to us.

The story continues in *Red Herrings Can't Swim*.

To read the first chapter for free, please head to: https://www.nextchapter.pub/books/red-herrings-cant-swim-hard-boiled-mystery

Discover more books by Doug Lamoreux at https://www.nextchapter.pub/authors/doug-lamoreux-horror-mystery-author

Want to know when one of our books is free or discounted? Join the newsletter at http://eepurl.com/bqqB3H

Best regards,
Doug Lamoreux and the Next Chapter Team

About the Author

Doug Lamoreux is a father of three, a grandfather, a writer, and actor. A former professional fire fighter, he is the author of four novels and a contributor to anthologies and non-fiction works including the Rondo Award nominated Horror 101, and its companion, Hidden Horror. He has been nominated for a Rondo, a Lord Ruthven Award, and is the first-ever recipient of The Horror Society's Igor Award for fiction. Lamoreux starred in the 2006 Peter O'Keefe film, Infidel, and appeared in the Mark Anthony Vadik horror films The Thirsting (aka Lilith) and Hag.

Other Books by the Author:

- The Devil's Bed

- Dracula's Demeter

- The Melting Dead

Co-authored:

- Apparition Lake (with Daniel D. Lamoreux)

Contributed:

- Horror 101: The A-List of Horror Films and Monster Movies (Edited by Aaron Christensen)

- The Best of the Horror Society 2013 (Edited by Carson Buckingham)

- Hidden Horror: A Celebration of 101 Underrated and Overlooked Fright Flicks (Edited by Aaron Christensen)

Corpses Say the Darndest Things
ISBN: 978-4-86745-416-9

Published by
Next Chapter
1-60-20 Minami-Otsuka
170-0005 Toshima-Ku, Tokyo
+818035793528
29th April 2021

Lightning Source UK Ltd.
Milton Keynes UK
UKHW011922180822
407522UK00002B/73